GETTING OFF EASY

BOYS OF THE BIG EASY

ERIN NICHOLAS

ISBN: 978-1-7338901-6-8

Editor: Lindsey Faber

Cover design: Angela Waters

Cover photography: Wander Aguiar

❀ Created with Vellum

1

―――

"I don't suppose you know anything about babies," James said as Harper Broussard swung her door open.

He watched her gaze go from his to the white blanket in his arms. Her eyes widened. "A baby *what*?" she asked, her tone and expression wary as she leaned back.

Holy shit, he almost laughed.

He had not expected that.

From the moment his boot had hit the landing at the top of the steps, his night had been completely off kilter. The second his eyes had landed on the pale blue laundry basket outside his apartment door, he'd known that his plan to pick up where he and Harper had left off two nights ago was out the window. But he'd been expecting a basketful of kittens. He really had. Which had immediately led to him thinking that he'd be able to cross the landing to Harper's door to ask for help with yet another life that needed intervention. This was hardly their first rodeo.

They'd probably curl up on her super-comfy couch and watch reruns of *NCIS: New Orleans*—her addiction—while they bottle-fed a lapful of kittens. He'd watch her tuck her hair behind her ear and lick her lips, and every time she shifted on the cushions, he'd see her shirt pull up to expose that strip of skin on her side he was obsessed with.

But when he'd looked down into the basket and saw the face of a human, he'd felt his world tip and a very deep, sincere sense of *oh fucking hell* go through him.

In the past, the tree, the lizard, the drunk girl, and the dog had all been reasons to talk to and interact with the out-of-his-league woman who lived across the landing from him. He'd sauntered over, knocked, flashed her a grin, and asked for her help each time, slowly wearing her down with his charm and his see-I'm-a-good-guy-that-people-trust-with-other-living-things shtick.

Tonight he'd *sprinted* to her door and pounded on it like his ass was on fire.

Her soft, French-accented voice always worked to make him feel calmer—and yeah, horny. At the moment, his heart was thudding so hard he hadn't believed either of those emotions could possibly make it through the ones swirling in his system. But they did.

He actually felt the corner of his mouth curl just slightly. "A baby boy."

Her eyes flew to his. "How did you get this baby?"

Okay, that was a fair question. He didn't think for a second she was insinuating he'd stolen the kid. He was certain she knew fire stations were safe havens—specified places where people could leave infants without question or penalty—which begged the question: why hadn't *this* person left *this* baby at the fire station?

"He was in that." James leaned to the side so she could see the basket still sitting outside his door. "I just got home and found him."

Her eyes, amazingly, got even rounder. "Oh my God!" She

reached out, grabbed James's arm and pulled him into her apartment.

James couldn't help but compare that reaction to the first time he'd ever knocked on her door and asked for her help with something.

Six months ago

"I don't suppose you know anything about ficus-ing?"

James Reynaud watched his across-the-hall neighbor raise a single eyebrow. God, she'd even come to the door with her hair up in a messy bun and the red-framed glasses perched on her nose. He felt his cock stir. He didn't go for staying-in-reading-in-my-favorite-chair-with-a-cup-of-tea types. But his body wasn't listening. Every time he saw Harper Broussard —*Professor* Harper Broussard—across the outdoor landing that separated their front doors on the third floor of their building, he thought *damn.*

She was a freaking linguistics professor at Loyola, for fuck's sake. He wasn't even entirely sure what linguistics was. She had the librarian thing going strong though. She was a little older than him. Definitely classier and smarter than him. And entirely unimpressed by him. In spite of the fact he'd left his work boots out by his door so she'd note he was a firefighter. In spite of the fact that he'd fixed stuff in her apartment with his shirt off. Twice. In spite of the fact that he'd left his window open so she'd hear him practicing on the piano. He was good, dammit. Really good. But none of that had seemed to do much for her.

Yet here he was, asking her about trees.

He might have been running out of ideas to get the professor to notice him.

And he never had trouble getting women to notice him.

So why did he care if she noticed him? He didn't go for the bookworm type anyway.

It was a challenge, pure and simple. Probably. That had to be it.

"Pardon me?" Harper asked.

"Ficus-ing. Taking care of ficus trees." He leaned to the side so she could see the four-foot-tall potted tree behind him. "I've become a father to a tree. And I don't know much about them. I don't suppose you do?"

She tipped her head, took in the tree, then looked back up at him. She had to look up about four inches. "I do, actually."

He grinned. "Awesome."

"Did you think that ficus-ing sounded like innuendo and would come off as flirtatious?" she asked.

James felt his grin dim. "Uh... yeah. Maybe a little."

"It didn't."

Got it. "Duly noted."

"Ficusing isn't a word, of course," she went on. "And it doesn't really sound anything like fooling—as in fooling around—or fucking."

He blinked at her. Had the seemingly uptight professor just said the word *fucking*?

"Just because the words start with the same letter, doesn't mean that inserting ficus into that sentence makes it seductive."

James sighed. "Okay. Thanks for... that."

She just looked at him.

He had no idea why he was going to pursue this, but he said, "Will you help me with it?"

"Will I help you take care of a ficus tree?" she clarified.

"Yeah."

"Sure. Let me know when you get one."

He blinked at her, then looked over his shoulder. "That's not a ficus?"

"That is an olive tree," she told him. "An Arbequina olive tree, to be precise."

She had this lilting voice, with a soft French accent around the edges, that made his gut tighten. His grandmother was a French immigrant and spoke her native language ninety percent of the time. He supposed he associated that accent with love and comfort and exasperated affection. And that was as far as he was going to go into why he thought this woman and her accent turned him on, thank you very much, Dr. Freud.

"I like olives."

She nodded. "Probably a good thing."

"I don't suppose you know anything about taking care of an Albuquerque olive tree?"

"No."

"Is that different from taking care of a ficus?"

"I don't know what an Albuquerque olive tree even is," she said.

He looked at the tree again then back to her.

She just watched him, patiently-ish. Wow, this woman didn't give an inch. "What's it called again?" he asked.

"An Arbequina olive tree."

"Arbequina. I was close."

"Because there was an A and a Q in both words?" she asked.

"And an R and an E," he said. Okay, he was assuming about the E, but he was ninety percent sure about the R.

Yeah, that unimpressed look was firmly in place. "Words and names matter," she said. "It's disrespectful to not make every attempt to get them right when speaking to or of a person, place, or thing."

James blew out a little breath. She was a ballbuster. Definitely not his type. He was used to women who were inclined to say or think, "Oh, you're a cute, charming firefighter who's also a musician? Here are my panties." Not women who were inclined to lecture him about being disrespectful in how he referred to trees.

Still, he said, "I didn't mean anything disrespectful by it."

"I can't take seriously your desire to take care of this tree if you can't even take seriously what kind of tree it is."

He was half expecting her to give him detention. And not the naughty-professor-and-bad-boy-student type of detention that, with any other woman, he would have teasingly suggested.

He found himself straightening. "Right. Okay, point taken. Do you know anything about taking care of an Arbequina olive tree?"

"I assume there is sun and water involved," she said. "I also assume that there is information all over the internet about it."

And, of course, the professor was going to give him homework rather than answers. "Want me to write a three-page paper about it?" he quipped before he thought about the fact that this woman actually kind of intimidated him.

She took a step back and put her hand on the door, clearly indicating she was about to close it. "Yes. And as soon as you turn it in, I will use it to help care for the tree while you're at work." Then she shut her door. More or less in his face.

But she'd offered to help. While acknowledging that she'd noticed his work schedule. A twenty-four-hours-on, forty-eight-hours-off firefighter's schedule was odd to most people, but James loved it. It gave him time to indulge in his love for jazz music and take care of the plethora of activities, errands, and responsibilities that filled up his life. But, yeah, if he was going to keep something alive while also being gone for twenty-four hours straight and having an erratic schedule during the forty-eight hours he wasn't at the station, he might need some help. It was just a tree but... he wanted to take care of it. It had been Amos's tree, and Amos had given it to James to look after.

It had been in Amos's room at the nursing home as long as James had been visiting him. The older man had played with the jazz band James joined on his nights off. Amos had played trombone for eighty of his ninety-two years. He'd been amazing. When he'd gone through surgery and then chemo for pancreatic cancer and had been too weak to play with them all night, he'd still come to the club, do a couple of numbers, and then sit at one of the front tables and listen while nursing a gin and tonic. When he'd gotten sick again and finally had to go to the nursing home, James had visited twice a week. And that tree had always been there.

Amos's funeral had been yesterday.

This morning, Amos's favorite nurse had brought over the trombone and the tree with a note that just said, "Give these to James. He'll take care of them." A trombone didn't need special care. It was in a place of honor in James's living room, but it could be left there for days without trouble. But a tree needed a little more effort.

He didn't know why he'd thought of asking Harper first thing. Maybe because she gave off an air of knowing everything. A theory that definitely had not been disproved by her knowing the tree was an Albeq—no... James thought and came up with Arbequina after just a second—an *Arbequina* olive tree and not a ficus.

He smiled. He'd gone over because it had been a reason to talk to her. Not a fantastic reason, but he was out of his depth with her. He didn't have to come up with reasons to talk to women. They came to talk to him. Every single night at the jazz club, but also at Trahan's Tavern, the bar and restaurant up the street from the station where some of his buddies hung out. He'd gotten to know the Trahan brothers, who owned the place, and it was a great stop after a long shift for food and drink. And yeah, women.

Hell, the only thing easier than meeting women in New Orleans was getting drunk in New Orleans. Especially for a local guy who was a firefighter and a musician. He didn't do any of that to seduce women. He loved it for his own sake. But the willingness with which women took their clothes off for him was absolutely a perk.

He headed back inside his apartment, hoisting the tree with him. He had a paper to write.

For the buttoned-up professor across the hall who was in no hurry to take anything off. Even those I-don't-give-extra-credit glasses of hers.

Five months ago

"I don't suppose you know anything about lizards?"

Harper looked at the tank James held up.

"Do you know what kind of lizard that is?" she asked.

James noted she didn't grimace looking at the animal. He hadn't known what to expect and had to admit he'd been curious about her reaction to it.

He had been expecting her to ask that, though, so he'd made sure he had the answer. "It's a bearded dragon."

She crossed her arms but gave him a look that was a little skeptical but also a little intrigued. "Why do you have a bearded dragon?"

"It was sitting in front of my door."

Her eyes widened slightly at that.

"In this tank," he added.

"So someone brought it to you?"

"Yes."

"Like the tree."

"Yes."

"With a note?"

He'd told her all about Amos in bits and pieces over the past month. "Yes. It said, 'I know you'll take care of Henry.'"

"The dragon's name is Henry?" she asked.

"Apparently." He held up one hand as if to stop what she

was going to say next. "And I know that you have a thing about names and words. The kids named him, so I don't feel like I can change it even if there is something possibly more meaningful out there."

"The kids?"

"Yes."

She narrowed her eyes. "Were the kids the ones who brought him over?"

"Well, I'm guessing it was Simon."

"Who's Simon?"

"One of the little boys in the third-grade class I spoke to the other day," he said.

He liked that she seemed a little interested in this and planned to milk it for all he could. He was great with kids, and people trusted him to take care of things, and he'd never miss a chance to remind her that he was a firefighter. "I do classroom talks about fire safety," he said. "Simon is a kid I met last year. He thinks I'm amazing."

She pursed her lips almost as if she were fighting a smile. "I see."

"When I was there a couple of days ago, he was telling me that their regular teacher is out for the rest of the year having a baby and the substitute hates Henry and wants to get rid of him. She's been asking the other teachers if they'll take him and even told the students that one of them could have him. No one wants him, and Simon's mom and dad won't let him keep Henry. He then asked me if I like bearded dragons."

"And you said yes."

"I said I had never met a bearded dragon that I *didn't* like. Which is true."

"You've met other bearded dragons?"

"No." He gave her a grin.

"So Simon got it into his head that you would take Henry, and the teacher is desperate enough to be rid of him that she went along with it, and somehow someone talked Simon's mom and dad into bringing him over here to you?"

"They actually brought him down to the station. But we were out on a call, and our smart-ass dispatcher said there was no way in hell she was letting Henry hang out with *her*, so she gave them my address and said it was fine to drop him off here."

Harper pressed her lips together and shook her head slowly. "Wow."

"So... can you take care of Henry when I work?"

"What are Henry's other options?" Harper's eyes were back on the tank now.

"Hunger, neglect, probably years of therapy."

She sighed. "Can't let that happen."

James grinned, feeling like he'd just gotten an A from the toughest professor on campus. "I'll bring him over on my workdays."

"No."

"No?"

"You go into the station at the crack of dawn," she said.

"You've noticed."

"You're noisy."

Uh-huh. She'd noticed. "I gotta go protect the people of our great city."

She gave a little eye roll. "Just get me a key to your place, and I'll go over and check on Henry on *my* schedule."

Give her a key to his place, huh? Was Professor Broussard the type to go through his drawers? He'd like to think so. "Okay," he said. "Will you know what to do once you're in my bedroom?"

Ah, there was that you're-not-nearly-as-charming-as-you-think-you-are look she was so good at. And that made her look so fucking hot for some reason. "I assume that was supposed to be flirtatious, too? And then I was supposed to say something about you having a dragon in your bedroom to which you would quip, 'already do'?"

He flat out laughed at that. She called him on his shit, and he liked it. He would not have expected that. The liking-it part. He'd expected the other from the very first time she'd done it. "Yeah, probably something like that."

She rolled her eyes. "This time, when you write up the paper about the care and feeding of a bearded dragon, use spell-check, and I'd appreciate a twelve-point font and double spacing. Also, bearded is b-e-*a*-r, not b-e-*e*-r."

Then she shut the door in his face. Again.

Yeah, she was really hot.

"I don't suppose you know anything about..." James sighed and swung the door open to reveal the woman who was slumped against his front door. Sobbing her eyes out.

Harper looked up at him. "What did you do?"

He huffed out a little laugh. "She's not mine."

Harper had to admit she liked hearing that. She hadn't seen a lot of—okay, any—women in and out of James Reynaud's apartment over the two months she'd been living here, and she'd fully expected to. But she had absolutely no doubt the man had as many as he wanted, whenever he wanted them. And there was no way he was celibate.

He was the kind of guy who just oozed sex appeal and confidence that said he knew every one of the ways he appealed to the opposite sex. Hell, even to a few of his own sex, she was sure. From the dark scruff on his jaw, to the swagger, to the tattoo that wrapped around his upper arm, to the fact he wasn't just a firefighter—oh, no, he couldn't have just one sexy profession—but also a musician. The guy was an alpha cliché from the tips of his work boots to the tips of his perfectly-styled-to-look-mussed dark hair.

Not that it was always perfectly styled. When he'd just gotten home from a shift at the fire station, his hair was definitely mussed. Just like his normally cocky swagger was traded for a fatigued trudge, and his quick, mischievous smile was a tired, solemn expression. She only ever saw any of that through her window, though. He never came over until he was freshly showered, smelling great, and full of cockiness.

The first time she'd laid eyes on the guy and thought *hot, young, and arrogant*, she'd figured living across from him was going to be either a parade of women, a parade of kegs, or both.

It had been neither.

It had been the sounds of his door opening and shutting, the sounds of those boots on the wrought-iron steps that led up from the brick courtyard below, the sounds of his piano drifting out of his window and into hers, the sounds of him calling down from over the edge of their shared balcony to Clyde and Billy, the two old men who worked in the kitchen of the praline shop that made up the first floor of their building, and then, every once in a while, the sound of him knocking on her door. Followed by his somewhat lame yet stupidly funny attempts at flirting with her.

She was now a co-parent to an olive tree and a bearded dragon. How had that happened?

But it had. And now it looked like she might be on the verge of... what? Adopting a sobbing twentysomething woman?

"What's going on?"

"She's drunk and heartbroken and hates men," James explained.

"Is she aware that you're a man?"

"I've never proven it to her in any meaningful way, but I assume so," he said dryly.

Harper really did like his sense of humor. "So, then, why is she on *your* doorstep?"

"Because this is where her sister dropped her."

Harper hadn't quite reconciled the fact that this man, who kept strange hours and had one of the most laid-back attitudes she'd ever met, was someone who others brought things to for caregiving. It was... fascinating.

And she wasn't a woman who used that word—or, really, any word—lightly.

Harper crossed her arms and propped her shoulder against her doorframe as she settled in for *this* story. There was always a story. And she found them... yes, fascinating.

"Okay."

"This is Courtney," he said, gesturing toward the woman.

She was sitting against his door, her knees pulled up to her chest, clearly not caring that with her short, bright red skirt, they could see she was wearing an equally bright red pair of panties. Her blonde hair looked like she'd run her hands through it repeatedly, and her mascara was streaked down her cheeks. Her eyes were red and swollen, and she looked quite miserable.

"Courtney was dating a guy in the band," James said. "He broke up with her last night. Her sister took her out to drown her sorrows. Then Courtney wanted to go to his house to talk to him. Her sister knew that was a terrible idea, but the only other person Courtney would agree to talk to was me."

"Her sister just left her here?"

"She figured this might take a while, and she had to go home because she's got a sitter with her kids."

"What, exactly, might take a while?" Harper asked.

"Me making her feel better."

Harper felt her eyebrows rise. "I see."

"Not like that." He gave her a look that seemed sincerely offended. "Her sister thought since I know Scott really well, I could convince her that Scott was serious about the breakup and that he's not worth her time and tears anymore."

Harper leaned to look around him at Courtney. "You think you can do that?"

"I will give it my best shot."

"What do you need from me?"

"A place for her to stay tonight."

Harper straightened away from the door. "What?"

"I can't talk to her about it tonight. She's blitzed. She won't remember a thing. She needs to sleep it off. Then we ply her with coffee and greasy food and ibuprofen in the morning and have a Come to Jesus."

"A Come to Jesus?"

"A talk that's serious and blunt and lays it all out."

"But you're going to be nice, yes?" Harper asked with a frown. "I mean, you're going to be gentle about it."

"Of course."

"But not too gentle. You'll be honest, and make sure she understands that she needs to move on."

"Sure."

"And you'll definitely be sure she drinks a lot of water and gets home safely and everything?"

He shrugged. "Yeah."

She sighed. She actually thought he *would* do all of those things. He was a good guy. He liked to walk around with his shirt off—not that she minded—and he *always* made sure his windows were open when he was playing piano because he clearly thought he was very talented—which he was—but he was a good guy. Guys didn't take in olive trees for old men and bearded dragons for little kids if they weren't, and, of course, he was a firefighter. There was no way she could forget that. Seriously. There was no way. He pointed it out constantly, besides leaving his boots out and NOLA FD T-shirts and hoodies draped over the outside railing.

"She can't sleep on your couch?"

"I'd rather she didn't. What with her being blitzed and hating men and possibly in the mood for revenge."

"You think she'd come after you with a knife or something?"

"Or naked lady parts."

Harper almost snorted at that. And she did *not* snort. "You wouldn't be able to resist?"

"Of course I would," he said, again, clearly a little offended. "I don't do things to people they're not going to remember in the morning."

"Got it."

"But I'd have to reject her, which would probably not be good for her right now and I'd have to touch her, which I'd rather not do if she's naked, lest we have some kind of misunderstanding about where my hands landed while trying to peel her off of me."

Harper studied him. He not only seemed sincere, he also had a point. It was possible things could go pretty wrong over in his apartment. "All right. She can sleep on my couch."

Her agreement had nothing to do with the fact she really didn't want James to see Courtney naked. She had no claim on James Reynaud. Nor did she want one. She was helping her neighbor and this poor vulnerable woman avoid a potentially messy situation. That was her story, and she was sticking to it. "You need to run and get some Gatorade, and I'll need more eggs for the morning. And chocolate chips."

"I'm not eating chocolate chips in my eggs."

"Did I invite you for breakfast?"

He flashed her a smile. "You're gonna want to."

"You seem certain of that." The idea of having James across her kitchen table for breakfast really shouldn't be so tempting.

"Courtney is a *talker,* and she's... loud. And inappropriate. I have a feeling five minutes into breakfast, and *you'll* be knocking on *my* door."

Harper felt herself fighting a smile. "Fine. You can come to breakfast."

"No chocolate chips in my eggs, Professor. That's disgusting."

"Don't be ridiculous. The chocolate chips are for the cookie dough tonight."

"Cookies?"

"Cookie *dough*. Best falling-asleep-with-heartbreak snack there is."

"You've had your heart broken?" he asked, his gaze suddenly laser focused.

Oh boy. She knew a lot about him, but she'd been careful not to share much about herself with him.

Like the fact she hadn't, actually, had her heart broken.

She'd dated. She'd had a few relationships. But none of them had ever broken her heart. When she and the men parted, they'd been very amicable. So much so, she'd wondered how deep everyone's feelings—including hers—had really been all along.

Which, stupidly, made her wonder about her romantic life at large. By the time a woman was her age, shouldn't she have been in love? Not a little in love or lust. Not just had a few crushes. But truly, passionately in love? Enough to have had her heart broken and cried herself to sleep at least once?

That's what the romance novels she read told her, anyway, and she read nearly one a day. Contemporary romance, romantic suspense, erotic romance, historical. She read it all.

She'd wondered briefly if those novels were making her set her standards too high. But then she'd realized that no, actually, what those stories had done was help her not confuse lust and crushes and simple attraction and I-kind-of-like-him with something deeper and more passionate. And they'd helped her decide to wait for the real thing. She knew what love looked like. It just hadn't come along for her. Yet.

Finally, she answered flippantly, "Of course. Hasn't everyone at some point?" Because she didn't really want to get into all of that with James tonight.

"Well, damn, what a dumbass," James said simply. Then he turned and headed over to gather Courtney up.

Harper watched him talk softly to the sad girl as he lifted her into his arms and carried her over to Harper's apartment.

Damn. Hot, young, cocky, and a good guy.

Yeah, her romance novels definitely talked about guys like him. All the time.

THREE MONTHS AGO

"I don't suppose you know anything about dogs?"

Oh, man. He'd just shown up with a dog.

Her hot-flirty-firefighter-jazz-musician neighbor who was also a good guy and took care of whatever and whoever showed up on his doorstep.

Harper helped. Some. But she often suspected that if it weren't for his crazy work hours, James wouldn't need her at all. He wasn't exactly a nurturer, perhaps, but he did what needed to be done, stepped up, met challenges.

The essays he'd written for her on olive trees, bearded dragons, and how alcohol effected men and women differently had all been surprisingly thorough. Not that he hadn't added his own flair and commentary to it—commentary, she, of course, deducted points for—but it had been obvious he'd actually looked into the topics and found the pertinent information to deal with taking care of the things that had been thrust into his path. Rather than giving them away or ignoring them, he'd done what he'd needed to do to help them not just survive, but actually thrive.

Their—*his*—olives were delicious. Henry was doing well, and now that he was past the stage where he needed insects regularly and could eat fruit and veggies during her shifts, she found him to be a surprisingly curious and interesting creature. Courtney had not only sworn off men over the past month, she also hadn't had a drink since the night she'd passed out on Harper's sofa—and puked on Harper's favorite throw blanket.

And now... Harper and James were clearly about to become co-parents to a dog.

A cute, shaggy little dog, whose breed was hard to determine and whose entire body was wiggling and vibrating with happiness.

She sighed. She didn't *really* want to sleep with James Reynaud, but it was extremely hard to remember why sometimes.

Too young.

Too laid back.

Too irreverent.

Too young.

James was at least five years her junior, and more, he was hardly interested in the same things she was. She loved to cook and read and knit and stay in. He loved jazz—playing and listening to it—and the nightlife and going out. He ate out a lot, and she certainly didn't know what he liked to read or even *if* he liked to read.

So, yes, he was younger than she was, but they were also so obviously mismatched, it was laughable.

But he was gorgeous.

And he was holding a dog.

She was only so strong.

"Where did the dog come from?" Harper asked, unable to resist reaching out to touch its head.

The dog pivoted quickly, swiping his tongue over her hand

before she could touch his soft head. She smiled. He was a cutie.

"He brought himself to the fire station," James said.

He'd worked for the past twenty-four hours and was just getting home. His hair was mussed, and he definitely looked tired, but he had an air of happiness around him that just seemed untouchable. Harper suspected it had to do with the love he had for his job. She knew how it felt to do something that just felt right, like you were made for it.

"He's been hanging around for a few days, I guess," he said.

"And, of course, as you were leaving, the guys all said that you should bring him home."

He grinned at her, and, as always, her heart gave a little extra thump.

Which was ridiculous. She was thirty-two years old. She was intelligent, highly educated, fully independent. She'd lived in France, Canada, and now the United States. Had had short-term affairs with a Frenchman *and* with an Italian. Never had her heart *thumped* over a man. It was not just ridiculous. It was annoying. She was better than to fall for a pair of deep-brown eyes, or a slow Louisiana drawl, or a set of six-pack abs. Because, of course, he had all of those. He looked every bit the part of a walking, talking romance-novel hero.

The real problem with James Reynaud, however, was that she was getting to know him. And he didn't just *look* the part. He definitely *acted* like a romance hero, too. Willing to rush into buildings, risking his life to save others? Check. Sweet with the elderly, vulnerable, and neglected? Check. Creative and talented? Check. Able to be self-deprecating and charming at the same time? Check.

And now he had a dog.

That was like a triple check mark.

"Do you like dogs?" he asked.

"Of course I like dogs."

James leaned in and ruffled the top of the dog's head with his nose in maybe the cutest gesture Harper had ever seen. "You're in, buddy," he told the pup.

The dog pivoted again and licked James's chin.

Harper propped a hand on her hip. "But he's going to have to live here full time, and *you* can come visit on your days off."

James lifted a brow. "Why's that?"

"Because he needs stability." *She* did, too.

This guy was messing with her emotions. Maybe not intentionally, but he was getting to her. She knew these things—the trees and drunk girls—weren't things he'd planned, so she couldn't say he was wearing her down with all of this on purpose, but the fact he attracted and *welcomed* all of these needy creatures and then helped them get even better than when they'd first come to him, was making her feel things she didn't want to feel.

So she couldn't be a co-parent. She needed to have a dog that her neighbor sometimes played with. With his shirt *on*. She needed to start drawing some lines before he further sucked her in.

"He needs someone who's here on a consistent schedule. Not being shuffled back and forth." She reached out and took the dog from James.

They didn't need to worry about the dog together or buy toys for the dog together or have Christmas with the dog together. Because of the *together* part of all that. The more time she spent with him, the more she figured out about him, the more she liked him. She was going to end up falling for him and then getting her heart broken. She did not want to find herself propped up against his front door with her mascara running down her cheeks.

He let it go, but he was watching her with a bewildered expression. "You want the dog full time?"

"Yes. And maybe sometimes on your days off you can take him to the dog park while I work. Sometimes."

James's brows drew together slightly. "Sometimes."

She lifted her chin. "Yes."

He seemed to think about that for a moment then said, "I guess I'll need a key to your place, then, too."

She frowned. "Why?"

"So I can come over and get him when I'm off. When you're in class. Unless you want me to wake you up early before I sack out after my shift."

He was right. He left early, which meant he got off his shift and back to the apartment early—twenty-four hours later. He'd need a key to her place if they had a dog together. No, if he was *dog sitting* once in a while. She'd gotten the key to his place because of Henry.

"Fine," she agreed. "I'll have one made."

"Great."

"Okay."

"Okay."

He reached out and ruffled the dog's head again. "Lucky guy," he said. "Be sure to snuggle her good." Then he gave Harper a wink and turned and sauntered off to his apartment.

Two nights ago...

Harper's phone rang as she was leaving her classroom. She'd had a department meeting run late and then needed to finish up some paperwork and was now hurrying home. James had been off today, but he had plans with his friends tonight, and she didn't want to leave Ami alone for too long tonight.

Okay, truthfully, she would just always rather be at home with the dog... and James... than pretty much anywhere else.

Her shaggy, devious, matchmaking dog.

She smiled as she reached into her jacket pocket for her

phone. It really seemed that James also enjoyed being at home more when she and the dog were there, too. The dog he called Fred even though she'd officially named him Ami, which meant *friend* in French. He insisted on saying it *Amy* and claiming it was a girl's name. Harper knew damned well that he knew French and knew how to pronounce it. But he didn't know she knew that he knew French. Because he didn't know she'd overheard him speaking French, fluently, to one of the tourists in the praline shop one afternoon or that she'd heard him swearing in French one day through his open apartment window or that she'd heard him talking on the phone to someone fully in French on the balcony another day.

Why he was pretending not to know the language, she wasn't sure, but she was playing along for now. And rolling her eyes every time he called their dog Fred.

Yes, the dog was officially *theirs* in spite of her best efforts to not get even closer to James. Her arguments that they were confusing the poor thing by using two names didn't hold water either. The mutt responded, happily, to both. He was smart and very much preferred when James and Harper were both with him. If he knew one was home but was in the other apartment, he whined and paced and lay by the door looking completely forlorn. It was how, over the past month, Harper and James had started spending more time together whenever they were both home.

It was all very domestic and, she knew, very dangerous. Because, while it seemed wholly platonic, she was constantly noticing things like how one of his middle fingers was crooked, as if it had been broken, and it made her aware of how much she wanted his fingers stroking her body. Or that he always started his slow, flirtatious smiles with the right side of his mouth, which made her aware of how much she wanted to feel those lips on hers. Or how the low, deep chuckle of affection he'd give for something Ami-Fred did made her stomach flip in a different way than the surprised, entertained chuckle he'd give when she one-upped him. Oh, her stomach flipped with that chuckle, too. It was just a different sensation. Strange she'd never noticed stomach flips could vary.

She glanced at her screen as she headed for her car.

It was James.

She stopped in the middle of the grassy square she was crossing and shifted her bag to her other shoulder.

He had plans with his friends tonight. Why would he be calling her? Was Ami-Fred okay? Was Henry okay? She couldn't believe she was actually concerned about a lizard, but here she was.

"James? What's wrong?"

"Hey, Professor. Nothing's wrong."

She could hear the grin in his voice. Was he drunk dialing her? She frowned. "Then why are you calling me?"

"I have a question."

There was music in the background along with the clinking of glassware and boisterous conversation. He was definitely still out somewhere with his friends.

She narrowed her eyes. "Okay."

"If a guy ties a girl up in bed—"

Immediately she realized he'd been talking to his friends about the conversation they'd had the other day. He'd noticed the books on the table next to her sofa and had asked about them. They'd had a mature conversation about romance fiction and erotic fiction and had even talked about some of the pieces of the BDSM lifestyle.

But now he was either calling to tease her or calling to get more information that he could share with his friends. She was going to make him regret either of those. "Oh my God, James. Does she have a safe word?"

He paused. "Who?"

"The girl you're tying up," Harper said. She didn't really think he was tying anyone up, she realized.

Interesting.

He'd, of course, noticed the stack of books was made up of five romances—two contemporaries, two erotic, and one suspense—and a book about female self-esteem. Because, at times, James was a thirteen-year-old boy in a twenty-seven-year-old man's body, he'd made the mistake of sharing his perception of all that. Harper had taken the opportunity to educate him—for twenty minutes—on the genres of romance, erotic romance, and erotica, in addition to the topic of women's sexual fantasies and empowerment and men's erroneous assumptions about all of the above, including women's self-esteem issues.

She'd fully expected it to turn him off that topic, and possibly talking to her again about anything ever, but he'd been surprisingly interested and attentive.

The man simply would not stop surprising her.

Which was probably even more dangerous than owning a dog together.

"You're *sure* she wanted you to do that?" Harper went on, resuming her walk, intent on giving him a hard time. "You have to *talk* about this stuff." She got to her car and unlocked the door. "I'm coming over."

"You'd come over if I have a girl tied up in bed?" He sounded a little baffled but also amused.

That was often how he looked at her in person as well. For some reason, it always made her feel warm.

In her real life, people looked at her as they would a well-respected professor and colleague, with admiration and respect and just enough intimidation to keep them from saying something inappropriate.

James looked at her warmly. That was the best word to describe it. It was almost as if there was affection mixed in when he talked to her or listened to her. He was not inappropriate or disrespectful, but there was an underlying air to him that said he wanted to be. That he was waiting for a time or a circumstance when he could be. And that when that time came, she'd very much enjoy it.

That all made her feel warm, too. But in a very different way.

"Do I need to bring scissors?" Harper asked, slamming her door shut behind her.

"You think I tied her up and can't get it undone?" James asked. He was clearly enjoying this.

"*Zut!* I don't know where my scissors are," Harper said. "I have a knife. That will work. But tell her not to freak out when I come in."

She had to admit, it often felt as if James had the upper hand when it came to flirting and teasing. For some reason, tonight she felt like turning the tables. Maybe because after their conversation about erotic romance, he'd seemed not only interested in the subject matter but very intrigued by the fact she read it extensively. Was there a side to her that he hadn't expected? Good. Because there were many layers to this man and every one she discovered made her feel more and more out of her element.

"Not to freak out that you're carrying a *knife* when you come storming into my apartment where she's tied to the bed and can't get undone?"

She heard the humor in his tone.

"Wow, Professor. Take it down a notch."

"Open the door, James," Harper said.

"I'm not home."

"Where are you? I need to drive this knife over to you?" Harper realized she was grinning. She was teasing a very hot, young, fully-accomplished-and-very-experienced tease and seemed to be doing a good job at it.

"Put the knife down, Harper," James said firmly. "I'm not home. I don't have a woman tied up. I was asking... for a friend."

"Did she know it would be *two* of you?" Harper asked, a surge of adrenaline pumping through her. Yeah, this teasing stuff was fun. Especially when it had to do with sex rather than ficus trees that weren't really ficus trees and adorable dogs that made her feel warm and fuzzy rather than warm and... sexy. She loved Ami, of course. And sharing him with James had brought them a new level of intimacy that was definitely sexy. Seeing a man in love with a dog did something to a woman's insides. No matter how much that woman wished that wasn't the case. But it all felt like... foreplay. There was another word she didn't use lightly. Yes, everything with Ami and even Henry, in spite of him being a lizard, and the olive tree, and even Courtney, had felt like foreplay. This felt like they were finally talking about sex. And she wanted him to come home. Right now. "You *really* have to talk this stuff out ahead of time," she went on. "Avocado makes a good safe word."

James blew out a breath. "You aren't standing outside my door, are you?"

"No."

"You're also not holding a knife, are you?"

"I'm not even at my apartment," she said. "But I'll have you know that I know exactly where my scissors are."

There was a pause. "You think you're pretty smart, don't you?"

She thought she knew this man better than she'd realized, actually. She liked that. "If you called to tell me that you had a woman tied up in your apartment and couldn't get the knots undone, I'd call 9-1-1," Harper said.

"Because you couldn't stand the thought of seeing another woman in my bed?" James asked. A sexy, teasing tone had slipped into his voice now.

For the first time, Harper let the warm tickle of awareness trip down her spine and didn't try to suppress it. "Because all of your firefighter and cop buddies would show up and would torture you over it forever," she said.

She heard the quick huff of laughter from him and felt her grin stretch.

"I'm taking this outside," he said to someone he was with.

Harper found herself squeezing the steering wheel in what felt like anticipation.

James was making their conversation more private. She didn't doubt for one second that James flirted, outright and blatantly, more often than not. He was not a guy who hid a lot of emotion, period. There was no way people would keep dumping things on his doorstep for care if they didn't know he was a loving, fun, warm person. So what did he need to say to her in private that his friends couldn't hear? For some reason, that made her feel like something *more* was about to come.

"Professor?"

His voice was low and rough. Over the line, she could hear he must have moved outside. There was still noise—there was always noise in the Quarter—but this was traffic noise, and the conversation was more muted, as if the people were moving past him rather than gathered around.

She swallowed, shocked to find her nipples beading just from that single word, his nickname for her. Of course, other people called her Professor. But there was something in the way James said it that made it sound sexy and affectionate at the same time. It made her think of him saying it, low and husky, against her ear, as their naked bodies slid against one another and on her cool linen sheets...

"Harper?"

She snapped out of that little fantasy. "Um, yes?"

"You said you're not at home."

"I'm not."

"When will you be?"

Her breathing sped up. He hadn't said anything like, *meet me in bed, naked, in fifteen minutes*, but somehow her body had heard something very much like that.

"I'm on my way home from campus."

"You're going directly there?"

"Yes."

"Me too."

"You're on your way home?" she asked. Could he hear that her voice was breathless now? Did she care?

"Now I am."

She smiled in spite of the fact her heart was pounding so hard she could feel it thumping through her whole body. She'd seduced the playboy by teasing him over the phone. Yeah, she felt good about that. She wasn't a seductress by any stretch of the imagination, but maybe the tree, lizard, drunk girl, and dog had been working on James, too.

"I'll... meet you there."

"Yeah, you will."

His voice was gruff, and a there was a touch of demand in the way he said that. Harper had never dated a man who was sexually dominant, but she'd read about a lot of them. Strangely, she'd always assumed she'd go for the scholarly, professor or scientist type herself. A little older than her. More mature. Confident. Not intimidated by her degrees or her own confidence.

But a little-bit-demanding, kind-of-a-big-kid, heart-of-gold-under-the-super-hot-exterior firefighter-jazz-musician type was okay, too.

"And Professor?"

"Yeah?"

"Make sure Fred's fed and watered and walked and... not needing anything for a while."

Harper felt her whole body go hot. "Okay."

They disconnected without another word.

Harper drove home, her mind on everything but the city streets and things like speed zones. Of course, living in the Quarter meant she couldn't go fast even when she wanted to. There was far too much foot traffic. She finally made it to their building, parked, got upstairs, and was in the midst of taking care of Ami when her phone dinged with a text.

Got called in. Warehouse fire. Don't know when I'll be home.

Her disappointment was shockingly intense.

Really fucking sorry, he added.

She believed him. *Me too. Please be safe.*

No worries. I've got a rain check with you to live for.

In spite of the disappointment, that made her smile. He was pretty sure of himself. But yes, she was definitely giving him a rain check on tonight. *Don't let that distract you while you're supposed to be working.*

It'll be tough, but I'm a professional.

Yes, a professional, badass, life-saving firefighter. As if she could ever forget.

She was still smiling as she took a deep breath and looked around her apartment, realizing she didn't have to worry about digging any lingerie out from the very back of her drawer tonight after all.

Dammit.

But she was fine. This was fine. She would do what she always did in the evenings after work. She'd make a little dinner, she'd hang out with Ami, and read for a while.

But as she went through her evening routine, she avoided her stack of erotic romance like it was a pile of poisonous snakes.

She hardly needed any further fodder for the heat that still coursed through her body just thinking about their conversation on the phone.

2

———

Now...

"It's a baby *boy*?" Harper demanded, her gorgeous brown eyes wide.

James tipped the baby so she could look at him. "I'm no expert, but... yeah."

She put her hand over her mouth in a kind of dramatic, but pretty adorable, gesture that definitely conveyed *oh, shit*, but in a classier way. That was Harper. Real, but classy.

God, two nights ago, he'd been on his way over here to finally kiss her. Oh, yeah, he'd intended to kiss her. And she'd known it. They'd had this whole sexy, teasing, foreplay thing on the phone, and he'd known that finally, *finally* she was ready. They'd been flirting for six months. He'd never spent that long seducing a woman.

Of course, he'd never used olive trees and crying drunk girls to seduce a woman before, either. But it had somehow felt like that's what he was doing. Every time Harper answered her door, her demeanor was a little softer, she lingered a little longer, her smiles were quicker, her eyes warmer. Yeah, he'd been winning her over. *Slowly,* but surely. He'd been willing to take the time, too.

Sure, some of that time it had seemed like she was trying to figure out how much of him was real and how much of him was just I-want-in-your-panties teasing bullshit. The answer to that with most women was fifty-fifty. But with Harper he'd felt less and less like he was teasing her to get her into bed and more like he was teasing her just to make her smile, because it made *him* smile. He hadn't even kissed the woman, yet coming home and seeing her was the best part of his day.

He knew that was a red flag for a confirmed bachelor who didn't want to get involved. But he was starting to wonder what was so damned great about being a bachelor. He'd been watching his guy friends fall in love one by one, and when he hung out with them and the guys from down on the bayou— who were all still single and living the weekend-fling-with-hot-tourists-who-love-Southern-boys life—he had to admit the guys who were actually sharing their lives with one woman they were crazy about seemed happier and just *better* somehow.

And hell, Harper Broussard was hardly just some girl. She was sassy, but in this very classy, almost elegant way. She was onto him. She didn't fall for his lines. Yet she kept opening her door. That mattered. She could have told him to leave her alone. She could have told him to shove his olive tree. She could have killed his olive tree. He knew women who would have done that. But she'd kept the thing alive and made him olive tapenade with the olives.

She liked him.

And she hadn't even seen him naked yet.

Most women who'd seen him naked liked him.

Most women who'd seen him naked hadn't spent a lot of time talking to him about books and dogs and his job.

None of the women who'd seen him naked had made him olive tapenade.

Harper liked him in spite of the fact that he'd kept his clothes on, and she'd never heard him play the piano in the club.

It was interesting. Not that he thought that was all he had to offer a woman. He wasn't sad. He was just a little out of his element with her.

That made him want to take her to bed even more. While the thought of it intimidated the hell out of him.

And now, when he was finally here when she was, both able to take their clothes off and he could carry her into her frilly, mostly-white-with-touches-of-green-and-yellow bedroom and lay her down on the fluffy, white comforter that he'd wanted to mess up since the first time he'd seen it... he was holding a baby.

A freaking *baby*.

"How do you know it's a boy?" she asked tentatively.

"The note says *I know you'll take good care of him*," James said. Repeating those words made his heart thump as it all seemed even more real. He really was holding a baby that had been left on his doorstep.

Harper was still gripping his arm. Tightly.

"Oh my God, he was just out there? Outside your door?" she asked. "Oh my God, I had no idea. I didn't hear anything! Someone could have come and taken him! He could have starved or gotten too hot or—"

"Harper," James cut in firmly.

Her eyes came to his.

"He's sleeping. I don't think he's been out there very long."

"But..." She frowned. "How do you know?"

James shrugged. "He's asleep. Babies fuss when they're hungry and wet and hot and cold and stuff, right?"

He watched her take a deep breath, appreciating for the

moment that he was the calm one. Harper Broussard had her shit together. He'd challenge anyone to say any differently. But it seemed that perhaps babies were one area where she was less than fully confident.

Of course, this baby was a huge surprise. To say the least.

"That's a good point," she conceded. She leaned in a little closer to peer at the baby.

Her demeanor was more that of a woman leaning in to check out an armful of rotten vegetables—very hesitant and with a scrunched-up nose and frown that made her look very put off—than one looking at an infant. But it gave James a chance to smell her hair. One of his favorite scents in the world. He took a deep lungful. Might as well. If he was going to be holding a baby, he might not get her very close very often. Seemingly.

Something about Harper being even less enthusiastic about the baby than she had been about the bearded dragon made James feel a shot of I-want-to-take-care-of-this. He liked her confidence and her sharp wit and her intelligence. But he also liked the little flickers of surprise he saw in her eyes from time to time when he said or did something that she clearly hadn't been expecting. Like when they'd talked about music. He'd given *her* a lesson on the history and rise of jazz music. Or when Clyde had come up asking for assistance on a pretty bad burn he'd gotten in the candy store kitchen, and James had taken quick care of it.

He should maybe feel insulted that she thought he didn't know anything about anything, but instead it made him want to tell her—and show her—*all* of the things he was good at.

"Can you take him while I run to the store?" James asked.

He said it mostly to see what her reaction would be, because it had only just now occurred to him that he'd need supplies for the baby.

Her eyes went round, and she took a huge step back from him and the baby. "Take him?"

"Yes, watch him." James bit back his smile. So Professor Broussard wasn't maternal. Okay. She was downright gorgeous when she was cuddling and playing with Fred, and that loving, warm side of her was a huge fucking turn-on, but babies might be a different story. "I can't leave him in my apartment alone, obviously, and I don't have a car seat or anything for the truck to take him with me."

He could, of course, have some things delivered. Or call any one of his friends to bring him stuff. Hell, all of his closest friends were also dads. But he wanted to do this with Harper.

He wanted to do everything with Harper.

Yep, red flag.

If he wanted to stay single and unattached and with a different woman every night.

But that was becoming less and less appealing.

While the woman standing in front of him in soft cotton flannel pants and fitted tank top with her hair up in a messy bun and no makeup on, looking like the baby in his arms was about to leap out and bite her, was more and more appealing every damned time he saw her. Especially now that they'd had a date for sex.

Because that was absolutely what the other night had been, and he wasn't going to let her forget it.

As soon as he didn't have a baby to deal with.

He looked down. When would that be? Who was this? Why was this baby on his doorstep? What the actual hell?

He felt his heart rate kick up again as his amusement over Harper's reaction gave way to the reality of what was actually going on.

"I'll go." Harper stepped to the side, carefully, as if to avoid touching the baby. Like having a baby in his arms was contagious or something. She slipped into her sandals that were always by the door and grabbed her little purse and keys. "I'll get stuff. You stay here with... him."

But she couldn't go anywhere because James and the baby were very much in the way.

"You're going to go?" he asked.

"Sure. Why not?"

So she was clearly freaked out by the idea of the baby— understandably, honestly—but she was still willing to jump in and help James. Maybe not *touch* the baby, but she was there for James.

God, he wanted to kiss her. Badly. Not because she was dressed in a short, tight dress in a club, moving her hips and rubbing against him, saying dirty things and giving him fuck-me eyes. But because she was going to help him, even with something she was clearly very uncomfortable with.

"Do you know what to get?" he asked.

"Diapers, food, formula."

He nodded. "A car seat. A crib. Probably some... toys?" He looked down again.

"Toys?" she repeated. "What kinds of toys?"

"I don't know."

"How old is he?"

"I have no idea." When he looked up, he saw her watching him with one eyebrow lifted. "What?"

"You have *no* idea?"

"How would I know that?" he asked. "I mean, somewhere between a few days and a year?"

Harper actually propped a hand on her hip. "You can't narrow it down, even a little? There have been *that* many?"

He frowned. "That many what?"

"Women."

"What the hell are you talking about?" The baby squirmed in his arms, and James realized he'd tightened his hold a little. He relaxed.

"Well, he's yours, yes?"

Her words punched him in the gut. *He's yours.* James stared down at the baby. Why hadn't that occurred to him? Because he hadn't had sex with anyone in six months. Not since Harper Broussard had first opened her apartment door and given him homework on olive trees.

But babies took longer than that to make. Well, not to *make.* That only took a few minutes if you wanted to get scientific about it. But the whole pregnancy thing took more than six months. So really any of the women in the maybe three or four months before Harper could be the mother of this baby.

Holy shit.

It wasn't like that was hundreds. But it was... more than one or two.

He heard Harper take a deep breath and he looked up.

"The baby is less than six months old. Forty weeks of pregnancy. That means it's someone you slept with about sixteen months ago who also knows where you live." She moved closer and then nudged him out of the way. "I'll be back."

She slipped out of the door before James could say anything.

———

SHE COULD *NOT* BE UPSET ABOUT THIS.

But she was.

Harper pushed her cart up and down the aisles of the twenty-four-hour shopping center that had everything from fresh produce to diapers to car seats to wine.

She had a little bit of all of that in her cart. Except the produce. She didn't need fresh veggies. She needed diapers. And wine.

How the hell had that happened?

An hour ago she'd been sitting in her apartment trying to

read over papers her students had turned in that morning, unable to keep from glancing at the clock over and over, wondering if James would be home tonight. And if so, whether he'd come over. And if he did, would he want to pick right up where they'd left off with the phone flirtation the other night?

He'd gotten home while she'd been at class yesterday, and she knew he was likely sacked out from the long night at the fire, so she hadn't gone over. But she'd thought about him all night. She'd woken up to find him gone again. When his schedule got thrown off by a big fire where extra personnel was called in, it took a bit for him to get back into routine. But she'd assumed he'd be home at his usual time tonight. She'd hoped.

When he'd come pounding on her door, he'd scared the daylights out of her. She'd rushed to the door, half worried and half hoping it was all because of pent-up desire and he was going to storm in, sweep her up in his arms, and stalk into her bedroom.

She hadn't expected him to look panicked.

She had definitely *not* been expecting a *baby*.

Harper turned around at the end of the wine aisle and went back to add another bottle.

A *baby*.

She was fine with babies. Pretty much. In theory. She didn't have much experience with them. But she was fine with them. As far as she knew, anyway.

She supposed it was like what James had said about Henry... she'd never met a baby she didn't like. She just hadn't met a lot of babies.

What she *hadn't* expected was a hard punch of jealousy.

She wasn't opposed to dating a guy with a kid. But dating a guy who was divorced or widowed or had already figured out the co-parenting thing with the mom was completely different than... this. This chaotic situation with a guy who she wasn't even officially dating and who'd now had a baby anonymously left on his doorstep. There were no established roles, no custody agreements, no structure, no plan. This was very outside her comfort zone.

There was also a woman out there somewhere who James didn't exactly have closure with. Which meant that he needed to see her again and work some things out. To say the least.

Just when things were maybe changing between *her* and him.

Harper blew out a breath and grabbed another bottle of wine.

She never should have let him and his stupid olive tree into her life.

She checked out, paying an exorbitant amount for a car seat that she wasn't even sure would work. She had no idea how old the baby was, but there was no way he was too big for this car seat. Still, she was glad that James would be the one to worry about it.

But as she loaded everything—being especially careful with the wine—she admitted that bugged her, actually. She'd love to leave him and his accidental offspring to themselves. They'd bond. They'd wait for mom to show up—or he'd figure out who she was and call her—and then they'd proceed to be whatever kind of family they decided to be.

And her staying the hell out of it, starting the second she got back to the building and delivered the supplies, would keep her heart from getting broken when the woman realized that James was absolutely the full package and there was no way she could walk away. And James, being James, would take her in and support her and help her and... hell, he might even fall in love with her. Harper knew from their conversations that he had several friends who were not just married or in very serious relationships but who were also dads. If she'd ever met a man who was a natural dad, it was James.

That might sound like a strange way to describe a hot

young bachelor who played jazz and partied in the French Quarter when he wasn't strutting around with his big old fire truck, saving lives. But he had a nurturing side that seemed second nature.

She wasn't the only one who saw it—as evidenced by the number of people who kept dropping things off on his doorstep. Once something was there, it didn't leave. He brought it in and took care of it. More, he enjoyed it. Sure, she'd made him look things up about olive trees and bearded dragons, but he'd gone with it. Not many guys would have. Especially when she didn't drop her panties when he turned that first paper in. He'd done it good-naturedly and had actually seemed amazed when the tree started producing. And when he'd found out that he could leash-train Henry, he'd been like a kid on Christmas morning. Ami loved him, Courtney thought he was "the absolute best," and… Harper had very little evidence to the contrary.

He'd be a great dad. He just would. Any woman would think that was hot, especially if it was with *her* baby.

Harper frowned at the wine bottles settled on the floor behind the driver's seat.

She should have gotten one more.

———

When she got back to the apartment, it took Harper a little extra time to climb the stairs. Not because of the heavy load of wine and diapers, but because she was really reluctant to go up there. She liked him. She really liked him. She should have known better. She didn't *know* him. She knew he didn't bring a lot of women—okay, any women—to his apartment, but she had no idea what his social life looked like. She didn't know if he had a couple of casual women he saw from time to time or if he was with a different woman every weekend. She didn't know how he felt about kids, if he had younger siblings, or truly *anything* about any of that.

Now she was about to face him and a baby, and all of those unknowns were now front and center and very important.

She didn't really want to know any of them. Because she was afraid she wouldn't like the answers.

But there were only so many steps between the courtyard and their landing, and she found herself outside his door far sooner than she wanted to. Thankfully, he'd moved from her apartment to his. Thankfully, it had been obvious to him that the baby supplies were going in *his* apartment not hers.

Harper raised her hand to knock but heard the squawk of a baby, the bark of a dog, and the sound of a man trying to calm them both. She took a deep breath and turned the knob, stepping into James's apartment.

"Thank God," he greeted her. He gave their dog a look. "Fred's jealous."

Harper looked at Ami. "Ami, come here." She dropped her bags by the door.

The dog gave a little bark at James but trotted over to her. Harper knelt and scooped the dog up, thankful to have something else to focus on than the big firefighter holding the tiny baby.

Now that the baby was out of the blanket and awake, it was easy to see that he was not very old at all. He couldn't support his own head, and he was small, especially held in James's big hands. He had the baby against his chest, cradled in both hands, one under his butt, one behind his head. The baby wasn't wailing, but he was fussing, trying to get his hands to his mouth, moving his head back and forth, clearly seeking something to put in his mouth. Preferably something with food in it, Harper assumed.

Great, that was something else she could concentrate on, rather than James. Or talking. Or this situation as a whole big picture. One thing at a time, one detail at a time. That's what she could do now.

"I'll put Fred over at my place and be right back," she said, also grabbing the bag with the wine in it. James didn't need to know about how she'd intended to cope.

"You must be as shaken as I am."

She looked over her shoulder at James. "What?" Had he seen the wine?

"You just called him Fred."

She looked down at the dog. Oh, wow. Yeah, she must be shaken. What a small word for what she was feeling. "It's a weird night," she admitted. There was no reason she needed to act put-together and fine about all this. That wasn't realistic.

"Yeah," was James's simple answer.

"I have the car seat in the car but thought this stuff was more important to bring up first," she said. "There are diapers and wipes in there." She nudged one of the bags with her foot. "You might want to try that until I get back to help with a bottle."

Harper paused for a second, blinking. She was talking with James Reynaud about diapers and bottles. That was really happening. Wow. Weird was an understatement.

"I'll do that," he said, starting toward the bag.

She hurried out of the apartment with Ami. "You have to cool it," she told him as she set him down inside her apartment and filled his food and water dishes. She gave him a treat and sat down on the floor with him, petting him and giving him a few cuddles to calm him. "None of us planned this, and we're not thrilled either, okay? But you can't be a pain about it. We're going to... *he's* going to figure it out."

Harper sighed. James needed to figure this out. How he felt, what he wanted, who the mother was, what he was going to do about the situation when he figured that out—or, she supposed, what he was going to do about it if he couldn't figure that out. But this wasn't an olive tree or a bearded dragon. This wasn't something he could just ask her to stop in once in a while and look after. It also wasn't a dog. She'd wanted a dog for years.

"Okay, behave," she said, stretching to her feet. She put one bottle of wine in the fridge knowing she was probably going to need it later. She shut the door. Then opened it again and moved the bottle to the freezer. She didn't intend to be over at James's place very long, and the faster that bottle got cold, the better.

She let herself back in. James was in the bedroom, talking to the baby. At least, she assumed he was talking to the baby. Or himself. Either that, or he was on the phone with one of his dad friends. Which was a fabulous idea, now that she thought of it. He had a ton of resources. He should definitely call one of them and ask them to come over. Whoever it was could bring his wife, too. Then she could definitely slip out and get back to her dog. Dogs she knew.

She eyed the door. If she left now and just didn't come back, he'd think of calling them. He was a resourceful guy. It wouldn't take him long to think of that. Or if he showed up in her doorway with the baby in a few minutes, she'd suggest it to him. Then her gaze fell on the shopping bag with the formula and bottles in it. Okay, the baby probably needed to eat. It would take a bit for any of his friends to get over here. She could at least help with this first bottle.

Carrying the bag to the kitchen counter, Harper pulled a can of formula out and eyed it. She'd spent an inordinate amount of time looking over the variety offered at the store, comparing what was there to what she had pulled up on her phone. She wasn't writing a paper for James on this, but she could do the research. She had no idea, of course, if the baby had any GI issues that would require special formula, so for now she'd gone with the basic kind for newborns and was going to hope for the best.

By the time James came into the kitchen area carrying the baby, who was now calmer, and again, cradled against James's chest—which would certainly make Harper feel better, so she could relate—she had a bottle ready to go. She held it out.

He took it, but his eyes were on her.

"You okay?" he asked.

He looked really good. It was crazy. She knew that he had to be a little upset or at least frazzled by this. But he didn't look it. He looked like he was just taking it in stride. Maybe that was the firefighter in him. He never knew what a work shift was going to bring. Maybe he was just really good at rolling with the circumstances as they presented themselves.

Something else they did *not* have in common. She was a planner. Organized to a fault.

"Professor?"

He was the one holding a tiny life that he'd created with someone he barely remembered, a tiny life that was going to need him for literally everything for the next, well, who knew how long? Eighteen years give or take in some capacity. But he was just holding the baby as if it were another tree or lizard or drunk girl...

"Harper?"

She finally snapped out of her thoughts and looked up at him. "What?"

"Are you okay?" He looked sincerely concerned.

She decided to be honest. She shook her head. "Not really."

"Not a baby person?"

He said it lightly, but she could see that he was suddenly tense.

Oh, *her* not liking babies made him tense? But him *having* a baby all of a sudden was just a roll-with-it kind of thing? She frowned. "I guess I thought maybe we'd at least go dancing before we were making baby bottles together."

Something flickered in his gaze. "You want to go dancing with me, Professor?"

His voice was deep and a little gruff, and that damned drawl made tingles trip up her spine.

Yes, she wanted to go dancing with him. Dammit.

She lifted her chin. "Guess that doesn't really matter now, does it?"

"There's such a thing as babysitters."

She lifted a brow. "You've been a dad for two hours, and you're already thinking about leaving him with a babysitter?"

"For a chance to get you up against me? Absolutely."

Harper didn't know if it was because there was a tiny human between them or because he sensed there was a widening emotional distance between them, but that was as direct as he'd ever been about the chemistry, the... *thing*... going on with them. Harper didn't like calling it a thing. That was such a nonspecific word that wasn't really descriptive at all. But that was the problem. She, with all of her words and definitions, didn't know how to describe her and James.

That was probably for the best. The fact they hadn't gotten to the phase where there was a clear definition meant it would be easier to end it.

"You have your hands full now," she said, looking pointedly at the thing that was literally filling his hands. "Dancing might not be your top priority."

"I can have more than one priority, Harper."

She wet her lips. She'd always found it flirtatious and sexy when he called her Professor, but when he said her first name like that, it was sexy in a different way. It wasn't teasing. It was hot. It made her catch her breath a little.

"The baby's mother should probably be one of those," she said softly, taking a step toward the door.

"The baby's mother and I don't have a relationship."

Yes, because he didn't even know who she was.

"But you need to now." Harper reached the door, gripping the knob in her hand.

She wanted him to say something that would change all this, but what could that be, really? She wasn't against being with a guy who had a son. But she was against getting involved with a guy who would be muddling through the messiness of… well, any messiness.

If she met a guy who was already through this part, that was one thing. Or if James wanted to take her dancing after all of this was sorted out, that was different. But right now, he needed to focus on that, and she didn't want to be hanging out on the periphery waiting to see what happened.

She also didn't want to be in the thick of it, getting attached to a man and—she blew out a breath. Yeah, she was scared of getting attached to the baby that belonged to a mystery woman with mystery motives who could show up again at any point and change everything just as they were making something work.

Because she and James made things work. Surprisingly easily. Olive trees and lizards might not seem like much, but they'd found a routine. Courtney wasn't a daughter or a sister, but they'd helped her, together, beyond the hangover and broken heart. But they had an easy partnership, a way of working together that was comfortable and natural, and it seemed like they'd known one another much longer than they had.

And if the lizard and a reformed party girl weren't enough to convince her, there was the dog.

The dog was something else. Ami needed a lot more attention and care. He loved them both. He wanted them both. He needed discipline and love and feeding and companionship and guidance. They'd become fabulous co-parents to that dog. The dog had made her feel bonded to James.

If the dog could do that, then caring for a child together... The idea terrified her.

She'd known better than to let James help out with that dog so much.

She should have stuck to her guns.

So she was going to now.

"Harper," James stopped her as she pulled the door open.

She sighed. "Yes?"

"I don't want this to change things."

She looked back. Big mistake. Hot guy, holding a tiny baby, looking concerned about *her*. Ugh.

"I'm sorry," she said quietly.

"I need you."

She squeezed the doorknob. He meant for help with the baby, but still those three words tugged at her.

Harper shook her head. "You need his mother."

"Har—"

"I have to go."

She slipped through the door, pulling it shut behind her, before she could think about it any harder. Leaving James, knowing he needed help with something, felt strangely foreign. That was ridiculous. She'd known him for six months, and she'd made him learn everything about olive trees and bearded dragons and dogs. She hadn't held his hand or taught him. She'd just... helped.

Shaking off the feeling that she was letting him down and hurting him, she headed straight for the freezer and the wine.

Ami came into the kitchen and looked up at her, cocking his head as she unscrewed the top and took a swig straight from the bottle.

"What?" she asked.

He gave a soft woof and then went to the door.

"No, we're not going to James's."

Ami lifted a paw to scratch at the door. Harper lifted the bottle.

Ami whined. Harper wanted to whine, too. Instead she… wined.

But she only took another drink. Then she recapped it and put it in the fridge.

Ami came back over to her.

"I'm not putting it away because I'm going over there. But if something happens in the night, he might need help, and he might not think of Caleb first," she explained, referring to his friend and fellow firefighter, Caleb Moureu.

Ami woofed.

"Well, of course he should think of me first," she said. She loved that he did, in fact. "I'm *right here*. And I'm usually here for him." She swallowed hard. "But this is different."

Ami whined.

"He's fine. You should have seen him. He looked totally in control. And he can Google stuff. Or call his friends. Or call the nurse hotline." She straightened. "I wonder if he knows there's a twenty-four-hour nurse hotline." She started for the door but stopped with her hand on it. Ami was wagging his tail so hard at the thought of getting out and going across the landing that his whole body was shaking. "Of course he knows," she told the dog. "He's a firefighter. He's a first responder. I'm *certain* he knows how to give a baby CPR and the signs of fever and infection. If the baby isn't eating, he'll know to take him to the ER." She crossed the kitchen again, this time pulling a bottle of water from the fridge.

She still couldn't get drunk. She definitely felt the need to stay sober. Which kind of pissed her off. But it was his first night with the baby. Maybe after a couple of nights, when he was settled in and she knew he wouldn't need anything, she could pull that bottle back out.

"Oh!" She spun toward the door. Ami started wagging again. "The car seat is in my car! What if he needs it to take the baby to the ER?"

But again she stopped halfway to the door.

She took a deep breath.

"He's not going to need to take the baby to the ER."

Ami scratched at the door.

"He'll call 9-1-1 if he really needs to," she reasoned.

Ami whined and looked over at her.

"Or he'll come get me. We'll get in my car anyway. He won't be able to handle the baby and the car and everything alone."

Ami finally gave up and lay down, his nose against the door, as if resigned to staying in but not willing to get any farther away from James than he had to.

Harper stubbornly turned in the direction of her bedroom. She washed her face, brushed her teeth, and headed for bed.

But she only stood next to it.

She'd probably hear James knock if he came over. He could pound on her door like a madman if he needed to. As he'd done earlier tonight.

But in the end, she sighed, pulled her pillow off the bed, and went to the couch. She settled down, pulled her favorite throw blanket over her and patted the cushion next to her. "Come on, Ami."

The dog looked over at her, then seemingly turned up his nose, before putting his chin on his paws and facing the door again.

She didn't think Ami actually liked James more, but he didn't have as many chances to sleep over there, so he usually spent James's night off on the foot of James's bed.

But she wanted the dog with her tonight. She couldn't say why exactly, but she thought it might be bitterness over the tiny person who was with him tonight because of the female person who had been *with him* in order to make that tiny person.

James didn't need to have the dog, too.

Harper stared at the ceiling. He'd made a baby with another woman, and he wasn't even sure who she was. Or rather, *which one* she was. That woman hadn't felt close enough to him to come to him during the pregnancy or even actually with the child herself. She'd just left the baby on the landing.

Who did that?

And did Harper really want to be counted in a number so large that James had to really think hard about who this woman could even be? Would he be able to come up with more than a first name? Had he known her for more than one night? Was she from here or had she been a tourist? Was he going to have to deal with someone local who could, potentially, be around all the time? Or would he have to figure out something with someone long distance? Or would he even have a prayer of tracking her down at all? Even if she was local, if he only had a first name and a few hours of... *impressions* of her, it might be difficult finding her at all. Especially if she didn't want to be found.

A woman who left her baby on the doorstep of its father with nothing more than an unsigned note didn't seem like someone who was interested in Mother's Day brunches and parent-teacher conferences.

Harper pressed her hand over her heart. The whole thing was so crazy. She'd been right inside this very apartment while that woman had climbed the steps and put that baby—*her* baby—in a *basket* outside James's door for him to discover when he got home. Harper believed him when James said the baby probably hadn't been there long. It was even possible the woman had hung around in the shadows downstairs to be sure that James kept him rather than calling the cops or taking him straight to a safe haven location.

Harper swallowed hard. The woman could have taken the baby to James at the fire station. But she'd brought him here.

She'd brought him *to* James specifically. With a note. So yes, she'd known who James was and had wanted the baby to be with *him*. Not just safe. Not just out of her hands. But with James.

Harper forced herself to relax, breathe deep, and shut her eyes.

This was all now, officially, not her problem. The baby wasn't *hers,* and the guy who she'd thought could maybe, possibly, eventually, be hers a little bit, was now *really* off limits. So she might as well get some sleep so she could figure out how to share a dog with a guy she had an enormous, stupid crush on who now had an infant son and a whole lot of mess to figure out.

On. His. Own.

3

Harper blinked and looked around.

Why was she on the couch? And what was that noise?

It was Ami. Scratching at the door.

But why was the door right *there*?

Oh, right, she was on the couch.

Why was she on the couch?

She reached for her phone on the coffee table and squinted at the time.

Three a.m.

Why was Ami asking to go out at three a.m.?

Then it all came flooding back. Why she was on the couch, why Ami was out here in the living room, why she'd been dreaming about showing up for a parent-teacher conference dressed in her flannel pajama bottoms and a tank top that said *I run on cuss words and caffeine.*

Neither of which was true. She tried to curtail her cursing, and when she did it, she did it in French. It sounded better that way. Everything sounded better in French. She also drank tea. On the rare occasion she had coffee, she doctored it with enough cream that she wasn't sure it counted as coffee anymore. Yes, her morning tea had caffeine, but she switched to decaf after that first cup.

So the shirt made no sense. Of course, that was only one thing in the dream that didn't. The parent-teacher conference, for instance.

What was...

Ami gave a short bark and Harper frowned.

The dog wanted James.

Yeah, well, join the club.

But now that she was awake it was impossible to ignore the fact that James was across the hall with a baby boy and that she was worried about them both and wondering how they were and feeling horribly guilty for leaving them alone and feeling jealous but also slightly possessive and more than slightly irritable about the whole thing.

Yes, possessive. She'd been here. Helping him. Liking him. Taking care of his olives.

Where had this other woman been?

Sure, growing his baby. But not *here*.

Harper was trying very hard not to judge the woman for leaving the baby. She didn't know this woman's situation or motives or emotional state. For all she knew, this was the most selfless thing she could have done for her child and possibly the hardest thing she'd ever do in her life.

But the fact remained that Harper had more of a relationship with James than that woman did. In spite of the little life they'd accidentally made together, which meant that Harper did have a sort of right to be over there. If not for the baby, then for James.

It all sounded perfectly reasonable in her head as she pushed up from the couch and went to slip her feet into her flip-flops.

She couldn't blame wine for her sudden one-eighty on this.

But it was three a.m. No one was totally rational at three a.m. She could blame that if needed.

Ami was about to burst into happy bubbles of joy, she was certain, as she unchained the door and opened it. She peeked out. She wasn't sure what she was expecting to see. Or afraid of seeing. But one never really knew what might be waiting on that landing.

It was clear and quiet. She cocked her head but could hear nothing from James's apartment, and there were no lights shining from his windows.

She grabbed her key to his apartment from the porcelain bowl on the table by the door and crept across the landing and put her ear to his door. Ami gave a short bark.

"Quiet," she hissed, pointing her finger at the dog.

He minded, but his tongue was hanging out, his tail going a mile a minute, and she knew that if she loitered for too long outside the door, the dog would lose his patience.

"Okay, but you have to be quiet," she told him. She inserted the key and let them in, opening the door slowly.

The apartment was dark and quiet.

That was probably a good sign. No crying babies. No harried men.

Harper rolled her eyes. Of course James would be good even with babies. He might not have known a ficus from an olive tree, but once he'd learned, he'd been great with the tree. And Henry. And Courtney. And Ami. And her.

Harper had to admit that he'd been really good with *her*, too. He'd teased and flirted. He'd flaunted his firefighting, He'd shown off his musical talents. But it had always been with a touch of humor and good-natured confidence. He'd never pushed. Never been inappropriate. Never overstayed his welcome at her apartment. Not that there had ever been a time when she'd been fully ready for him to leave.

But it really didn't surprise her to find that in a few hours' time, he was already handling the dad thing with ease.

Was there anything the guy *wasn't* good at?

The question brought to mind a number of things that she'd definitely wondered about over the past few months that involved things like mouths and hands and naked bodies and slippery sheets. Which was not at all appropriate considering she was here to check on him and his infant son.

She tiptoed to the bedroom. The door wasn't shut, and she found herself in the doorway staring.

James was stretched out on top of the mattress, the sheet over one leg. He was wearing only boxer briefs. And a baby.

The baby was on his chest. Sleeping soundly.

James had an arm slung up over his head, the other cradled the baby's diapered butt.

Harper wasn't sure she'd ever been more stunned to be attracted to someone.

Truly, without the baby, this was the sexiest scene she'd ever walked in on. The briefs did nothing to hide a thing about James's big, hard body. They molded to his hips, thighs, and cock lovingly. Even in sleep, and presumably unaroused, the man had *so many* impressive inches, she paused a moment just to take it all in. All of it. From the sexily mussed dark hair to the scruff on his jaw to the wide chest to the hard abs to *all of that* below, Harper was thrilled that he was asleep, and she could just look her fill.

Day-um. Yes, with a y. She had an appreciation for language, and that definitely extended to the use of local color to emphasize emotion in ways simple words couldn't at times.

This guy. He might be wrong for her in a number of ways, but there was no denying her body heated whenever he was around and that for the past six months, whenever she read her erotic romances, James was the guy she was picturing for every hero.

But add that baby in and the way James was protectively holding him, keeping him safe and warm, making him feel comforted... Harper sighed. She'd thought James was sexy when he was holding and playing with Ami.

That was nothing compared to this.

She watched them for another moment. Then realized she had two choices. She could turn around and leave, assured that things seemed fine here. Or she could help. She had no idea how James usually slept, but there was no stretching or rolling or turning in this situation. Or if he did, he risked rolling on top of the baby. Or what if his arm relaxed and slid away from the baby and then the baby rolled or slid off?

Suddenly Harper saw beyond the sexiness and she instantly moved. She could take the baby. She could cuddle, keep him warm, make sure he slept safely since she had forgotten to get a crib. Another realization that was just hitting her.

She'd been distracted at the store. There were so many kinds of formula. So many different types of diapers. She'd been stressed about getting the right car seat. And her mind had been spinning with thoughts of James as a father and the other woman and what all this meant and her own feelings about the whole thing, and yes, she'd forgotten a crib. *Merde!*

Well, she couldn't do anything about that right now, so she moved toward the bed. She'd take the baby, and then James could stretch or roll or whatever and get comfortable. Surely, subconsciously, he'd recognize he could move and he'd reposition.

She looked down at them from beside the bed. They weren't right on the edge. Again, she wondered if James always slept in the middle or if he'd specifically moved over so there was mattress on either side in case the baby did roll off. Still, that was risky. The baby couldn't lift his own head yet. He could suffocate if he rolled into the blankets. Her heart suddenly pounding, Harper reached out to lift the baby off of James.

But just as her hand touched his back, James stirred.

She froze.

"Professor?"

His voice was husky from sleep, low and gravelly, and Harper's belly flipped, heat sliding from her stomach lower, between her legs. They were in his bedroom. One of them was *in* bed. And that voice. And the nickname. She could hardly be blamed for her reaction.

"Hey," she said softly.

"You okay?"

It was the middle of the night, and he was the one asleep with the thing that had just turned his life upside down, but he was asking about her? She never came to him with needs. He came to her. She nodded. "I thought I'd take him so you could get more comfortable."

He looked down at the baby, and seemingly instinctively, his hand slid from the baby's butt to his back. James's hand was huge on the tiny baby, and Harper swallowed hard at the sweet picture. "He's okay."

"You sure? I don't mind."

He looked up at her. He was clearly still sleepy, maybe not fully awake. "You wanna help?" he asked.

She nodded. "Yeah." She felt terrible for leaving earlier. It had gone against every instinct except the one that screamed at her to protect her heart no matter the cost. But she was afraid she was far past the point of that being possible.

"Then come here."

Harper wet her lips. "Come... there?"

"Yeah." He reached for her with his free hand and caught her around the wrist, tugging her forward.

She could have easily pulled back, broken free, resisted. But she let him urge her onto the mattress.

Harper knelt with a knee next to his hip. "How does this help?"

"Gets you up against me," he said, his voice still sleep roughened.

Her heart skittered. "That's helpful?"

"Can't imagine how it will hurt." He gave her a sleepy, but still devastatingly sexy smile. "This way you're here if he does need something."

Well, he had a point.

Harper stretched out on the mattress beside James. He put his arm up above his head again, not holding her, but definitely exposing plenty of surface area for her to be *up against*.

Oh, what the hell. She wouldn't sleep well at her place now, wondering what was going on over here. This way she was very much here for whatever went on. And she'd wanted to be up against him for a few months now. Lord only knew what the next few days were going to bring with the baby and everything. She might as well enjoy this moment while she had it.

She scooted closer. His body was hot and hard. She swallowed with some difficulty.

Then the baby made a little grunting sound and curled and stretched against James.

This was so not how she'd ever pictured being in bed with James Reynaud. That was for sure.

———

THIS WAS SO NOT HOW HE'D EVER PICTURED BEING IN BED WITH Harper Broussard.

But damn, he'd take it.

James was stiff, and his arm was asleep, and he wasn't sure he'd ever get the kink out of his neck, but he had a baby boy sleeping like a rock on his chest and a gorgeous woman sleeping like a rock up against his side, her cheek on his chest, some of her hair clutched in the baby's fist, and a shaggy dog sleeping like a rock on his left foot. James wouldn't have moved for a million dollars.

As consciousness slowly returned, he took a further inventory of what was going on. Specifically, Harper. He'd woken up with Fred before, and he had a feeling he'd be waking up like this with the baby a few more times. If not *a lot* more times. But his chance to lay next to Harper as the morning sun streamed in through his window, before the day started, before he really had to deal with any craziness, was something he wasn't willing to rush through. It might not happen again.

Her soft curves were pressed up against his side, her breasts against his ribs, her pelvis against his hip, one of her legs draped over his. She was warm and smelled amazing. He wanted nothing more than to slide his hand down, cup her ass and roll her over and underneath him, kissing her awake.

One definite reason to get a crib *today*.

The baby had slept through the night, which even James knew was miraculous and something that didn't happen much with babies. He remembered Caleb talking about Jack, Lexi's little boy, as a baby, being awake every two hours, hungry and wet.

That concerned James on one level. Maybe something was wrong with the baby. Maybe he shouldn't be sleeping this much. But he hadn't been feverish. He'd seemed appropriately alert and engaged when he'd been awake. James had gone through the basic tests that he knew from the field. Of course, most of his stuff had to do with triaging emergency situations, but they couldn't be too far off even in this situation. And today he'd get some real, actual medical input on the kid.

The kid. Possibly *his* kid.

That had honestly not occurred to him until Harper said it.

Now he couldn't *stop* thinking about it.

Was this little boy his son?

His heart kicked when he thought about that. It was possible, yes.

He hadn't been with a woman since he'd first introduced Harper Broussard to his olive tree. But yes, it was possible that this little one was his, and that's why he'd shown up on James's step.

That hadn't been his first thought when he'd seen the baby, though. He wasn't sure why. In part, because he was a fanatic about condoms. And because, while he might not know the birthdays and favorite flower of all the women he'd slept with, he couldn't imagine any of them being scared of coming to him with a pregnancy. Or at least sticking around *with* the baby when she brought him over.

Then again, it wasn't like he'd delved deeply into the psyches of all his flings.

Harper took a deep breath in her sleep and let it out softly, snuggling closer. James's body responded because, well, he'd wanted this woman for six months, and her ugly flannel pants, and the fact this whole situation was pretty complicated right now had zero negative effect on his libido. But there was an infant on his chest. One that was starting to squirm and would soon need attention, no doubt, and that would break up anything resembling a sexy moment.

James looked from the soft brown of Harper's head to the darker tuft of hair on top of the baby's head. Yes, it was very similar in color to his own hair. He blew out a breath. Well, fuck. This was not exactly how he'd expected to wake up next to Harper for the first time, but he might as well make the best of it. There was little he could do to change it right now. The baby—his or not—had been entrusted to him, and James was going to take care of him.

He was going to take care of Harper, too.

They'd had a date for sex the other night. The four-alarm fire had gotten in the way, but it *had* been a date. For sex. It had been clear. And he wasn't about to let her forget about that. Yes, he now had a baby. Maybe. Well, he *had* a baby in his care, whether or not the kid was actually *his* biologically. But that didn't mean he didn't still want Harper. She'd been freaked out by it, understandably. But he'd seen two important things in her eyes along with the shock. He'd seen concern. For him. She'd been worried about him as she realized things had just gotten more complicated in his life. He'd also seen jealousy. There was another woman on her mind now. The baby obviously had a mother, and who she was to James mattered to Harper. He was sure she'd try to deny that, but he'd seen it.

Concern and jealousy. Those weren't things that a woman felt for her across-the-landing neighbor. Those were things a woman felt for a guy she was interested in. A guy she cared about. He wasn't going to let her just ignore those things or pretend they weren't there.

Him having a kid didn't change how he felt about her. He wanted Harper. He hadn't even kissed her. Hadn't seen her in a sexy dress. Hadn't danced with her. But he'd never wanted a woman more.

And she wanted to dance with him.

That was going to happen.

Baby or not.

Speaking of whom—at that moment, the baby stretched and then screwed up his face, gave a little squawk, farted, and then threw up.

On Harper.

That woke Fred, who lifted his head and gave a little woof. James wasn't sure if the dog was telling the baby to knock it off or if he was inquiring if the kid was okay. Fred was going to have to adjust to this whole thing quick, or he was going to be sleeping at Harper's full time.

Harper stirred. Whether it was Fred's noise or the warm goo on her neck, she frowned then opened her eyes, blinked and looked around, clearly trying to figure out where she was. James started to sit up as Harper lifted a hand to her neck where there was warm, sticky baby puke. Her eyes focused on his stomach then slid up to the baby, who had just let out another squawk and who was clearly gearing up for more noise as she pulled her hand away from her neck and looked at the white slime.

James was trying very hard to just keep his mouth shut. There wasn't much good to say just then, and he was, frankly, having a hard time understanding why he found Harper so fucking hot when she looked so confused and disheveled. She had baby puke on her neck, and he would have put her up against the nearest firm surface in a heartbeat. If he didn't have a baby in his hands, of course.

His rustling around disturbed Fred, who woofed and then got up, stretching and shaking. He focused on them all and gave a little bark.

The noise made the baby jerk and screw up his face, preparing to cry. James patted his back. "Shhh," he cooed softly.

"Ami, quiet," Harper admonished. "You're okay."

Fred snorted and jumped off the bed.

Yeah, off the bed might be good before the baby made more of a mess. James scooted to the opposite side and stood. With a sigh, Harper sat up on the side she was on, wiping at her neck, looking more resigned than disgusted, and James had to admit that was pretty great. She was a classy linguistics professor, but she wasn't freaking out about being puked on.

He couldn't help but pause in front of her as he rounded the bed on the way to the bathroom where he'd laid out a stack of towels to use as a diaper-changing station. "'Mornin'."

Her gaze started at his knees and traveled upward. Slowly.

James became aware that he was only wearing his underwear. It was how he always slept, but he hadn't woken up with a woman in a very long time so hadn't thought much of it.

But hell, he'd gone to bed without a woman. This woman had come to him. In the middle of the night. Yeah, he couldn't forget that, and he wasn't going to let her forget that either.

Concern. That's what had brought her across the landing. He knew it. But he thought maybe more than that had led her to climbing into bed with him.

The fitted underwear that didn't have much space to accommodate the way his body responded to her perusal. It was too late to grab a blanket or pants or to shift to cover his growing erection with his hands. His hands were full anyway. Of a baby who was getting louder and squirmier. So he let her look.

Not that he minded. What he minded was not being able to do anything about the fact he was in only his underwear, and she was in pajamas, including a thin top that was slipping off one shoulder, while she was clearly braless, her creamy skin just begging to be touched, and there was a bed *right there*.

He had a new appreciation for his friends with kids and all the times they must have been cock blocked.

Just then the baby made a funny little squeal sound and suddenly farted again. But this time there was more than just noise.

"Oh!" Harper's hand flew up to cover her mouth.

James grimaced as he felt warm slime cover his hand and slide onto his chest. He knew what it was. He didn't need—or want—to look.

At least his erection and lusty thoughts were effectively dead now.

"Um... shit," he said, in a feeble attempt at humor.

Harper made a choked, laughing sound behind her hand and squeezed her eyes shut. "This is so not how I envisioned our first morning in bed together."

She'd envisioned a morning in bed together?

Even with baby poop on his hand and chest, he couldn't just

skip over *that* tidbit of information. "Tell me, in graphic detail, how you *did* envision it."

She shook her head, smiling behind her hand, eyes still shut. "I can't. Not with that smell and the knowledge that I have spit-up in my hair." She took her hand away, pointing in the direction of the bathroom. "Go clean up. I'm going to grab a shower, too."

She was leaving. "Wait. Don't... go."

Her eyes opened. "What?"

"Don't leave." The baby was squirming and fussing, and yeah, the smell was becoming impossible to ignore. James started for the bathroom. "Just... wait."

"I really am just going to shower quick," she assured him. "I'll come back over. I don't have a class until two."

He spun. "You have to work today?"

"Well, yes." She frowned. "Hey, you're off today?"

"Yeah."

Harper stood, and James took in the sight quickly. The thin pants hung loose on her hips, and it wouldn't take much to push them to the floor. Did she wear panties to bed? Then she moved in front of the window, and the morning sun shone through the thin material of her top, showing the delicious outline of her perfect, perky breasts.

"Do you think she knew that? Do you think she planned to bring him over on a night when you'd be off the next day, on purpose?"

Her words jerked him back to the conversation. And the foul-smelling, slimy, wiggling baby in his hands. He stepped into the bathroom. "Hey, bud, it's okay," he said softly to the baby. The baby did *not* agree. He started yelling louder about how bad his backside felt and probably how hungry he was.

James looked around the bathroom. How was he going to do this? If he cleaned the baby up first, he'd get the kid dirty again when he picked him back up. He couldn't very well just lay him on the bathmat while James showered. Plus then *he'd* get dirty again when he picked the baby back up.

"Uh..."

Suddenly Harper was in the bathroom doorway. "So it's someone who knows you're a firefighter. Does that help narrow down who she might be?"

He reached for the roll of toilet paper, tearing off a long strip and trying to wipe... something. Anything. The baby was squawking now, and James knew they were maybe a minute away from outright crying. "All the women I've been with know I'm a firefighter, Harper," he said absently over the noise.

"You use that as a pickup line all the time?"

"It's one of my strongest selling points." He tried to wipe at his hand, but it was difficult to support the baby and wipe at the same time.

"That is so not true," she muttered.

"What?"

But before he could ask her what she meant by that, she stepped around him and leaned in to turn on the shower. He was momentarily distracted by how great her ass looked, and how, if he'd been on the other side of her, he would have been able to see down her shirt.

Damn, even a squalling, poop-covered baby couldn't get in the way of his attraction to this woman.

"Get in." She stepped back, clearly meaning he should get into the shower.

He glanced down at the baby. "Uh."

"Take him in with you."

James shrugged. That would work. He flashed her a grin. "You wanna take my underwear down or hold the poopy baby so I can?"

She lifted a brow. "I think you can get in with them on."

"Worth a try." He stepped over the edge of the tub, turning

so the spray would hit his back, blocking it from the baby at first.

With her nose wrinkled up in an incredibly adorable way, Harper reached in to unfasten his diaper.

James held the baby firmly against his chest, supporting his head and butt, so it took several swipes of her fingers over his chest, ribs, and abs to get the diaper off. It was the most she'd ever touched him, and it was the most ridiculous thing ever, but he was newly aroused by the time the poopy diaper was free, and Harper was holding it in by the very, very edge with one finger and thumb on each hand, looking like she'd never been so disgusted.

It was pretty bad.

And James still wanted her.

Which said a lot about his state of lust for this woman.

"You want to get in with us?" he asked with a grin. "You need to clean up, too."

"Sure, I'll just strip down and shower with you and this baby that just showed up on your doorstep last night," she said. "That wouldn't be the weirdest thing I've ever done."

He chuckled. The first time he'd seen her, she'd had her hair up in a neat bun, her glasses on, had been wearing a cream-colored skirt that flared at the bottom, a button-up baby-blue shirt, and a shawl. He hadn't even realized that women still wore shawls. But sure as fuck, the hot, young, God-I-hope-she's-a-librarian across the landing had been wearing a shawl. And he'd gotten hard.

"It's not like my hands are gonna be wandering anywhere they shouldn't," he said. The water was warm but not too hot, and he eased back a little, letting some of it run over his shoulders and down his chest, getting the baby just a little wet. The baby's eyes widened, and he quieted at this new stimulation.

"Yeah, well, I think maybe I need to do something with *this*." Harper started for the door.

"There's a garbage bag outside on the landing. I'll take them all down later. We have a lot of stuff we need to get." A diaper pail was only one thing.

She glanced back. "We?"

Right. Him. This was *his* thing. The baby had been left for him. Even if it wasn't *his*. Which it really might be. He shrugged. "Me."

But her shoulders relaxed, and she blew out a breath. "I'll help," she said. "Of course."

She would. Even if this meant that another woman would be coming into his life. He wasn't too thrilled to think that he'd made a baby with someone who would just drop the kid off in a basket. He was pretty fucking pissed about that, when he thought about it, no matter who she was, and especially if he *knew* this woman. But if he *had* gotten someone pregnant, who had freaked out about it to the point that she'd felt she had no other options, then he had some work to do convincing her otherwise. If he could figure out who she was.

But that didn't change what he wanted to happen with Harper.

Somehow he was going to have to prove that to her.

Making her tend to dirty diapers and waking up with baby puke on her neck might not be the best way of talking her into giving this all a try, though.

James concentrated on the baby in his arms rather than the woman who was tending to the dirty diapers. It would be easy for her to slip across the landing and shower in her own apartment. She could get dressed, make coffee, a whole bunch of stuff that would make her more prepared to face all this before she had to go to work.

Or she might not come back over here at all.

Ever.

He wouldn't blame her. This was a strange—at best—situation and not one of *her* making. This wasn't an olive tree or a bearded dragon. This was... big.

With his hand over the baby's head, blocking his face from the direct spray, James moved back a little farther into the water, letting it run over the baby's back. He squirmed but didn't seem unhappy. James turned, so the water would clean the dirty parts and miss the little one's face. He ran his hand up and down the baby's back, trying to help remove the mess, but as the kid got wetter, he also got slipperier. The baby squirmed, and James tightened his grip. He couldn't hold him too firmly, and he couldn't let go of his head, so he couldn't really move his hand away from his lower back and butt. He hoped the spray would get all the stuff that needed to wash away.

A moment later, Harper was back in the bathroom, shutting the door behind her. "Is he warm enough?" she asked.

She had her phone out.

"Are you Googling how to give a baby a shower?" James asked.

"Well, I just thought—" She'd pulled the shower curtain back and stopped midsentence, staring.

James lifted his eyebrows. "Harper?"

"Uh." It took her a second, but her gaze found his... "Yeah?"

"Everything okay?" He looked down.

"I just..." She swallowed. "I didn't think that those could get any clingier."

He looked down again. To his boxer briefs. They were black, so they hadn't turned see-through in the water like white might have, but the water had definitely caused them to mold to his body like a second skin. He looked up at her and grinned. "I guess you could have just taken them off of me after all."

She pulled in a breath through her nose, not even pretending not to take a good, long look. "All of this is just so..."

"Huge?" he supplied. Helpfully. Kind of. If he hadn't meant

it with every single ounce of innuendo he was sure she could hear it in his tone.

She snorted at that. And James fell a little harder for her. This side of Harper, when he knew the polished, sophisticated side was so much more natural for her, was fucking sexy as hell. It was intimate. She was vulnerable here, not put together, in no way on her usual turf. This was stuff she didn't show most people. He loved it.

"I was going to say unexpected," she said. She lifted her eyes to meet his gaze. "But yes, huge does apply."

He gave her a wicked grin. Then the baby decided to stretch and wiggle.

James felt his hand slip slightly, and he instantly focused back on the slick bundle in his arms.

"Oh my gosh!" Harper's hand came out instinctively, and she pressed it over James's on the baby's back.

"He's slippery," James said. "I was just trying to figure out to actually wash him and hang on at the same time."

Harper paused for a moment, then she muttered, "Well, dammit," and stepped over the side of the tub.

James was sure his surprise showed on his face. But he was also sure it was instantly replaced by delight.

She looked up at him. "So you got me in the shower with you."

"That was actually pretty easy."

She gave a soft laugh. "All you needed was a baby."

"You think I didn't notice that it happened *after* you'd fully ogled me, Professor?" he asked.

Her cheeks got a little pink, but her lips still curled. "A gentleman would have never mentioned that."

"Who the fuck said there was a gentleman here?" he said, dropping his voice to a husky near-growl.

She was in his shower. After having been in his bed overnight. And he'd yet to really touch her. This was testing him in ways he'd never imagined, yet he was having a hell of a good time.

Baby poop aside.

Her eyes widened. "You can't swear in front of the baby."

James looked down. "If this kid's first word is fuck, I'll give you fifty bucks."

She smiled. Her hand was still on top of his on the baby's back. "You hold him, and I'll wash him."

Okay, that was going to be torturous. Her hands were going to be brushing all over James's chest and torso too as she did this. There would be no real way to avoid that. "Or you could hold him, and I could do the washing," he said.

Harper looked up at him, and he saw a glint of mischief there that shot an arrow of heat straight to his cock.

"You think I don't realize that to wash him I'll be getting you pretty soapy, too?" she asked.

James shook his head slowly. "I'm going to have to take that to mean you're good with that situation?"

"Maybe." Her gaze slid over him again.

Maybe, his ass.

James had no hope of hiding his erection, but he was totally fine with that.

Suddenly the buttoned-up, gorgeous, too-good-for-him professor from Apartment 3B had turned into a vixen. Who was standing in his shower in her pajamas. With baby spit-up in her hair.

"Well, Professor, you're not going to hear any complaints about you soaping me up," he said. "Especially as you get wetter and wetter."

Her eyes flew to his, and he gave her a knowing grin. So she was *wet*. Very, very good to know.

"What?" she asked, her voice a little choked and her cheeks a lot pinker.

He looked down at the front of her pajama top. She wasn't

directly in the shower spray—yet—but the front of her shirt was getting wet all the same. And it was thin. And a light green color. That wasn't quite as good as white would have been, but he could see skin and the darker pink of her nipples. The nipples that were nice and tight. From the water or the situation or his gaze, he didn't know, or care. The fabric was every bit as clingy as his briefs were, and she looked like a hot coed who'd just been doused at a fund-raising car wash rather than the linguistics professor handing out term papers in a lecture hall.

Harper glanced down, too, and her eyes went wide. She covered herself with her hands instinctively, and James chuckled. "You're gonna need those hands for soaping."

She drew in a quick breath, squeezed her eyes shut, then dropped her hands.

His body reacted, but he forced himself to focus.

"Soap's behind me."

"We need to get baby soap," she said absently, as she attempted to reach past him without leaning in.

Because if she leaned in, she'd touch him.

Of course she couldn't reach, and she had to not only lean but take a step forward.

"We can do that later," he said of the baby soap. He didn't use anything too crazy, though. Nothing with major perfumes or anything in it, so he thought for one bath they'd be okay.

He loved that Harper was reacting to him and obviously feeling some of the heat and want that he was, but he had to grit his teeth and look up at the ceiling as she finally reached past him, her breast grazing his side— her hard-tipped, nearly-naked-in-that-pajama-top breast.

She leaned back with the bar of soap in hand and looked up at him. She was right there, her sweet, wet body nearly against his. If not for the baby in his arms, he'd have her up against the tile wall and be driving deep in minutes.

But if not for the baby in his arms, she might not be here in the first place.

Except...

"Just so it's perfectly clear, in case there is any doubt for either of us, the other night when I was on my way over here from the bar," he said, "I fully intended to come to your front door and knock like I always did. But when you answered, I wasn't going to say anything except, 'put your glasses on,' if you had them off. Then I was going to kiss the hell out of you, strip you naked, and take you on your kitchen table."

She sucked in a sharp breath, her eyes widened, and her lips parted.

"And if that fire hadn't broken out and I'd had the pleasure of giving you five orgasms in one night, this baby still would have showed up, and we would still have to be figuring this out. I would just already know how sweet you taste and how fucking good you feel and how you sound when you come and if you prefer all fours or riding me." He couldn't move his hands to touch her, so he simply leaned in, putting his forehead on hers. "So what I'm saying is that the only thing different *now* is that we're going to need to buy a crib *today* and get this kid to sleep early, and you're going to have to be a little quieter than I'd like when you come so that we don't wake him up."

She was breathing fast, the puffs of air coming quickly against his lips. But she didn't step back or push him away. And she didn't deny anything he'd just said. So James tipped his head and met her lips.

He couldn't kiss her the way he really wanted to, but he felt that it was vital in that moment to show her that *not* kissing her simply wasn't an option anymore. Baby or not.

She made a sweet little whimpering sound against his lips and pressed close for just a moment.

And that was enough.

For now.

She wanted it. She knew he wanted it. And they were, by God, going to make this happen.

After baby soap and cribs and stuff.

James straightened, leaned back, and then turned the baby to face her.

Looking slightly dazed, Harper focused on the baby. A tiny smile curled her lips as she looked at him, and that kicked James in the gut. The baby was freaking her out a little—well, the *idea* of the baby and the complications that were going to come with him—but the way she smiled at the little guy made James melt a little.

Yes, melt.

That wasn't manly.

He didn't care.

It was the same way he'd felt when he'd seen her feed Henry bugs the first time. She hadn't liked doing it. She hadn't chosen to have to do it. But she'd done it. For him. For Henry, mostly. But because James had brought a lizard and bugs into her life, and instead of telling him to go to hell, she'd just done what needed to be done.

It was the same way he'd felt when he'd first seen her with Fred. She sure didn't seem like the type to encourage puppy kisses, but the first time she'd picked him up from James after the dog had spent the day with him, she'd squatted in a pale yellow dress and heels and let the dog climb up into her lap, licking and wiggling, clearly over the moon to see her. She'd not only allowed the kisses, she'd leaned in for them.

A woman had never made him melt before.

Not because that wasn't a manly thing to feel or acknowledge or whatever, but because there just hadn't been a woman who had been like Harper before.

Women in the past made him laugh. They turned him on. They sometimes even did things like make him breakfast or show up at the station with brownies.

Harper had never once shown up at the station. She'd also never made him brownies. But he still liked everything about her more than he'd ever liked another woman. This was a softer feeling, something that he'd actually *seen* on the faces of the men he knew who had become husbands and fathers.

Harper Broussard was the one for him.

But he knew she didn't know that yet.

Harper smiled and talked to the baby as she soaped his feet and legs. James held him firmly as she ran her hands over the baby's belly and arms and then used just the pads of her fingers on his face, even soaping his hair. James turned when she was done, letting the water rinse the soap bubbles away, then pivoted back and was about to turn the baby so she could get his back.

Just then, however, he peed.

On Harper.

Since they were in the shower it was much less messy than it would have been otherwise. But because she was still wearing clothes, they did end up with more than shower water on them.

"You should definitely take those off the next time we do this," James said, trying not to laugh.

She sighed. "We need to buy a baby bathtub today, too."

They probably did. "They make those?" Of course they did. But he thought this shower thing had turned out okay in a few ways.

"They do."

"Damn. The guy who invented those clearly hadn't had the pleasure of female help showering with a baby."

"It was probably a woman."

He grinned and turned the baby's back to her.

Finally, the kid was clean, and Harper stepped out first, grabbing a towel and holding it open. He handed the baby over, and she wrapped him up. James ducked his head back under the spray and quickly shampooed and soaped, even with his underwear on. He was tempted to strip them off now. What would she do? She'd freaking ogle him again, and he'd walk around all day with a hard-on, but that was pretty much already where they were with things.

He shut the water off and pulled the curtain back completely.

Harper was just standing there holding the towel-wrapped infant.

He lifted a brow.

She watched the water running off his body.

He lifted a hand and ran it through his wet hair.

She swallowed hard.

"I'm going to need that towel," he said. He hadn't thought to bring another in from the closet in the hall.

"He might pee... or worse... on me."

"He might."

"Also..."

"Also what?"

"Five orgasms in one night?"

He grinned and stepped out of the tub. He moved toward her, and she backed up until she was against the door with nowhere to go.

He was dripping all over the floor, and the bundle of baby and terrycloth was between them, but James braced a hand on the door over her head, stretching his wet, mostly naked body over her, and leaned in. "Oh, yeah," he said. Then he took her chin with his finger and thumb and kissed her again.

He was able to go a little deeper and a little longer this time, sliding his tongue over her bottom lip and then in along her tongue, when she opened with a needy moan.

He pulled back after just a few seconds, though. He took the baby from her, enjoying the dazed look on her face again and then taking the towel from around the baby and laying him down on the pile of towels he'd been using as a changing area.

He quickly put a new diaper on the baby to prevent any more accidents then dried off before picking the baby up and standing. He turned to Harper.

Who had been, apparently, watching the entire thing.

"I need to get out of this wet underwear," he said. He dragged his gaze over her and the nearly see-through top, the tantalizingly hard-tipped breasts, the pants that clung to her legs.

"I'm, um..." She crossed her arms over her chest. Then dropped her arms. Then sighed. "I'm going to go shower and change clothes."

"Okay." He could let her go now, because he felt more confident that she'd be back.

"Can one of your friends go to the store with you today?"

"One of my friends?"

"You have a ton of friends who are dads," she pointed out. "They'd be great resources about what you need to get, yes? Plus another pair of hands for him." Her gaze dropped to the baby.

Yeah, he did have friends who would be great resources.

He didn't want them. He wanted Harper.

"I can't bother them," he said.

That was completely untrue. Any of them would jump to help him. Hell, all of them would. At once.

"You... can't?" she asked. "Or you don't want to?"

"I don't want to."

"You want to play house with me. You think that will make me more likely to... what? Sleep with you?"

"Oh, I think the chances of you sleeping with me are one hundred percent," James told her honestly but also with a teasing grin.

"Then why do you think I should hang out with you and the baby today?"

"Because it's been fun so far."

"You've been pooped on, and I've been puked and peed on," she pointed out.

"And I've gotten to wake up next to you, see your almost naked nipples, and finally kiss you," he said. "I'd take as much of the other stuff as needed to have those things happen."

Her cheeks got pink. "Finally?" she asked softly.

"You're lying if you say you don't know that I've wanted to kiss you for a long time, Professor."

She pressed her lips together, studying his face. "I have to teach that class, and I have a meeting after. But I can shop with you before that, and I can come over as soon as I'm done."

He nodded. "I'll take it."

She didn't say anything else. She just chewed on her bottom lip—the lip that he wanted to suck on almost as badly as he wanted to suck on her nipples—and then she turned and left the apartment.

He looked down at the baby. "I don't know who you are, exactly," he said. "And I realize I'm changing your diapers and feeding you and stuff. But I might just owe you one."

The baby hiccupped then farted.

James laughed. Best wingman ever, and he couldn't even talk.

4

———

She was crazy.

She wanted to be at home with James changing diapers rather than lecturing to bright young minds about the connection between language and societal change.

They'd gone shopping earlier and had gotten everything they needed, including a carrier for the baby that James could strap to his body and still take Ami for a walk. They'd all seemed very happy and settled, and Harper had found it difficult to leave them.

That was crazy.

Almost as crazy as how quickly James had settled into all of this.

"Harper!"

She turned as she was almost to her office door. Her friend and fellow professor, Dr. Celia Ownsby, was coming toward her with a huge smile.

"Hi, Celia."

"Hi. Hoping you're free for lunch." Celia gave her a grin. "I haven't heard how the big date with James went."

Harper had been expecting her friend to find her and ask

for details. She'd been so disappointed that their date had been interrupted, that she hadn't texted or called her one true girlfriend about it. And then James had brought a baby home.

It seemed like that had happened a week ago in some ways.

Harper really wanted to get back to the apartment. But she knew that was ridiculous. She had a meeting in a little over an hour. Going home in between class and that meeting was silly. By the time she got there, she'd only have a few minutes to check in on everything.

Just last night she'd been worried about getting too involved anyway.

Of course, it had only been six months ago that she'd been thinking she should avoid getting involved with James Reynaud altogether.

Now, here she was.

Her phone dinged with a text, and she swiped to open the message.

It was a photo of the baby lying on James's couch, bracketed between a denim-clad thigh, that had to be James, and a shaggy little dog lying with his back pressed to the baby's other side.

Harper felt her heart swell and everything in her demand she go directly home.

Except her mouth. Thankfully.

She looked up at Celia. "Lunch would be great."

Harper tucked her phone into her purse without sending so much as a heart-eyes emoji back. In spite of the fact that she couldn't quite shake the thought that James had just sent her a perfect photo. Three things she could quite easily fall madly in love with.

She was already in love with the dog.

And the guy who belonged to that thigh... well, he'd been wearing her down for a few months now.

It was the affection and protectiveness she felt for that little bundle in the middle that was startling. It was just a natural maternal instinct she hadn't been in touch with before this. It didn't *mean* anything other than her estrogen levels were high or something.

Harper and Celia walked to the campus cafeteria. It wasn't glamorous but it was close and had very good chicken salad. They picked out their food, scanned their faculty badges, and chose a table near the windows, away from the noisier groups of eaters.

"So, how was it?" Celia asked without preamble, stirring sugar into her tea.

Harper sipped her water and thought about the entire evening with James. How had it been? Crazy. Unexpected in every single way. Sweet. Scary. They'd bonded. She'd thought they were already bonded over Ami, but the baby? That had been a new level. Partly because he was a human being and that put everything on a new *holy-crap* level. But also because he was more work. And neither of them knew what they were doing. It was different with the dog. She knew now that James had had dogs growing up, and her grandmother had owned a dog and—

"Harper?"

She focused on Celia. "What? Oh… yes?"

"Wow, that must have been some date." Celia put her spoon down and leaned in. "It was that good? I mean, did he just put you up against the wall and knock the plaster down or what?"

Harper felt her cheeks heat. She wasn't a prude. She read very erotic fiction, and she was a huge proponent of women's sexuality being open and honest and fully satisfying. She wasn't a virgin. She talked about men and sex with her friends.

But she'd never felt this way about a man. Especially one she wasn't really dating and hadn't slept with.

She felt like she and James were intimate on another level, and they hadn't even seen each other fully naked. Yet.

Of course that sent her thoughts spinning to the shower

and how the water had made his boxer briefs mold to his body —his big, hard body. And how he'd told her he'd intended to give her *five* orgasms. And how he'd kissed her.

"Holy. Crap." Celia was staring at her.

Harper could feel her cheeks were hot.

"I swear if I didn't know better, I'd think you *just* had sex with him before walking over here with me. You're flushed, and you looked dazed and happy and like you're totally floating."

Floating? She'd spent the morning cleaning up baby poop and puke and pee. The three P's. Then shopping for pacifiers and a crib and more diapers and all kinds of overwhelming necessities that filled James's apartment and made the whole thing feel even bigger than it had before.

Harper put her hands against her cheeks. "Do I?"

"He was good, huh?" Celia asked. "Wow. I mean, he *looks* like he'd be good. The firefighter body, the piano player fingers..." She shook her head and cut her grilled chicken sandwich in half. "I'm so jealous of you right now."

Harper laughed. She was tired. They hadn't really slept deeply or very long. She'd had puke in her hair and pee on her pants. She and the guy she had a huge crush on had been cleaning up poop together. Poop. But Celia was jealous of her.

"We didn't do the date," she confessed.

Celia finished chewing and swallowed. "Well, it wasn't a date, I guess. But you..." She frowned, really looking at Harper now. "Wait, you didn't *do* it? At all?"

Harper shook her head. She sighed. "He got called to a fire."

"But that was at least a couple of days ago."

"I know. He was there all night, slept a lot of the next day, went to work yesterday."

"Which leaves last night." Celia leaned in. "Don't tell me you changed your mind."

Harper shook her head quickly, reliving the feel of James's lips against hers. "No. Not at all."

"So what happened? Why haven't you jumped him yet?" Celia asked, biting into her sandwich.

Harper realized she needed to eat, or her break was going to be over and she'd be starving in her meeting. She took a bite of her chicken salad and washed it down. "His baby son showed up."

Celia froze midchew. She stared at Harper. Then frowned. Then chewed quickly, swallowing, wiping her lips and then said, *"What?"*

Harper twirled her fork in her chicken and mayo. "Yeah. There was just suddenly this baby on his doorstep last night, and, obviously, that took up a lot of our time and attention."

"He has a *baby*?"

Harper lifted a shoulder. "Yes."

Celia set her sandwich down. She leaned in. "Does this change things?"

Harper nodded. "Yeah."

Celia looked disappointed. "That's too bad. I know you really liked him."

Harper tipped her head. "You think so?"

Her friend smiled. "You talk about him all the time. He makes you laugh. You always have this affectionately exasperated air when you talk about him, but you definitely like him. And I know you were looking forward to getting him naked."

Harper gave a little choked laugh. Celia had told her that she should sleep with James after the olive tree situation. She said she had never seen Harper that delighted.

Delighted. That was the word Celia had used.

Celia taught English composition. The woman shared a love of words and agreed that words mattered and that people should choose them carefully. It was something that had first forged their friendship over salads in this very cafeteria shortly after Harper had joined the faculty. They'd only known one another a little over a year, but Harper felt that if Celia said something like she'd seemed "delighted" then that was worth considering.

"Well, it has changed how I feel." Harper pressed her lips together and shook her head. Admitting it out loud made it more real. But finally she said, "After seeing him taking care of the baby, I like him even more."

She'd been prepared—so she'd thought—to date a man who was a father, perhaps. Or to date one who was open to adoption. But to be attracted to him *being* a father... she hadn't experienced that before. It wasn't just the protectiveness that came out either. James already had showed that side. He was a firefighter. He protected people every single day. It wasn't the sweet side. She'd seen that, too. With Ami. Even with Henry. With *her*, honestly.

It was actually the way he'd just done what needed to be done. He'd picked the baby up and come straight to her, out of habit. But when it had become clear this was *not* her forte, he'd taken over. He'd been the decision maker between them. He'd been the one to assume the responsibility.

That was really damned attractive. Especially when his youth and laid-back attitude and tendency to—seemingly, anyway—need help with things were some of what was making her hold back from him.

He'd blasted right through those hesitations in less than twenty-four hours.

Celia's grin was big and bright and immediate. "Oh, that's amazing."

"You don't think that's crazy?"

"No. You've always been attracted to his caregiver side."

Harper took a deep breath and nodded. "And the kisses were pretty great, too."

Celia's eyes went round. "You *kissed*?"

"Yes." Harper couldn't help her huge smile now. "I mean, they were pretty short, but they were sweet. And hot." Had she just sighed? That was strange. But that had to have been her. "And he says that we're still going to do everything he'd planned on the other night."

"Well, yeah," Celia said, picking her sandwich up. "I mean, just 'cuz there's a baby, doesn't mean there's no sex to be had. Babies sleep. Married couples manage to have sex after they have kids. It can be done."

Babies slept. Of course they did. This one had slept really well last night, in fact. Maybe he would again tonight... And when had she gotten so hot and horny?

Oh yeah, about the time the firefighter across the hall had brought her an olive tree.

"Harper?"

"Huh?"

Celia laughed. "Wow. I hope James can measure up to whatever you have going on in your head. Good thing he knows about the books. Hope he's read a couple."

Harper blushed hard at that. He had, in fact, borrowed a couple. A couple based on her recommendations. A couple of her favorites. He said he was an avid reader and that they often had a lot of downtime at the station. She hadn't asked if he'd finished them, but they'd been back on her table. And two more had been missing.

If he now had an idea of what she found sexy in books and was willing to...

"Dr. Broussard? Hi."

Harper's thoughts were interrupted by one of her students approaching from the main counter.

"Sophie! Hi!" Harper was thrilled to see the girl.

Sophie Duncan had been in her class last semester. She was nineteen and was putting herself through school. She was one of Harper's brightest students and had been one of Harper's favorites. Intelligent. Studious. Always in the front row. A copious notetaker. Sophie was a driven, type-A perfectionist who had her eyes already set on grad school, even as a fresh-man. Harper also knew that she was doing this all on her own. Harper didn't know much about the girl's parents, but she knew that Sophie was here on a full-ride scholarship, which was the only reason she was managing Loyola at all, and she took it extremely seriously.

"How are you?" Harper asked. "I haven't seen you much this semester." In fact, she hadn't seen the girl at all, and she'd been concerned enough to check with the registrar's office to be sure Sophie was still enrolled. She'd wanted to do something to keep in touch with the girl this semester when she didn't have her in class. She was bright, but putting herself through school far from home was a strain, and Harper had seen students like her burn out.

"Oh, fine," Sophie said. "Really busy. Crazy, really. But things are back on track now." She smiled. "How about you? Anything new?"

Harper almost laughed. What a question. "I'm okay," she finally answered. "Busy. A little crazy, too."

Sophie nodded. "Well, if anyone can handle it, you can. I've always really admired you." She blushed and ducked her head slightly as if she hadn't meant to say that. "I hope to be like you someday."

Sophie's words surprised Harper. Not the admiration in general, maybe. She knew the younger woman looked up to her. But to hear, directly, that she was a role model made Harper feel good. Of course. But it also came with a sense of responsibility.

What kind of person did she want Sophie to see when she looked at Harper? Was there any part of her life that she *wouldn't* want the younger woman to know about?

No.

Including being there for James—as a friend, at least, and

possibly more—when he needed support. She should be proud of being there for him. And the baby.

Harper smiled at Sophie. "I'm really flattered by that. Thank you."

"Of course." Sophie looked mildly embarrassed, but she returned Harper's smile. "I'm eager to be in your class again next semester."

"Oh, I'm glad I'll have you again," Harper said sincerely. The girl was clearly enthusiastic about subject matter that Harper loved. "I was actually hoping to run into you and chat."

She hadn't wanted to call Sophie directly. That felt too familiar without Sophie giving Harper her phone number personally. But it was a small enough campus that Harper had expected to see Sophie and had hoped that Sophie would come to her at some point even though she wasn't in Harper's class.

Harper went on. "I'm in need of a research assistant. It would only be a few hours, but I have some grant dollars to use to pay a small stipend. It would give you a little money and could be done on your own time. The deadline is several months down the road, so it's not a big rush. And it would look good on your résumé. I was wondering if you'd be interested? I can't think of anyone who's more willing to talk and read and write about all the stuff I love than you are." And Harper would have a chance to keep an eye on the girl.

Not that Sophie needed babysitting, exactly, but Harper sensed that Sophie could use someone asking her how she was once in a while and making sure she got enough sleep and maybe buying her a sandwich now and then. And if Sophie was in her office on a regular basis, Harper could make sure Sophie was hearing that she was bright and doing a great job and that Harper admired her, too.

Sophie's face lit up. "Oh my gosh! Thank you. I'd love to talk more about that!"

Harper gave Sophie a huge, sincere smile. "Wonderful. Come by my office any time. I'll keep the spot open for you."

Sophie looked sincerely touched. "Thank you so much, Professor Broussard." She smiled at Celia then at Harper again. "Well, I'd better get going."

"See you soon."

"You have some grant dollars to pay a stipend for a research assistant?" Celia asked.

Harper nodded. "I will have some grant dollars for the project, and paying a research assistant could be part of that. Once I add that in."

Celia gave her a knowing smile. "Do you really need a research assistant?"

"Hey, I have a baby at home now. I could definitely use an assistant," Harper said, giving her friend a little shrug. And a smile. Giving an enthusiastic student some of her work would benefit them both. It was a win win.

Celia laughed softly. "And it looks like you're taking care of a nineteen-year-old at the same time."

Harper watched Sophie walking away, and she felt her heart swell. She might not know how to buy a car seat for a baby, but she knew how to encourage a young woman who was just getting started going after her passion and looking at her future.

Maybe she had a little nurturing in her after all.

"WELL, YOU CAN'T TAKE HIM TO THE ER IF YOU DON'T WANT COPS involved."

James turned to look at Logan and Caleb. The two men were lounging on opposite ends of his sofa while he paced the living room with the baby. Who was no longer sleeping peacefully. He also wasn't wet. Or hungry. He was just yelling for no apparent reason.

It made James want Harper. Which was funny, actually. Last night had, in no way, convinced him that she was a baby person. In fact, for the most part, she'd seemed befuddled and had been following *his* lead. Which had given him a shot of confidence and was stupidly hot. She was easily the most capable woman he'd ever been attracted to, yet last night she'd needed *his* guidance. He liked that. He liked feeling like they were more on the same level. He found her sophistication hot as hell. He also found her vulnerability hot as hell.

He was pretty well enamored with her all around. And he was fine with that.

But right now, as the baby cried, and his friends acted amused and lifted not one finger to help, he wished she was here, for sure.

"I definitely don't want the cops involved." He'd already explained that. Whoever left the baby with him had chosen James. He was willing to give her a chance to explain herself before he said anything to the cops

He looked down at the baby.

Except that he wasn't going to say anything to the cops. He had this handled.

The baby gave a particularly loud squawk and he amended the thought to *he had this handled with Harper's help.*

"Should I just call a pediatrician's office?" he asked.

Logan shook his head. "How are you going to do that? You don't know his birthday. You know nothing about his actual birth. You don't know anything about his mother—even if you knew who she was. Which you don't."

Caleb chuckled.

Yeah, his friends were very entertained by the fact he now had a baby that presumably belonged to him, and that he was having trouble narrowing down who the mother could possibly be.

He thought he had it down to two.

He'd need help tracking down one who had been a tourist, and he thought maybe she was from Wisconsin. Or Wyoming. And it didn't really matter because both were pretty big states.

The other was the sister of one of his firefighter brothers. It wasn't a fellow firefighter he was particularly friendly with, and James was sure that would be even more the case once Ethan found out James had showed his sister some true Southern hospitality. But he'd been hoping Caleb might poke around and find out if Ethan's sister had been expecting in the past few months. Of course, Caleb had pointed out that she probably wouldn't have just left the baby on a doorstep if her family knew she was pregnant. The baby's sudden absence would have been hard to explain. Which had reminded James that Ethan's sister had been in town from Oklahoma. Ethan might not have known she was pregnant. Possibly. Maybe. But she was last on James's list. And not just because he wanted to avoid any hint to Ethan that he'd slept with his sister. But mostly because he wanted to avoid any hint to Ethan that he'd slept with his sister.

Logan and Caleb thought it was all hilarious. But they could also empathize. They'd both had plenty of those kinds of flings. And Logan had, actually, knocked up a one-night stand. He was now happily married to her and the father of her two girls from her first marriage and their own baby girl. But it had all started with one hot night that wasn't supposed to be more than that.

"That's going to be a problem," James agreed.

"Yeah, that will raise a ton of red flags," Caleb said. "You can't just waltz in there with a baby you know nothing about. You don't even know his name."

James looked down. No, he didn't. "What if he doesn't have a name?"

"He needs a name," Logan agreed.

"He looks like a Nathan to me," Caleb said.

James frowned. "We're not just going to slap some name on him."

Caleb lifted a brow. "We're not?"

"Names should mean something." Was he channeling Harper? Yep. But if they were going to give the baby a name, then she should be a part of it.

And she'd probably kill him if she wasn't.

And then change the name anyway.

The dog's name meant something. Harper had even insisted on knowing the actual type of olive tree he'd brought over. She would definitely want to be a part of this. And he wanted her to be.

"Anyway, back to the ER thing," James said, shifting the baby so he was propped up against his left shoulder.

"I guess you *can* waltz *in* with the baby," Caleb said. "But you probably won't waltz back *out* with him. Even if you try to tell them he's yours, they'll want proof before they let you take him back home with you, if you can't give them any other information. A doctor's office will be the same way. You'll be throwing red flags up all over the place."

"So what should I do? I want to be sure he's okay. He seems all right from what I can tell, but I'd like to have a professional opinion. And at some point he'll need to go to the doctor for *something*."

Just then there was a knock on the door. James frowned and started in that direction, but Caleb stretched to his feet and beat James there. He opened the door for his girlfriend, Lexi.

"Hey, guys," she said with a big smile as Caleb pulled her in and kissed the top of her head.

James's eyes widened. "Hey."

Her attention zeroed in on the baby, and she came toward James, holding her arms out. "Let's see him."

"You told Lexi?" James asked, surrendering the unhappy infant to her.

She started cooing and patting him, bouncing him as she walked.

Caleb shrugged. "Of course."

"I didn't really think that I'd let everyone in on this until—"

"She's a nurse," Caleb reminded him. "And she's a mom. She can give you some good advice and info here. Plus she knows a pediatrician who will trust her to vouch for you and keep things on the down low until we figure it all out."

James let all protests die with that. In fact, he felt a rush of relief. "Right. Okay."

Lexi smiled at him. "Also, I need to swab you."

"You need to what?"

"DNA test."

"*What* is going on?"

They all swung to face the doorway, where Harper had just come in. She was staring at everyone, looking confused and a little irritated.

"Hey, Professor," James said, stupidly happy to see her.

"What is going on?" she repeated. Her eyes were on Lexi and the baby. She looked worried and wary. "Who are these people?"

She'd met Caleb only once, when he'd stopped by to grab some tools from James. She had no idea who these people were, and the possessiveness in her eyes when she looked at Lexi made James want to smile. He didn't know if it was because of the baby or because of *him*, but Harper felt like there was another woman on *her* turf. He liked that.

"This is Lexi, Caleb's..." James looked at his friend. "Girlfriend?"

"For sure," Caleb said, his eyes on Lexi.

Lexi gave him a smile that was hot and sweet at the same time. "Yeah."

"This is Caleb," James said with a slight eye roll. Caleb and Lexi were a fantastic couple. In fact, they'd been a fantastic couple long before either of them admitted they even *were* a couple.

James was envious of them. But as he looked at Harper, he realized that if he knew she was as crazy about him as Lexi was about Caleb, he'd be strutting around and making sure everyone knew it, too.

"And this is Logan," he said, gesturing to the other man. "A couple of the dads that you suggested I call," he reminded her.

Harper came into the room, still frowning. "I see." Her eyes were still on Lexi. "Seems like even with all the advice, things aren't exactly smooth sailing."

James stifled a grin. Yeah, she was feeling possessive.

Even though Lexi was younger than Harper by probably a good eight years, she got a knowing look on her face. She came over to Harper and offered the baby to her. "He's fussy."

Harper took him without the look of trepidation in her eyes that had seemed constant last night. She cuddled him up against her neck, talking to him softly and rocking him back and forth, even as she continued to study Lexi.

James went hard instantly.

Damn.

And damn if the baby didn't start to settle down as Harper stroked his back.

Lexi gave her a smile. "I'm a registered nurse," she said. "I work in the ER, but I feel confident in doing an exam. If that's okay with you. Then if there's anything to be concerned about, I have some resources we can tap into."

Harper looked over at James.

"We were just discussing that it will seem strange, and likely problematic, for the ER staff or a physician if we don't know more about him when we take him in."

"Well, we can't just never take him to the doctor," Harper said. "How old do you think he is?" she asked Lexi.

"Maybe a couple weeks?" Lexi said. "Not much over that. He's not smiling yet, but James said he's sleeping eight hours at night and eating well. He's turning his head, but not lifting it. And he's maybe seven or eight pounds? We need to weigh him." She shrugged. "It's hard to pinpoint, of course. Babies are different, just like adults are. But he isn't more than a month."

Harper frowned. "But if we don't know how old he is, it's hard to know if he's on track. The sleeping thing, for instance. We won't know if that's normal or something to be concerned about."

"He seems fine otherwise," Lexi said. "But yes. It would be better if we knew when he was born, if he was premature at all. We need to monitor his weight and growth from here on for sure, though."

"What we need is to get the information from his *mother,*" Harper said matter-of-factly. She looked at James. "You need to track this woman down. And have her sign over custody to you if she wants nothing to do with him. But you need to do everything you can to find her. We might want to think about hiring a private investigator. Then if you can't find her, we need to get an attorney and look into what comes next, if there's a way for us to become foster parents, or something. But we need to figure this out. Now."

James couldn't help it. He grinned. That firm, no-nonsense tone of voice was the Harper he knew. Plus her continued use of "we" made him happier than he would have expected. Not to mention that she had not suggested they turn the baby over to social services in the event they couldn't find his mother. She didn't seem to be entertaining the idea that he should be with anyone other than *them,* no matter whether they found his mom or not. He might be the one who could step in and handle things like blow-out diapers, but Harper was an intelligent, extremely capable woman who could help him with the other details. Like attorneys. And math homework. When it was time for that.

He really wanted her to still be around when it was time for that.

"We do," he agreed. He looked from her big brown eyes to the baby who was now sucking on his fist with his nose nuzzled against Harper's neck.

Yeah, he'd be pretty content right in that spot, too.

"What do you need to examine him?" Harper asked Lexi, breaking eye contact with James after a long moment.

"Let's get some towels and blankets to pad the table," Lexi said, shifting into professional gear. "Do you have a scale?" she asked James.

"A scale?" he repeated.

"To weigh things?" Lexi asked.

"I do," Harper said.

"You'll have to just step on it without him and then with him, and we'll use the difference," Lexi said.

Harper nodded and turned to head for her apartment. James started after her.

"Need help?"

Harper turned to him. "To step on a scale?"

He lifted a shoulder. "Yeah."

"No."

"I can... come anyway."

"I will not be telling you what I weigh, James," Harper said.

He let his gaze travel over her blatantly. "Not too much for me to lift up against the wall, Professor."

Instead of blushing or even shooting a glance in the direction of their audience, she said, "Good thing, since I've got some *shower*-wall ideas after last night." Then she looked at the doorknob.

Grinning, James twisted it and pulled the door open for her.

"Stay here," she told him as she headed across the landing.

He was still grinning when he turned back to his friends.

"She can totally handle you, can't she?" Lexi asked, her hand on her hip, looking pleased and amused.

"Totally," James agreed.

"Shower-wall ideas after last night?" Logan asked.

"You're a charming son of a bitch," James told him. "But *I* managed to make a woman want me even when there were poopy baby diapers involved."

Caleb laughed, but Lexi shrugged. "I wanted Caleb the minute he offered to take a look at my piece-of-crap car, but the first time I *really* wanted to tear my clothes off was when I walked in and found him cleaning up poop."

Caleb looked surprised. "Really?"

"Really. Jack had been fussy all day and clearly wasn't feeling well, but you insisted I bring him over anyway and go to class. I came to your house that evening, and you had him and Shay in the tub and were cleaning up the floor. For about five seconds I wondered what would happen if I just took my clothes off."

Caleb's eyes darkened. "I would have..." He paused then blew out a breath. "Dammit. I wouldn't have done anything because we couldn't have left the kids."

She nodded. "Probably ninety percent of the reason I didn't do it."

"The other ten percent?" Caleb asked, his voice a little gruff.

"I didn't know how you felt."

Caleb didn't say anything. His jaw tightened. Then he nodded. "I didn't know how I felt either."

Lexi gave him a soft smile. "I know."

James turned wide eyes to Logan. Logan sighed. "Yes, they're always like this now."

James saw Caleb a lot at the station but didn't see him and Lexi together that much. Logan saw them as a couple more often because of the support group they all attended. It had started as a single-parent support group and was where Lexi and Caleb had met. Dana, Logan's wife, and Logan's brother, Gabe, had met there as well, and Logan had come to some of the family events with his brother and nephew. The group continued to meet but had evolved into more of a group of friends who still shared their parenting struggles but also supported each other through everything else life threw their way—the good and the bad.

"That was a long time ago," Caleb said, clearly still thinking about what Lexi had said.

She laughed softly. "Yeah."

"You've been wanting to take your clothes off for me for *that* long?"

"For sure."

Caleb cleared his throat and looked at James. "Sometimes they just cry. For no reason. It's okay. No one will die. You can't really hold them too much, no matter what some people say. Sleep whenever you can. No one really knows what they're doing, so don't worry too much."

"What are you doing?" James asked.

"Giving you all my advice now. Lexi and I are heading out as soon as she's done with the exam."

Logan laughed. "Kids are with Bea?"

"Yep," Caleb said simply.

"Bea?" James asked.

"Bea is from the support group," Lexi explained, her cheeks a little pink. "She takes the kids when neither of us can."

Great. So Caleb and Lexi were heading home to have sex. He didn't need to know that.

"So, Lexi," James said, changing the subject. "If he's two or three weeks old, that means he was conceived nine months ago, right?"

Lexi shook her head. "It's not that easy. A typical pregnancy is forty weeks, actually. He doesn't show signs of being prema-ture—not that we can tell that for sure—but assuming he wasn't, then he could have been born anywhere from maybe three weeks early to two weeks late."

"So thirty-eight to forty-three weeks ago?" Caleb asked, doing the calculation quickly.

She nodded. "Yeah."

James rolled his neck. "Okay, so that's... what? A five-week window?"

"Give or take," Lexi agreed.

James sighed. "Give or take how much?"

"Another week or two on either side."

Dammit.

"How many women is that?" Logan asked with a grin.

James shook his head. He didn't know for sure. It's not like he penciled the women in on a planner or even on his phone. He met women. He flirted. If he wanted to sleep with them and they wanted to sleep with him and the opportunity arose, they did. But sometimes those things didn't all line up.

"I don't know. Two? Three?" He couldn't be sure. But that was probably a decent guess.

"That's it?" Logan gave him a fake shocked look.

"I actually sleep alone almost every night," James said. "And I do see women more than once. Sometimes." James *wasn't* grinning. This was going to be a pain in the ass. He was going to have to actually get a calendar out and try to remember what he'd been doing and where ten months ago.

"So not a woman a week?" Logan asked.

James shrugged. "Between the station and the club, I get busy." He also had a lot of family in the area, and he did several projects here and there during his time off. He loved women, but he had other interests, too. "At least we can narrow it down to that window of time." James shoved a hand through his hair. "If only Harper had moved in ten months ago."

"Why would that have mattered?" Lexi asked. "Have you guys been sleeping together this whole time?"

James shook his head. "We haven't slept together at all. Yet."

"Has she been scaring women off?" Lexi asked with a little devious smile. "I like that. Has she been coming over to borrow a cup of sugar and then telling the women that you have an STD or something?"

James lifted a brow. "No, she has not. And that's very specific."

"It would be a great plan," Lexi said, lifting a shoulder. "I would have totally done something like that to women Caleb was with, given the chance."

Caleb coughed and shifted on the sofa.

Caleb and Lexi had been "friends" who helped each other out with childcare while Caleb worked and Lexi had been going to nursing school. Caleb hadn't been serious about any other woman in the time he'd known Lexi, but he'd tried to convince himself that she was too young for him and too good for him and not interested in him, and he'd spent some time with other women. Just never around Lexi.

"Well, no, Harper hasn't been scaring any women off. I haven't..." James cleared his throat. But what the hell? What was the harm in admitting this? "I haven't brought any women home since she moved in."

"You haven't brought any women here since she moved in," Logan said. "Or you haven't *been* with any women since the professor moved in?"

"Both."

"You haven't slept with any women since Harper moved in," Logan said one more time.

"No."

"Really?"

James spun to find Harper standing in the doorway again.

And he rolled his eyes. Logan had seen her there and had made that clarification so she would hear it.

James wasn't sure how to feel about her knowing it now. Because it seemed like an overreaction to what had been going on between them? Maybe. What had been going on between them had been mostly nothing for the first few months. But even from the beginning, it had seemed like *something*. And he honestly just hadn't had a strong enough craving for anyone else. He'd kicked himself about it for two months. He'd called himself ridiculous. He'd *forced* himself to hit on a few girls at the club. But when it came to the end of the night and the want-to-come-back-to-my-place moment, he hadn't been able to say the words.

Now, though, looking at Harper with her hair mussed, a little bit of worry and a lot of surprise crinkling the corners of her eyes, and the baby on her shoulder, he realized he didn't regret a thing.

"Yeah, really," he said with a shrug.

"That's..."

"I know," he agreed.

Everyone was quiet for a moment. Then Logan said, "So how are you planning to find them?"

"Them who?" Harper asked.

"The two or three women who could be the little man's mom," Logan said with a grin.

He was enjoying the fact that James was going to have to play detective to find the women he'd been with in the window of time the baby could have been conceived. James was going to tell Dana, Logan's wife, on him. Logan had been as much a playboy as James ever was.

"You have it narrowed down to two or three?" Harper asked.

She'd thought it might be more? For some reason that bugged him.

He hadn't brought any women home during the time he'd lived across from her.

"Would it have been better if there was just one, who I was really serious about?" he asked crossly.

She blinked at him, probably surprised that he'd been curt with her. He'd *never* been curt with her before. But honestly, did she *want* him to have had a serious relationship with another woman that could turn into something more now that there was a baby in the picture? Would this all be better if there was an ex that he might want to rekindle things with if they were going to co-parent?

"Uh, no," she said, shaking her head slowly. "I guess not."

The *uh* was a telltale sign. The professor with a doctorate in languages did not say, "uh." He nodded. "There's been no one serious in a really long time. And certainly not in the past year or so. I've gone out with a few women, yes, but I've been busy doing other things, too, Professor. So yeah, we've got a couple of women to track down and talk to."

She was watching him with wide eyes. "We?"

"Yeah, *we*. You're coming with me." He'd just made that decision.

"I am?" But she didn't look shocked. She looked intrigued.

"Yes. We're going to need passion and determination along with common sense and rational thinking to find this woman and get to the bottom of what's going on once and for all."

"You need me along for the common sense?"

"Oh, no, you're the passion and determination. I'll be there for the rational thinking," he said.

"You think *I've* got passion and determination about this?" she asked.

"I do."

"But *you* can be rational?"

"Of course. I don't have feelings for these women."

"But I do?"

He gave her a slow smile. "I think maybe you do, yeah."

She narrowed her eyes. "Because of the baby. I don't approve of her, whoever she is, just dropping him off on a doorstep."

That wasn't a denial of feeling passionate.

James nodded. "Sure. Protectiveness and possessiveness… of the baby."

Harper looked at him for a long moment. Then she said, "Okay. Maybe I should go along."

She should go along. They were in this together. He wanted her there to help ask the important questions, to see that he truly wasn't emotional about any of these women, and maybe to get a little peek into his life as they searched for this woman. Going back to the places where he'd met these ladies would show Harper a view of him outside his apartment and the landing between their places. And he suddenly wanted her to have that.

He was hoping to get a bigger view of her life and interests as well.

"And we need to stop referring to him as *the baby*," she said.

James couldn't hide his huge grin. He'd known it. "I agree. What should we name him?"

"Well, you know how I feel about names *meaning* something," Harper said.

He nodded. "I do."

"So his name should be meaningful. Something about him, or his situation, or this whole adventure."

James pretended to be thinking. "This is big. What means 'found by a handsome, sexy, musically gifted firefighter who learns to balance his heroic career and active social life with becoming an overnight super dad?'"

Harper lifted a brow. "Are you done?"

He shrugged. "I think that describes this kid's situation, don't you?"

She nodded. "That means the perfect name for him is Isaac."

James was surprised that she'd come up with that so quickly. Though he knew he probably shouldn't have been. "What does Isaac mean, Professor?" he asked.

She gave him a mischievous smile. "It means, 'God laughed.'"

Lexi, Caleb, and Logan snorted. James felt himself fall a little bit in love with her.

"I like it," he said. He looked at the baby boy. "Isaac it is."

Harper looked immensely pleased.

He couldn't wait to get her out on their date tomorrow night.

Was it strange to think of looking for the woman he might have knocked up in a one-night stand as *dates* with Harper? Maybe. But he was looking forward to them anyway.

5

———

She was definitely going to go along to find this woman with James.

Not because she wanted to see her in person and see just what kind of woman was James Reynaud's type, or because she wanted to confront this woman about how she could just abandon her baby in a basket. Not because she felt a stupid need to see James and this woman together to gauge if there maybe was something there besides a physical attraction that had lasted, apparently, only one night. Not because she was enough of a control freak to want to be sure James asked all the right questions. Not because she thought she was exceptionally good at reading people and thought she could maybe deter-mine how attached or unattached this woman really was to this baby that Harper was starting to feel very attached to. Not because...

She was full of crap. It was because of *all* those reasons. And because she wanted to see James outside of this apartment and the landing in between their places. Their relationship existed inside a bubble that encompassed two apartments and a ten-foot stretch of balcony between them. She wanted to see him out in his world. She had no doubt that the search for these women would take her into some of his favorite places. It wasn't as if he were picking women up in places he never went or enjoyed. She was certain at least one of them was someone he'd met at the club he played in on the weekends, and she suddenly wanted to see that club.

This was all probably a really bad idea.

They'd be looking for the woman he had a *baby* with. They'd be meeting women he'd slept with. Did she really want to do that?

No.

Still, Harper spun in front of her mirror in a new dress. A. New. Dress.

She never bought dresses like this. She wore jackets and skirts to work, professional dresses, slacks. She had a sundress or two for summertime in Louisiana, of course. She was going to need to get more of those because she'd only been here for one summer, and holy hell, the fewer clothes the better down here in the devil's armpit. But she didn't have date dresses. Because she didn't go on dates.

"You're not going on a date now either," she told herself firmly.

She and James were going out to a restaurant together tonight because the maybe-baby-mama was a waitress at this particular establishment. They were going to a restaurant together because they were trying to figure out if him having sex with this woman had resulted in a sweet baby boy. Because he *had* slept with this woman. That part was certain.

Her breath caught as she heard the knock on her door. That had to be James.

Not. A. Date.

But her stupid stuttering heart rate didn't quite believe it.

She pulled the door open.

"I don't suppose you know anything about—"

James had clearly prepared to greet her at the door the way he had so many other times. But he broke off midsentence. His gaze traveled over her. Head to toe. Twice.

"Damn," he finally said gruffly.

"Stop it." Him looking at her like that was doing nothing to slow her heart rate or convince her imagination that this wasn't what it appeared to be. A date.

She stepped out and pulled the door shut behind her.

"Seriously," he said, backing up only enough so that she could turn to lock her door. He didn't give her much space at all. "You look amazing."

See, *that* made it seem like a date, too.

"Is everything okay with Isaac?"

James had dropped him off with Bea just before coming over to get Harper. She'd been tempted to go along. He'd invited her. She'd wanted to. She'd wanted to meet Bea and be there to help give instructions for the baby's care. But that had been an overreaction. Bea was watching him because they were on their way to play Sherlock Holmes for the night and try to find his mom. He wasn't *theirs*. At least, he wasn't *hers*. She wasn't his mom. There was no reason for her to give Bea instructions. Besides, Bea was the grandmother of six. She'd not only helped raise some of those kids, but she'd raised three of her own and now babysat for several of the parents in the support group. She knew far more about babies—even this one —than Harper ever would.

Harper was really only a babysitter herself. A brand-new-to-all-of-this one, as a matter of fact.

Plus dropping the baby off together would have also made this feel like they were in a relationship and going on a date rather than what it was—a mission.

"Everything is great. And you look amazing," James repeated.

He did, too. He was dressed in dark jeans and a dark gray

button-up shirt. It was untucked, and the sleeves were rolled up to the elbows, and he looked sexy and relaxed and confident, and she wanted to lick the V of skin where the top two buttons were unfastened.

Finally, Harper made eye contact. "Thank you."

"Really. You don't look professor-y or librarian-y at all tonight."

"Those are not actual adjectives." It seemed easier to talk grammar than to talk about how his compliment made her feel.

"Sure they are. They have 'y' on the end and are describing a noun. You."

She couldn't help her little smile even as she shook her head. "That doesn't make them an adjective."

"Not sure you're right about that."

"What's that mean, anyway?" she asked, knowing from experience that these types of "arguments" were without end or victory with James. "It's a good thing that I don't look like I usually do? And sometimes I look like a librarian?"

"Oh, that's not what I'm saying at all," he told her, putting a hand on her lower back and steering her toward the steps. "Hot professor and naughty librarian totally work for me. But sweet girl-next-door does, too."

Harper stopped at the top of the stairs. She turned to him. "This isn't a date."

"I wasn't sure, either. Until I saw you."

Her heart flipped. In part, due to his words but even more because of the look in his eyes. It was hot, but there was also a touch of affection there.

"It's the hair, yes?" she asked, lifting a hand to touch the curls around her face.

She shouldn't have worn it down. She definitely shouldn't have curled it.

James lifted a hand and twisted one of those curls around his index finger. "Yeah. It's the hair."

"I had my straightener heated up but made a last-minute change to go with the curling iron instead."

"Well, don't beat yourself up, Professor. The curls are just going to get you an extra dance and a kiss or two. Something sweet like that. Nothing too dirty."

"Oh." She wasn't sure how to feel about that. She knew she shouldn't think of this as a date. She should discourage dancing, and they definitely shouldn't kiss. This was about finding a woman who he'd done that—and a hell of a lot more—with a few months ago. It seemed totally inappropriate to want this outing to end with Harper naked in his bed. His obvious casual approach to sex and "dating" was why they were in this situation.

"Of course, the legs and breasts are a whole other thing."

She looked down. The dress had a low neckline, but it didn't really show cleavage. It did hit midthigh, though. "What?"

He grinned. "It's always the legs. Especially in those suit things."

"Oh." She felt a little warm. "I didn't know that."

"And your ass." He checked out her skirt again.

This one flared slightly and would swirl if they danced. Not that they were going to dance.

"This one doesn't show off your sweet ass as much as those sexy professor skirts do, but I do like your boobs in this. Your jackets cover those up."

She swallowed hard.

"But the hair is the thing making me think *you're* thinking of this differently."

"I'm not," she tried to protest.

"You did your hair for me, Professor." His voice was low, and his smile was far too knowing.

She pressed her lips together. Yeah, she had. Dammit.

"Sorry."

He looked puzzled and amused. "Don't be sorry."

"It makes this all the more complicated."

"What does?"

"Us. Our feelings. Anything with... us." She was very rarely at a loss for words, and this was a bad time to not be able to express herself clearly.

James shook his head. "I disagree. This. Us. Makes everything easier. *You* always make everything easier."

"We might be meeting the baby's mom tonight," she said softly. She was hopeful that would be the case. She was also scared of it. Because that would introduce another woman into this situation. A woman who had every right to be there. It was selfish and wrong of her, but Harper didn't really want that.

She wanted James and the baby to herself.

"We might be," he agreed. Then he frowned. "And we'll be getting some fucking answers from her." He lifted a hand and cupped Harper's face. "But that's it. I mean, obviously, she'll get to have as much to do with him as she wants, but she's not moving in here. I'm not taking *her* on any dates. Nothing like that."

Harper nodded. "Okay."

This was all *such* a bad idea. She was getting way too involved in something she should be steering way clear of.

Instead, she lifted up on tiptoe and kissed his jaw. Then, with him too surprised to do anything else, she took his hand and started down the steps.

They walked the few blocks to the restaurant. They didn't really talk. The busy sidewalks of the Quarter made it difficult, and it was also unnecessary. They both knew where they were headed and why. They didn't have a plan, exactly. How did you plan for something like this? But they did hold hands the whole way.

"This is it," James said as they stopped in front of the restaurant.

It was like so many others in the French Quarter. It had long, tall windows, many of which were open to the night air. The front doors of the building were also open, and a chalkboard sign sat on the sidewalk in front proclaiming the evening's specialty was shrimp and spicy orzo. Gas lanterns hung on the outside bricks of the building, and clusters of people wove along the narrow sidewalks, pausing at the corner to let cars and the occasional carriage pass. Music from the streets floated on the air, spiced with cayenne and hickory, and laughter and conversation surrounded them.

The restaurant was busy. People stood around the bar, two deep, and all the tables were full. Harper took a deep breath. "Okay, let's do this."

James nodded and stepped back to let her go in first.

She stepped through the doorway. A woman at the hostess stand gave her a smile. "Hi. How many?"

"Two."

"We're here to talk to someone," James said over Harper's shoulder.

"Oh. A customer?" the hostess asked.

"An employee. A waitress," James told her.

Harper put her elbow in his side. He didn't need to be so assertive. She reached for James's hand and pinched the back of it in a warning she hoped he'd understand.

"There's a waitress that waited on us a few months ago when we were here," she explained, using the story she'd thought up as they walked from the apartment. They couldn't just barge in here demanding to see her. They couldn't just walk in, smile, and say, "Hey, did you have a baby a couple of weeks ago?" either. "We'd love to sit in her section again, if possible."

The hostess looked out over the bustling restaurant. "Who was it?"

Harper could see she was already dreading the idea of

trying to get an open table in a specific portion of the restaurant. That was fine. Harper's plan meant they didn't even need to actually talk to the waitress.

"You know, I don't remember her name."

"Megan."

Harper glanced up at James sharply. He was looking at her, not at the hostess.

"Her name was Megan."

Of course he knew her name. Harper hadn't asked. She also hadn't told him they shouldn't just ask for her right away. She had a plan, but it had just come to her, and she had hoped James would simply follow her lead. Clearly, he wasn't that good at reading her yet.

"Is she here tonight?" Harper asked the hostess, with a forced smile.

"She is," James said.

Harper sighed. He'd already seen her.

"Yeah, she is," the hostess confirmed. "But I can't tell you how long it might be. I have to take people in order on the list, so even if a table opens up in her section, I can't seat you until everyone in front of you is seated."

"We totally understand," Harper said quickly. "We're going to wait at the bar. Just do your best with the table. We're not in a hurry."

"Okay. If you're sure," the hostess said. Clearly, requests for specific waitresses were uncommon.

But this way, Harper's plan could still work out. Without James actually seeing or speaking to the waitress. To *Megan*.

Harper grabbed James's sleeve and pulled him toward the bar. She tucked them around the far end, away from the dining room, with at least fifty people between them and the middle of the room. She turned so that if James faced her, his back would be to the tables.

"What's with the story about being in here before and having her wait on us?" James asked.

"We can't just walk up to her and ask about the baby," Harper said.

"Why not? If it's her, then her reaction to seeing me will give her away."

Harper had absolutely thought of that. "Yes, and that's kind of unfair to do to her at work, in a public place full of people. Let's not be so confrontational. There's a reason that she didn't knock on the door and hand him to you."

James frowned. "Yeah, I intend to ask her about that."

"She didn't want you to know it's her, James," Harper said. "If you just show up and surprise her and get aggressive, she's going to panic and either lie or maybe run."

"Run? She's in the middle of work."

"She's not a heart surgeon in the middle of a double bypass," Harper said. "She can probably set her tray down and head out."

James ran a hand through his hair. "You think she'd do that?"

Harper stepped closer to him. "I have no idea. I don't know her. But I know that it probably takes a lot for a mother to drop her baby off in a basket on a doorstep. Clearly, she didn't see another good option. Including just *coming* to you."

He blew out a breath and for a moment looked truly miserable. "Yeah. I feel like shit about that."

"Well, she doesn't know you very well," Harper said. Then she shrugged. "Or maybe she does. She knew you'd take good care of him."

"But she didn't trust me enough to *face* me."

"It might not be about trust. You have no idea what she's going through. And that means being angry and confrontational isn't a good idea."

James took a deep breath. Then he nodded. "Charming. Friendly. I can do that."

Harper smiled. "I think maybe you need to do none of the above. To start."

If Megan was Isaac's mom, then they'd have to talk at some point, of course, but Harper had decided at some point between the outside sidewalk and the hostess stand there might be a way to rule this woman *out* as the mother before they even spoke to her, and if she was *not* Isaac's mom, then there was no reason for James and her to chat.

That did seem a little jealous and possessive, but Harper thought maybe she'd just deal with that later.

"None of the above?"

"Let's find out if Megan was even pregnant a month or two ago."

"How do we do that?"

"We ask her coworkers," Harper said. She glanced around. "If she was working here when you met her and is still here, that means she worked through her pregnancy. It's unlikely she took four to six months off work."

"Impossible, actually. She's working here and does ghost tours. It's how she pays her bills."

Harper lifted a brow. "You actually found out what she does for a living?"

"Brat," he said. "I do *talk* to the women I spend time with."

"Beyond what their favorite position is?" she teased.

But stupidly, there was a little part of her that didn't like that he'd gotten to know any of these women. The light, super-ficial, very short-term flings sat better with her. Which was stupid. Did she really want to get involved with a playboy? But there was something special about how *they* knew one another, how he knew things about her just because they'd spent time together over a period of time, day to day, doing routine things like taking care of their dog. And they had not had a physical relationship but that he still seemed to like her and want to spend time with her.

They'd covered a lot of territory over the six months of knowing each other when she really thought about it. James's easygoing attitude and ability to charm her before she was even aware of it at times made it seem that they mostly flirted and talked superficially, but the truth was, they'd talked about childhood memories, their friends, their parents, their work, and why they loved their careers.

"Well, we cover those important topics first," he teased in return. "But you have to say *something* besides, 'Hey, have you seen my pants?' later on."

Harper knew she should smile. She should laugh. She should joke. But she hated the idea of him saying that to anyone.

To anyone *else*.

He'd never said that to her. But she wanted him to.

She wanted to know what his favorite position was, wanted to tell him *her* favorite position, and she wanted to use them *all*.

"I want you to lose your pants on my bedroom floor."

His expression, his body language, his *breathing* changed. Immediately. He stepped forward. For some reason, she stepped back. Instinct maybe, because when a predator came for you, you stepped back. And James definitely looked predatory suddenly. But she bumped into the wall. And he kept coming.

He didn't say a word as both hands came up to cup her face. He tipped her head back and covered her mouth with his.

There was no squirming baby between them now. No clump of terrycloth. Nothing else demanding their attention or making this inappropriate. They were in public, but no one around them even noticed them, not to mention protested.

Not that she cared after about two seconds.

James's kiss consumed her. His lips moved over hers, steady

and firm, saying *you're mine,* as his thumbs stroked over her throat in a clear message of *and you're not going anywhere.*

Harper's entire body hummed with awareness and need and she moved to press closer, wanting to be *against* him, however she could.

He obliged by sliding a foot between hers then leaning in so his thigh was wedged between hers. She was straddling him, her skirt pulled up and the denim of his jeans rubbing enticingly against her inner thighs. He shifted her, and then her aching clit was pressed firmly against his thigh. He rocked her against his leg, and she made a whimpering sound. She didn't know if he heard her, but she didn't care. She didn't care if everyone heard her.

Still holding her head in place, he dragged his mouth to her ear. "I want so badly to slide a finger into your panties to feel how hot and wet you are right now."

Harper whimpered again, and that time she was sure he heard.

"I would do anything to pull the front of this dress down and suck on one of your nipples."

"James," she gasped as heat and lust flooded through her.

"I'm taking you home after this. We are going to pick up where we left off the night of the big fire. I'm going to lose my pants on your bedroom floor, and you're going to lose your mind in your bed."

She gripped his arms, her knees wobbling. "Yes."

"Louder, Professor."

"*Yes.*"

He leaned back, his dark eyes hot as he gazed down at her. "Fuck, yes."

Harper pulled in a deep breath. It was insane how quickly he did that to her. One second he was sweet and charming, then he was frustrated and emotional, then he was hot and dirty.

She wanted it all.

She was in a lot of trouble here.

"So what's this big plan of yours?" he asked, finally letting her go and stepping back. "Let's get this over with."

Harper breathed deep again and nodded. "Just let me take care of it. If she was pregnant while working here, her coworkers noticed." She glanced at the room behind him. "The uniforms they wear are fitted. There's no way she could hide a pregnancy, at least not by the seventh or eighth month."

James nodded. "Okay."

"Let me talk to someone. I'll find out if she was even pregnant. That's step one. If so, then I'll go have dinner at a table in her section, and we'll go from there."

"Just you?" he asked with a frown.

"She didn't want you to know," Harper reminded him gently. "We need to not spook her. We need information for Isaac."

It was clear James was frustrated, but he nodded. "Fine."

"Just stay here. And don't let her see you."

Harper didn't know which woman Megan was, and she didn't really want to. Or need to. At least not yet.

She wound her way through the crowd, pretending to be looking for the bathroom.

Crossing her fingers that she wasn't stopping Megan herself, she approached one of the waitresses. "Hi, can you tell me where the ladies' room is?"

"All the way to the back on the left." The waitress's name tag read Lucy.

"Thanks. And can I ask you something else?" Harper asked.

"Sure."

"Have you worked here for a while?"

"About a year."

Good. She would definitely know Megan, then.

"I was here with my boyfriend—well, ex-boyfriend now—

about three months ago, and we had this amazing waitress. He was being an asshole, and we got into a fight and left without tipping her. I thought of it when I came in tonight, and I'd love to make up for it."

"Oh, wow, that's, um... really nice," Lucy said.

"Yeah, but I don't remember her name." Harper smiled apologetically. "She was pregnant, though." Harper felt like she was holding her breath. "Do you know who that is?"

Lucy frowned. "Pregnant?"

"Yeah. This was a few months back."

Lucy shook her head. "We haven't had any pregnant waitresses."

"She might not be pregnant anymore."

"No one's been pregnant here at all."

"Really? You're sure?"

"All of the waitresses here have been here for a while," Lucy said. "And we know each other pretty well. No one's been pregnant. Are you sure you were *here* with your boyfriend?"

Harper shrugged. "Geez, maybe not. We're from out of town, so I guess maybe it's possible we were at another place. Sorry."

"No problem. But that's still really nice of you," Lucy told her with a smile.

Harper smiled and moved toward the bathroom. She let herself into a stall and locked it, just taking a moment to breathe deeply.

Okay, one girl down, three to go. Megan wasn't Isaac's mom. There was no reason for James to talk to a woman tonight that he'd found attractive enough to have a hot one-night stand with.

Harper put a hand against her forehead. She wasn't at all used to feeling like this about a guy. She wanted him. Not just physically—though they were definitely to the point where that was absolutely impossible to deny or ignore any longer—but she liked him. She wanted to help him with the baby and everything else that came along, and she wanted peeks into his life. Peeks that didn't involve other women.

They still needed to find Isaac's mom. But it wasn't going to be tonight. And it was still early.

Harper ran a hand through her hair, smoothed the front of her dress—the dress that James really liked and wanted to run his hand up underneath—and relished the shiver of desire that went through her, remembering his hot words against her ear, and then opened the stall door and headed back into the restaurant.

She slid in next to him where he was leaning on the bar, watching the game that was on the TV behind the bartender, cradling a glass of an amber liquid with one big hand.

"It's not her," she said, tipping her head to look up at him.

He didn't move to give her more room. He just slid an arm around her, tucking her up against his side, settling his other hand on her ass. "Good."

"Yeah?"

"Yeah. That means we can go dancing."

"Dancing?" She'd been thinking about straight back to the apartment.

"Dancing," he confirmed.

"What about Isaac?"

"He's fine for a little longer."

"You're sure?" They'd only made a plan to come to this one restaurant for this one woman, but she assumed the other women were in the general vicinity. They probably *should* try to do this as quickly as possible.

"The next girl I need to check with doesn't work nights, and I don't want to show up at her apartment," he said.

It occurred to Harper that she hadn't asked nearly enough questions about these women. She hadn't really wanted details. Like how attractive they were or how he'd met them or how funny or sexy or interesting they were. She was assuming he'd only spent a night with each of them. She didn't know that for sure. By his own admission, none of them had been serious or "long term," but she wasn't sure what that meant to James.

"Can we go somewhere else?" she asked. They were still in Megan's restaurant. She wasn't the mom, and it wasn't crazy to think James might come into this establishment again in his life and run into her. But Harper wouldn't mind if they never saw each other again.

"Yeah. We sure can." He straightened, taking his hand from her butt. He tossed a few bills onto the bar then threaded his fingers with hers and started for the door.

Okay, their mission—for tonight—was over. So maybe this was kind of a date. Now.

HE WANTED TO TAKE HER STRAIGHT HOME AND INTO THE bedroom. Which was why he was leading her across the street to Trahan's Tavern.

This was a date. Now.

Megan was off the list. Which was great. He remembered the bubbly blonde but not as anything more than a good time, and as soon as he'd seen Harper in the dress she was wearing, he couldn't have given less of a shit about Megan.

Yes, he wanted to find the baby's mom. Kind of. He wanted information. He wanted to make sure she was healthy, that Isaac was healthy, and that she wasn't going to be showing up to claim him in a few months, out of the blue. He wanted to make the kid legally his, and that would require, he assumed, at least a signature from her.

But that was it. He'd much prefer to not have her around for raising the kid. He was going to be fine with that. He had Harper. And his friends. And his friends' network of friends.

Bea was awesome, and James knew that Caleb and Logan and Gabe had an even bigger group of people who would welcome him and Harper. He intended to go to the next support group meeting to get to know everyone, and he was hoping Harper would go along.

Was this the way he'd intended to finally get Harper out on the town with him? In his bed? In his *life*? Of course not. But he was a smart guy, and he wasn't about to let this opportunity pass by. She was getting attached to the baby. And to him.

He was now going to make sure she knew this was about more than having a second pair of hands to change diapers and rock a fussy baby.

"Oh, this is Logan's place," she said, taking in the sign over the door.

"Yep. Best Pimm's cups in the city," James said, steering her into the restaurant. "And you have to have the seafood pot pie and the brown butter pecan pie."

She laughed. "That sounds amazing." She turned, stopping in the middle of the floor. "But I thought we were dancing."

"We will," he promised. "But dinner first."

Something in her face showed that was the right answer. She was already more relaxed than she'd been across the street. He realized she'd been nervous about seeing Megan and finding out if she was Isaac's mom. He lifted a hand to her face. "How did you rule Megan out?"

"I asked another waitress which of her coworkers had been pregnant three or four months ago."

"And?"

Harper lifted a shoulder. "None of them. She's been there a year, and no one's been pregnant."

"Okay, then."

She nodded with a smile. "Okay, then."

"Hey! James!"

He looked toward the bar to see Gabe Trahan waving him over.

"Let's have a drink."

"It's busy in here, too," she said, looking around.

"I have VIP status in here," he said. "And so do you." He put a hand on her lower back and nudged her toward the bar.

"I do?" she asked, starting forward.

"You're the reason we're starting the erotic book club. The guys love you."

She laughed. "That's real?"

"Very real. Our first meeting is in a couple of weeks."

"How's it going?" Gabe asked, wiping the bar in front of two stools at the end.

"Great. This is Harper. Professor Broussard," James told his friend, with a wink.

"Ah. Professor. So nice to meet you," Gabe said, giving her one of the grins that was one of the reasons Trahan's was incredibly popular with the female tourists.

Gabe and his brother, Logan, owned the bar and ran it with the help of a group of friends. They were well known for their amazing drinks, incredible food, and the Louisiana charm they exuded even in spite of both being happily married. Their wives knew they couldn't help it. It was, after all, exactly what had landed each of those ladies in their husband's bed the first time.

"You too," Harper said. "Let me know if you need any discussion questions for the book club."

"Oh, I think I'd love to hear your discussion questions," Gabe told her.

"You would," Harper told him. "But you'd like to hear my answers even more. Very insightful."

Gabe laughed and reached for a business card. He scrawled his email on the back and slid it across the bar. "Email me. You'll make me sound incredibly smart."

Harper took the card and tucked it into the little handbag she'd been carrying. "And all it will cost you is a piece of brown butter pecan pie."

"Done."

"Every time I come in."

Gabe laughed. "Done."

Harper grinned at him, and James wanted to dip her back on her barstool and kiss the hell out of her. He didn't know if she knew she was being flirtatious and fucking adorable, but she was, and he found the whole her-charming-his-friend move totally hot. For some reason. Maybe because he'd never imagined this scenario. He'd imagined plenty of scenarios of all kinds with Harper. Yeah, most of them involved her naked and on various pieces of his furniture. And hers. But a couple had involved them cooking dinner and taking the dog to the park. Normal things.

None had, however, involved her hanging out with his friends.

None had involved a baby.

And now both of those had happened before the cooking and dog park stuff, and it was... awesome.

"Okay, how about you back up and remember that you have a hot, amazing wife," James told Gabe as he slid up onto the stool next to Harper and leaned in. "And how about you remember that you're on a date with the hot guy from across the landing that you want to try showering with *naked* next time."

Harper's cheeks got pink even as she turned her head to grin at him. "I can't forget that."

"I won't let you." He said it with a gruff promise.

Her pupils were dilated, and she wet her lips, and yeah, he wanted to take her straight home.

Chuckling, Gabe made them two Pimm's cups without asking what they wanted. "You eating?"

"Definitely. Seafood pot pie," James said.

"Same," Harper agreed.

"You got it." Gabe moved off to put the order in and help more patrons farther down the bar.

Harper looked around, taking in the whole restaurant. "I love this place. It's so authentic, and everyone seems so happy."

"It's always packed," James told her. "Everyone who's been here even once makes a point of coming back."

She turned back to him. "So you grew up in New Orleans?"

He took a draw of his drink, the lemonade, liquor, and soda mixed perfectly. "Yep. All my life. Only child. Mom and Dad left after Katrina. But I've got aunts and uncles, cousins, a grandmother all still here."

"Where did your mom and dad go?" Harper asked, sipping her drink.

He watched her eyes widen and her take another bigger drink before setting her glass down. He grinned. "Baton Rouge. Not far. But Mom had a lot of anxiety after the storm."

"They lost their house?"

He nodded. "Lost almost everything. I think Dad would have stayed, but he was happy to go, too. My grandma that's still here is his mom, and they tried to talk her into going with them, but she's never leaving. She's actually a little pissed at them for going. It was tough on a lot of families."

Harper nodded. "I read all about it."

"Where did you grow up?"

"We lived in Provence until I was about eight," she said.

"France?" he asked.

She nodded. "My mother is French, my dad is American. We moved to Quebec when I was eight."

"You moved down here on your own, then?" He wanted to know all about her, he realized. He wanted to know what her fifth birthday had been like, what subject she had liked best in high school, what her favorite song was. And he was going to learn it on the piano if he didn't already know it.

"I did. We've traced some family lineage down here with the Cajun settlers, and I found that fascinating. So when the teaching position opened up, I decided to come find out more about this French heritage of mine."

"Do you miss Canada?"

"It's so much cooler there," she said with a smile, picking up her drink again.

He laughed. "I'll bet."

"But yes. I miss my parents, of course. And home. But they've always been great about adventures and seeing the world, so they're fully supportive, and they love coming to visit down here. The French culture here in Louisiana is so vibrant."

"*Tout a fait.*" James smirked as he lifted his glass as she registered that he'd said, "It sure is" in French.

She looked at him quickly. Then she narrowed her eyes. "*Tu connais le français?*"

He set his glass down. Yes, he knew French. He nodded. "*Oui.*" He was fluent. "*Je parle couramment.*"

"How?" she asked.

"My grandmother. Speaks French most of the time."

"Oh, it was your grandmother."

"Who?"

"The person I've heard you on the phone with. Speaking *fluent* French."

He was sincerely surprised. "You knew I spoke French?"

"*Oui.*"

"Why didn't you let on?"

"Thought there was a reason *you* weren't letting on."

He grinned. "You're right. There was. You're cute as hell when you swear in French, and I thought maybe you'd stop if you knew I understood."

She opened her mouth, as if to protest, but then shut it. "I might have."

James leaned closer. He was already sitting sideways, his knees on either side of her stool, one elbow on the bar, the other on his knee. Now he moved that hand to the back of her stool. Everyone in the bar saw in that body language that she was with him, but he wanted to make it very clear to *her* that she was with him. "Because you were trying to impress me in the beginning? With how sophisticated and upstanding and *pure* you are?"

She licked her bottom lip and nodded. "Yeah. I think so."

"Why?"

"Because I am all those things."

He gave her a slow grin. "Yeah. Which has gotta be why I've wanted to make you *impure* from the first time I saw you."

"Rebellious streak?"

"Wanted you on my level."

"You're impure?"

"You have no idea."

Her eyes were hot but she grinned. "I might have an idea. You know what I read."

He gave a low chuckle. "Good point. A lesser man might have a little bit of insecurity about measuring up."

"But not you?"

He leaned in. "You realize that I've read your favorite erotic romance three times, right? I know exactly what you like, Professor. And I'm very willing and able to deliver."

She swallowed hard. "How do you know it's my favorite?"

"The spine is the most bent on that one, and it's always in the top three on your stack. You reread it a lot."

Her voice was a soft whisper when she said, "Well, certain parts, yes."

James felt a jolt of heat shoot through him. "So I know some of your favorite dirty things," he said. He lifted a hand and dragged his thumb over her bottom lip. "But I also think that you haven't really done much of that—or maybe any of it."

Her tongue came out to trace the path that his thumb had just taken. Then she said, "I wanted you to think I was sophisticated and upstanding and pure so that you wouldn't be interested."

"You didn't want me to be interested?"

"Not at first."

"Why's that?" God he could look at this woman all night. Just look into her eyes, watch her mouth, study the length of her eyelashes and the sweep of her eyebrows and the line of her jaw.

"Because I might have a little insecurity about measuring up."

Surprise hit him almost as hard as the desire did. Jesus, she honestly had no idea how tied up she'd had him for months just with her humor and intelligence and the way she gathered her hair up into a bun and the way she always stood in the doorway with her right foot on top of her left.

"That is so not going to be a problem, Professor."

"I read a lot," she said. "I don't necessarily *do* a lot."

He took a moment to consider all the ways he could respond to that. He could say something dirty. He could assure her that he'd happily do all the work. He'd insist that coaching her through it would be his absolute pleasure. But in the end he said something that surprised him as much as it seemed to her.

"You forget that I've watched you step up. Over and over. With the baby," he said. "And Henry and Ami." Yes, he'd used her name for the dog. Because he wanted her to know he *meant* this. "I know that when you care about something, you put your whole self into it. And that's all I need, Harper." He leaned in. "Your whole self into this."

Yeah, he'd used her first name, too. Because he wasn't

teasing here. He just needed her naked, willing, and eager in his arms. It was absolutely that simple.

Her breathing was quick, and he could see the faint flush of pink move from her neck to her cheeks. She licked her lips. "I think we're going to need to take our food to go."

6

———

Gabe didn't ask any questions when he brought their food out and James immediately asked for to-go boxes.

In fact, Harper thought he knew exactly why they weren't eating in the restaurant.

They stepped out onto the busy street just off Jackson Square, and Harper's heart started pounding. Fear, maybe. Not of James, of course. If he didn't touch her *soon*—well, more than her hand and lower back, anyway—she truly might die. But there was a slight fear of what they were about to do. Because it was going to change everything. Which led her to the next strongest feeling. Anticipation. Everything had already changed, and she was ready for this next step. She'd been ready, but now with everything else going on, while it should probably feel like the perfect time and reason to pull back, she felt very much like getting closer. Very close. As close as she could be. To all of it, really.

But to his naked body. Right now. For sure.

They walked, again without talking, toward their building. Her mind was spinning with questions. Whose apartment would they go to? Should she ask him to take her straight to the shower because, yes, that had become a must-do fantasy, or should she let him take the lead? The book he was referring to didn't have a shower scene, but her favorite scene, the one where the hero made the heroine come with his tongue before bending her over and taking her from behind could be reenacted in any room, really.

Honestly, she didn't care. She just needed his hands and mouth on her. Anywhere. As soon as possible.

They turned up Chartres Street. There was a man on the next corner playing saxophone. The song was "A Kiss to Build a Dream On." James dug into his pocket and pulled out a few bills, tossing them into the man's guitar case. Then he set their food bags down and turned to Harper.

"Come here."

"Wha—"

He pulled her in, and they started dancing.

Dancing. On the street corner.

He'd said they were going to.

He grinned down at her as they moved together in a slow sway. "Love those curls."

She smiled then put her head against his chest. Where she'd wanted to have her head almost since she'd first met him. He was the perfect height for her to rest her ear right against his chest where his heart beat.

They'd talked about dancing a day or so ago—was it really just a couple of days ago?

"I can have more than one priority, Harper."

That's what he'd said when she'd told him he had his hands too full with the baby to think about taking her dancing. It seemed maybe he was right. Of course, fathers did that all the time—juggled kids and wives and jobs and hobbies. *People* did that all the time—had lives that included children. But she'd thought he'd have to adjust, get used to it, figure things out.

It turned out James Reynaud was an incredibly capable guy.

He was caring, laid back, and dependable. He did what he said he was going to do, and he did it with humor. He'd asked for help when he needed it. He'd recognized when he needed someone else's input. But he was the one getting things done.

He was also a great dancer.

The song ended, and the musician launched into another.

They continued to move together in the shadow cast from the balcony overhead. It felt like they were in their own little bubble and that she was truly his only priority at the moment. She appreciated that he did that, too. He'd made sure the baby was cared for. He'd taken her word for it that Megan wasn't the woman they were looking for, and he'd let it go. Now, at least for a little bit, they could just be together, the two of them.

This was romantic. Sweet.

She loved it.

And now she wanted him to take her up to her apartment—or his—and prove that he could put her up against the wall the way he'd said he could when she'd gone to weigh herself with the baby earlier.

She pulled back and tipped her head up. "James…"

He lifted a brow.

She blew out a breath.

"You okay?"

"I'm trying to channel one of my favorite heroines and figure out the best way to say this. But I don't know if I should be romantic and sweet and tell you how much I like you and admire you and how glad I am that you knocked on my door with that olive tree…"

With another guy, or even the guy she'd thought James was six months ago or so, she would have never thought that was the way to make him start taking his clothes off. But now she wasn't so sure. He had a sweet side. No doubt about it. And it was as hot as his flirtatious side.

"Or if I should be bold and dirty and tell you that I've never wanted anyone like I want you, and I've never wanted to take my panties off more than I do right now. But—" she said, pausing for a breath as heat washed over her at the look in his eyes.

He was letting her talk, taking it all in, but the waist of her dress was bunched in one of his fists, and his eyes were laser focused on hers, and his jaw was tight. He looked like he was fighting to stay still and quiet, letting her finish, and she appreciated it. Even while she really wished he'd just take over right now.

She had no idea how to finish her thought. She gave a little laugh. "I don't have anything else. That's it. Just... I love our olives, and I really need to take my panties off."

James blew out a breath. "Damn, Professor."

She could tell that was a good damn, and a shot of satisfaction went through her.

"You don't have to channel anyone," he said gruffly. "You're a fucking heroine all on your own."

She would not go that far. But she wanted to be. That was something. She loved the dirty, fun sex in the books she read and the way the women owned their sexuality and openly enjoyed it. But she also loved watching people learn things about themselves and do new things that challenged them and made them more than they were before. She wanted that, too. She liked to think the books were one reason she'd let James and the parade of needs through her doorway.

Including a baby boy.

That was a big one. But she was going to try to be heroic. Or heroic-ish, at least.

She was also going to take a chance at some dirty, fun sex with the hot firefighter-musician living across from her because, seriously? That was romance material for sure. Almost ridiculously so.

And if she could make it an erotic romance, all the better.

Harper gripped James's arm and lifted a foot. She didn't even glance around to see if there was anyone nearby. This was the French Quarter. No one blinked at things like a woman taking her panties off on a dark street corner. She reached up under her skirt and hooked the top of her panties. James watched. He surely knew what she was doing, and he definitely didn't make a move to stop her. Harper drew the panties down her leg and over her shoe then stepped out of them with her other foot. She handed them to him.

"Yeah, really needed to get out of these."

He crushed them in his fist, dragging in a deep breath. "Home. Now."

The firm almost growl, made her inner muscles clench, and she also sucked in a breath. "Yes."

They grabbed the bags of food and started up the street. They walked quickly and were climbing the steps to their apartments within minutes, Harper in front. She paused at the top of the steps, not sure which direction to turn. James didn't hesitate. Didn't speak. Didn't ask a question. He headed straight for her door. He pulled her key from his pocket. She didn't know if he'd brought it tonight with the idea that something like this might happen or if he always carried it—that wouldn't surprise her, actually—but he inserted it, turned it, and pushed the door open. Then he reached for her, pulled her into the apartment, and kicked the door shut behind them.

He backed her up against the door, and Harper's heart flipped. That was so hot whenever she read about it, and it was so much more so in real life.

James braced his hands on the door on either side of her head and stared down at her. "You are so fucking beautiful."

"So are you," she said honestly.

He gave her a half grin. "Thanks for curling your hair for me."

She nodded. "Anytime."

His eyes heated even as his smile grew. "And I really like this dress."

"I'm glad."

He lifted a hand and hooked his index finger in the neckline of the dress. Then he pulled it down. Her body flooded with heat as he also caught the cup of her bra and bared her breast. He'd said earlier he wanted to pull the front of the dress down and suck on her nipple. He didn't forget a thing, it seemed.

His gaze didn't leave hers immediately. He just stood, looking into her eyes, her naked breast exposed between them. Her nipple drew tight. Without looking down, he moved his thumb, brushing over the tip.

Harper sucked in a sharp breath as electricity shot from there to her clit.

He did it again, watching her face, not her breast or his hand. Her head fell back against the door, and she flattened one palm on the wood behind her while the other grasped his forearm. "James."

"Damn, I like that, Professor," he said huskily.

"More."

He thumbed her nipple again then added a finger, plucking at it gently.

Everything tingled from head to toe with a sweet ache settling between her thighs. She needed so much more, yet this buildup was so good.

He pulled a little harder, and she gasped.

"Fuck," he muttered.

Then he dipped his knees and took her nipple in his mouth.

Harper whimpered and had to grip his arm tighter as her knees got a little weak. It was all so crazy. She'd read these things but had chalked it up to fictional drama. People's knees didn't really get weak. People didn't really feel like they were on fire. People didn't really ache for one another.

She'd been so, so wrong.

"You're so fucking sweet," he said against her breast as he teased with his tongue then sucked hard.

Harper had never wanted to be naked more than she did right then. She'd never wanted another person's hands on her as much as she wanted James's on her in that moment. She now understood some of the more brazen heroines in the books.

"James, I need you," she said. "I need you to touch me. I need to touch you."

He didn't hesitate, didn't tease, didn't question. He straightened, reached behind her, unzipped her dress and pushed it to the floor. Then he unhooked her bra and pulled it down her arms. His hot eyes dragged over her as he stepped back and unbuttoned his shirt, shrugging out of it and tossing it aside.

With his shirt off, she forgot to think about the fact that she was completely naked now. She'd seen him shirtless before, and it had always been a pleasure. But it had never been a prelude to sex, and in this moment, everything about his body was so much *more*. He was hot and hard and big. His muscles rippled as he unzipped his jeans, and she was fascinated with every move. Those muscles were about to do all kinds of amazing things to her body. He moved with a confidence and a determination that made butterflies kick up in her stomach. She was nervous. She wanted this to be good. She wanted him to feel every bit of heat and want and *I'll never get enough* that she was feeling. But she also couldn't wait. She sensed this was going to be the kind of sex she read about, and she loved knowing that sex like that actually existed.

James pulled a condom out of his pocket before he shucked out of his jeans. He pushed his boxers down, and she saw him fully naked, and fully erect, for the first time.

In the shower, she'd gotten a pretty good idea of what this

would be like, and she hadn't been wrong. He was big. Of course he was big. He had that amazingly, how-can-that-be-real, hot V on either side of his abs. He had six-pack abs. He had hard, strong thighs, and a wide, hard chest. And dammit, this wasn't fiction. He was a firefighter. He had to work to stay in shape for his job, and every person in New Orleans who might need him to fight to save their families or their homes or businesses should be damned grateful.

She certainly was.

"Oh," she said softly.

He gave her a cocky smile. "Come here."

She stepped forward, out of her dress. He reached and snagged her hand, pulling her close. He pressed her against his hot, naked body, running his hands up and down her back. He lowered his head, taking her mouth in a hot, slow kiss.

Harper let her hands roam. There was no way she could help it. She ran her hands up and down his sides, over the bumps of his abs, down to his tight ass, squeezing and pulling him closer. His cock pressed into her stomach, and she felt her inner thighs tighten. She wanted him filling her. Now. She'd never been one to rush into sex. She'd never *had to have it*. She'd been fine with foreplay and a slow build. But now she *needed* him.

She reached between them and wrapped her hand around his cock. His sharp intake of breath gave her a heady rush. She squeezed then stroked, and he tore his mouth away from hers, pressing his forehead to hers, sucking in air.

"Holy shit, Harper."

Harper.

She loved when he called her Professor. She'd learned it was a term of endearment. When he was teasing her or even feeling affectionate. But when he used her first name it was when things were... more. He was feeling more right now and she loved that.

"God, you feel good," she told him. "I want you so much."

"You've got me. Whatever you want."

"Will you..." She swallowed. Her favorite heroines had put lots of thoughts in her head and had given her a little shot of confidence and *hell yeah* about having hot sex with her firefighter-single-dad-sort-of-roommate, but *saying* it was different. Words mattered. They should be carefully chosen and could have a big impact.

"Anything," he said gruffly.

The sincerity in his tone made her heart flip. She believed him. She also knew that she could say anything to him.

"The first night you were over here with Ami, you were sitting on the couch with him, and I wanted to climb into your lap and..."

James put a hand on her face and dragged his thumb over her bottom lip. "Say it, Harper. Please fucking say it."

He was begging. His voice was rough, and when she looked into his eyes she could see the swirling, hot emotions.

She swallowed. "I wanted to climb into your lap and ride you."

He blew out a little breath. But for some reason that didn't feel like enough. She hadn't gone far enough. She needed to be fully honest, fully raw here.

"I wanted to climb into your lap and fuck you. Right there, on my couch, just like that," she said.

James froze for a second, then he pulled back to look at her more directly. "Tell me you want that now."

Her hand was wrapped around his massive, hard-as-steel erection. She was bare naked, pressed up against him. He'd read her favorite erotic romance just because he'd wanted to know what she liked. They had a tree, a lizard, a dog, and a baby together. Sort of. But it was enough.

Fuck should be a graphic, not-romantic, not-meaningful-enough word.

Instead, it felt perfect. It was meaningful because it was not one she used regularly or casually. It was not one she'd ever used with another guy. It was raw and dirty and yes, graphic. It felt just right because of all that.

"I want to sit you down on that couch right now. I want to climb on top of you, and I want to fuck you right there where I first realized that you are a great guy inside this hot-as-hell-and-knows-how-to-use-it body. I want this"—she squeezed him—"filling me up and making me come hard. And then I want you to flip me over onto that couch cushion, and I want you to put one of my legs over your shoulder, and I want *you* to fuck *me* until you come harder than you ever have before."

So apparently once she opened her graphic-talk dam, it all came flooding out.

James made a little growling noise, reached between them, rolled the condom on, and then lifted her with his big hands under her ass.

Thrilled, Harper wrapped her arms and legs around him, his cock nudging and teasing her entrance as he stalked to the couch.

"I'm going to give you *all* of that," he told her, his voice low and rough. "I want to hear a 'Fuck yes, James,' when your sweet pussy comes all over my cock. And then when I flip you over and pound into you, I want to hear it again. Got that, Professor? Fuck. Yes. James."

She wasn't sure she could *help* saying all of that. Hearing him ask for it was so incredibly hot. She knew that he wanted it because it would mean that he'd gotten her to do something she normally resisted, something she was typically too reserved to say. He wanted her to give him something that wasn't easy or usual for her.

She could do that.

"Got it," she said breathlessly as he sat down on the middle cushion, his cock sliding up against her clit.

He squeezed her ass. "Your sweet, sophisticated, classy mouth saying *fuck* for me is the hottest damned thing. And that makes me an uncouth, vulgar bastard, and I don't really care."

"It doesn't—" she started to protest.

But he shifted her forward and took her nipple in his mouth again, sucking hard.

"Oh, God."

He pinched her other nipple, making her inner muscles ripple in anticipation.

"Reach down and play with yourself," he ordered gruffly.

She reached between them and ran a finger over her clit, her muscles clenching.

"Harder," he demanded.

Oh yes, he was going to be bossy, too. She loved that in the books. He knew that. She loved that he knew that. Reading what she read was a definite look into her fantasies, and she loved that he'd done that. She wanted to hear his, too. She wanted to *tell* him hers. She wanted to read a book for the first time together and talk about why it was hot.

But right now she wanted him inside her. Deep. Hard.

She circled her clit harder and faster with her finger, feeling the tension and pleasure building.

Then suddenly he shifted her back, and she slid down onto his cock.

She moaned. He groaned, deep and low. It was a tight fit, but it was exquisite. He stretched her deliciously, and she soaked it in, feeling the waves of pleasure coursing through her whole body.

"Dammit, Professor. You're fucking perfect."

He shifted, thrusting up, squeezing her ass, settling even deeper.

"Oh! *James.*"

"That's right." He squeezed her again. "Now ride me, Harper."

Harper. Damn, that made her hot.

She started to move. She lifted and lowered herself, the friction and heat and pressure glorious.

Her nipples beaded as goose bumps erupted over her skin, and her muscles clenched around him as if to hang on to the best thing they'd ever felt. But she couldn't stay still. She did it again. And again. Taking him deep, slowly, relishing every inch. Every hot, hard, holy-crap-that-is-so-so-good inch.

He just let her go for a few minutes, watching her, holding her hips tightly but letting her move and shift and circle. And enjoy. Because she was. She so was. This was amazing. His jaw was tight, his eyes hot, but he just let her do her thing.

Until he didn't.

"Harper, damn, girl. More, baby." He pressed her down on him hard as he thrust upward.

"Oh!" She loved that fullness and the feel of him getting even deeper. "Yes!"

He brought her forward, to kiss her, yes—and he did, hot and long, stroking her tongue with his—but also to bring her clit against him where a press and a rub shot tingles of heat and pleasure zinging through her. He squeezed her ass with one hand and lifted the other to a breast, rolling and tugging on a nipple making her inner muscles clench.

"James!"

"You know what I want to hear, Harper," he rasped against her mouth.

His rough voice added to all the sensations, and she felt the coiling of her orgasm, delicious and tight. "Yes," she told him breathlessly. She wanted him to hear it, too. She wanted to come hard, his name on her lips. But not quite yet. This was all so good. Just being connected like this, his big body around her, part of her, filling her.

He shifted her again, rolling her hips, rubbing her against him, pinching her nipple, and she felt herself on that precipice.

She moaned. She wanted to linger there. Enjoy it. Anticipate it all.

But he was having none of that. He surged up into her, pressing her down at the same time, kissing her deeply, breast in one hand.

"You are so damned sweet," he told her. "I love how you're just soaking this up. I've never seen someone just..." He blew out a breath. "I've never watched someone just freaking *enjoy* like this."

In spite of the heat and fullness, the way her whole body was insisting that she move and *take,* she laughed lightly. "I am very much *enjoying* this. Isn't that how it's supposed to work?"

"It's... different with you."

She looked at him. He seemed confused. Or amazed. Or something. It was usually easy for her to put words to things. It seemed significant that she couldn't just now. It also seemed right that they would be talking during sex. Words mattered to her. He knew that. The fact he was using them right now mattered.

He also had a point.

"Enjoyment is used in a lot of ways," she said. He was buried deep, their bodies were hot skin to hot skin. They were as intimate physically as two people could get at the moment, but she was going to give him a language lesson. Because this mattered. "It can definitely mean getting pleasure and satisfaction from something. But it can also mean fun. And my favorite meaning is gladness." She took his face in her hands and looked into his eyes. "I'm *glad* to be here. I also like the related words 'savor' and 'relish.' Both are related to enjoyment. Both apply here."

He stared at her. "Damn, I like you, Professor," he finally said.

That might have been the best thing he could have said in

that moment. Because she was certain he'd never said that to another woman in quite that way in this type of moment.

"I like you, too," she told him.

He got a hot, almost mischievous look in his eye. "I know you do. And you think me being a firefighter is hot."

She laughed. "Dammit, I do."

"You have from the very first day."

"Yes."

"Knew it."

"You know what else I find hot?"

"My lizard?" He gave her a wink.

She did like Henry, actually. But she wouldn't call him hot. She leaned in and put her mouth against his ear. "That you know what I mean when I say *baise-moi.*"

He gave a little groan, gripped her hips, and said, "Gladly." Then he lifted his hips, thrusting deep.

They might have taken a little break from the motion and friction, but the pleasure flared hot instantly, and Harper felt herself teetering on the edge of her orgasm again within only a few strokes. She also knew it was because of this man and her feelings for him and her experiences with him to this point rather than because of what they were doing physically.

Though when his big hands on her ass shifted her again just right and pressed deep, she couldn't deny it was also what they were doing physically.

"*James.*"

"Little more, Professor. I need a little"—he thrust up —"bit."—he thrust again—"more."

She came with a cry. "Fuck yes, James!"

His breath hissed out, and even as the waves were still crashing over her, he flipped her over and thrust deep. So deep. Harper thought maybe her eyes rolled back. Her brain definitely short-circuited for a second. He hiked one of her legs up, propping her calf on his shoulder, just as she'd asked, and then he *took her*. She'd never been taken. Not really. Not that she now knew what was possible.

She wasn't sure she even breathed during the next few minutes, but she couldn't think of something as mundane as that when she had James Reynaud doing the things he was doing to her.

Harper was shocked to feel herself climbing toward a second orgasm—something else she'd chalked up to fictional fantasies only—and she cried out and clamped down around him as he roared her name and came.

He let her leg down but didn't change much else about their positioning as he lowered himself to the couch and pulled her against him on the cushions.

Their labored breathing filled the air, and Harper *enjoyed* every bit of the heat and hardness of his big body against and mostly on top of her as they recovered.

———

As far as James was concerned, things were pretty fucking perfect.

Harper Broussard was amazing. Her sharp mind and humor and willingness to feed a bearded dragon flies, and the way she called him on his bullshit and was not really okay with but still stepped up when it came to baby poop. She was also the best sex he'd ever had.

Not just because she had a body he was sure he'd never get enough of, but because of the *way* she had sex. She had made sex with him seem like something she just absolutely *loved*. Everything from the slow way she'd moved, seeming to just absorb it all, to the look on her face, had been so different from any he'd ever had. Women liked sex with him. They had a good time. Orgasms were handed out, and everyone left with a smile on their face. But he'd never felt *relished*. She'd used that word, too. As if it were all something she just wanted to wallow in and remember for a long, long time.

In spite of the fun he'd had with other women, he wasn't *quite* cocky enough to think he was a never-forget-it guy to all of them. A couple, maybe. Possibly even several.

But none of them had ever looked the way Professor Harper Broussard had looked.

She was good for his ego.

He could tell himself it was because she was less experienced than the women he typically slept with. Or that it was because of her books and that she had a few fantasies she was bringing to life with him. Maybe that was part of it. He had no trouble being part of her fantasies. He knew the hot, gritty, dirty stuff she liked to read, and if she wanted *any* of that, he'd happily deliver.

But he thought the olives and shopping for baby car seats were also part of how all this felt. For both of them.

Strangely.

He loved it.

"We should go get Isaac," she finally said softly against his chest.

"Yep."

They lay for another few seconds.

"So you should probably get up." She stroked her hands up and down his back.

James felt his cock stir just from that.

She did, too. She laughed. "That's not what I meant by getting up."

He laughed and hugged her. "You might need to get used to that."

"I think I can handle it." She ran a hand down his side, but he trapped it under his hand before she got to wandering too far.

"I'll give you all kinds of chances to handle it, Professor," he said. "After we get the kid back and settled in his own bed for the night."

Harper didn't say anything right away, and he cranked his neck to look down at her. "You okay?"

"Yeah. That just sounded... really nice." She looked up. "I like all of this."

He did, too. Maybe too much. "Same."

"It's happened really fast."

"That's how it goes sometimes."

"That's probably the part I'm not as used to. I think things through. Plan. Analyze."

He nodded. "Which makes the way you're just rolling with this even more awesome."

She gave him a little smile. "It's mostly because I've been wanting to get you naked for months now."

He snorted. "Sure."

"I'm serious."

"You just had to ask, Professor. At any point. *Any* point."

She looked completely serious when she said, "I know. That's why I didn't."

That hit him a little harder in the chest than he would have expected. "You thought I was just fucking around."

"I did. At first," she admitted.

"And now?"

"You don't fuck around." She frowned slightly as if that had just occurred to her. "I guess I'm learning that there's a big difference between having fun and fucking around."

"You don't do either one?" That should surprise him, but it didn't. She seemed content. She seemed sure of herself and like she was living a life she chose and doing things she wanted to be doing, but she didn't present a picture of fun, exactly. Not by a traditional definition. Not by his definition as of six months ago.

Huh. His definition of fun had changed, too. Interesting.

"I... enjoy things." She gave him a little smile as she clearly thought back to her use of that word during sex.

Again, his body stirred.

"I enjoy things," she said again, as if more sure now that she'd given it a little thought. "But I suppose it all feels thoughtful and intentional. Not spontaneous and fly by the seat of my pants. That's never been me."

Thoughtful and intentional did seem like her. Those were great words, actually.

"But I think that you're a lot more thoughtful than you come across," she said. "You make an impression on people. People see the caregiver you are even in short interactions—like the little boy in his classroom with Henry," she said. "You are not frivolous. You're fun, but you don't fuck around." She seemed to have made a decision because she gave a little nod.

"So where's your thoughtfulness and intention come from?" he asked.

"I was an only child," she said. "And my parents were—are—very studious people. My mother was a teacher. My dad was a lawyer. When we took trips, it was for a purpose and well planned. We enjoyed it. But we didn't accidentally end up in the wrong town or spontaneously take a side trip or strike up random conversations.

We socialized, but it was never a last-minute decision, and it was never anywhere... chaotic." She seemed to be thinking hard about all of that, analyzing it.

"We never went to theme parks or amusement parks. We went to plays and movies and even ball games, but it was always something that we needed to plan for, have tickets for, that had start-and-end times. It was never to places that were just-show-up-and-do-whatever-comes-up-when-you-get-there places." She frowned.

"I never realized that until now," she said, looking up at him. "Or I never really thought about it. But everything was planned. So now, I feel most comfortable when I have a plan. I find the Quarter fascinating because it's full of such a mix of people and activities, and it's never the same day to day. So I kind of watch it from a distance. But my life in the midst of it is still very ordered. Classes start and end at a certain time. I'm in charge of what happens during those class periods. At least... until I get home." She gave him a little smile. "I never know what might show up outside my door."

James settled his hand on her ass in what he recognized as a possessive move. He wanted to keep her. Yes, right here with him on this couch, naked and satisfied and warm and soft and wet. But also just in general. He wanted to keep her. But he kept bringing chaos to her door. Was that really okay?

"Sorry 'bout that," he finally said.

"Don't be."

"No?"

"Nah. I've got a hot firefighter living across the landing to help me out."

He lifted a brow. "My job and schedule is definitely chaotic. I never know what's going to happen or truly how long it's going to last. Generally, of course, but as you've learned, things can change pretty quickly."

"And you deal with it," she said. "No matter what it is. Even when you've come over here for 'help,' you really just wanted to flirt. You would have dealt with all of it if I'd told you to get lost."

James felt warmth spread through his chest and gut. Not the heat this woman so often created in him but true warmth.

"I'm glad you didn't do that," he said.

"Me too." She gave him a soft smile.

A woman like Harper Broussard liking him mattered.

He gave her a little smack on the ass. "Stop trying to seduce me, Professor. I got a kid I gotta take care of before I bend you over the island in my kitchen and lick your pussy until you scream the way *I've* been thinking about since the day I found you feeding Henry mealworms there."

She clearly didn't know how to respond to any of that. She was staring at him, clearly shocked and turned on and amused and slightly scandalized and yeah, turned on. He leaned in and kissed her long and deep and full of promise that he hoped she understood.

He lifted his head, and she cleared her throat.

"Okay, yeah, we should definitely go get him."

She'd said *we*. He would have been okay with her just climbing into his bed and waiting for him to get back. Naked, of course. But she wanted to come along to pick the baby up from Bea? That was great.

"Then let's get going. I need you again. Soon."

She gave him a hot look. "Same."

Thirty minutes later, they were on Bea's front porch. James had a sleeping baby boy in his arms, and Harper had a chicken casserole in one hand and a pan of some kind of pasta in the other.

"The support group knows better than anyone what it's like to have a newborn at home," Bea said. "There's no time to do anything, it seems, and when you do have a break, you should be trying to sleep. So we've got these dinners for you, and we're sending dinner over from Trahan's on Sunday night. Also a couple of my granddaughters are going to come clean both of your apartments on Saturday. And I'll be coming by to pick up laundry on Thursday."

"You do not have do clean and do our laundry," Harper protested.

"Oh, don't be silly. I'm doing laundry that night anyway," Bea said. "And my grandson is grounded for missing curfew, so that gives him more folding to do, which is the perfect punishment. I make him do it in the living room with me while I watch my mystery shows."

"Mystery shows?" James asked.

"Oh yeah, you know the unsolved mystery ones. I always find the episodes where some teenager was a brat and went to a party and was never heard from again when he's watching with me."

"Wow," James said. He looked down at Isaac. "Should I be taking notes?"

"Nah," Bea told him. "Just come talk to me again when he's fourteen. I'll have all kinds of tips and tricks." She rolled her eyes. "Not that they're fail-proof. Obviously. Little shits. But I love them. And I tell them that my job isn't to make them happy, it's to make them people that the rest of the word is happy to have around. There is a difference. At least at this point in their lives."

James grinned. He loved the idea of the support group still being around and the people still friends, sharing advice, and helping each other out when Isaac was fourteen. The idea that Isaac would be fourteen *with him* also gave him a little jolt of emotion that felt like a mix of fear and happiness.

He looked at Harper.

He'd sure like to have her still around when Isaac was missing curfew and he was making punishments stick and dealing with heavy sighs and eye rolls and slamming bedroom doors.

It was too soon to tell her that. He knew that. But it was right on the tip of his tongue.

"Well, I'm never going to turn down home cooking from anyone," Harper said. "But we'll take the help with at least James's apartment." She looked up at him. "That's where we'll be now most of the time."

He gave her nod. "Yes, *we* will."

They got the baby and the food settled in the car, and he looked over at her. "Thank you."

"For?"

"For letting them help us out."

She nodded. "I'm learning that it's nice to have a team."

"Yeah?"

"I've never done a lot of that," she admitted. "Always been very self-sufficient. But it's nice to have someone who can be there for my dog when I can't be and someone who'll fix my dishwasher when it stops working."

He reached over then grabbed her hand, lifting it to his lips.

"It's also nice to have people who will come over and listen to you freak out about discovering you're suddenly a parent and someone who can come over and reassure you that the baby is healthy."

"Do you have people to listen to you freak out?" he asked. He didn't know anything about her friend group. She didn't have people over to the apartment, and if she went out, it had to have been on nights he was at work or the club because she was always home when he was.

She shook her head. "I meant your friends. They came straight over. They gave you a hard time, but they were there."

He nodded. "They're the best."

"You get good friends when you are a good friend."

He loved his friends. He was lucky to have them. "And when you introduce them to erotic romance," he said lightly.

She smiled. "I have one friend at school and she's great."

"Have you told her about me?" he asked, lifting her hand to his lips again and kissing it then dragged his lips back and forth, scraping lightly with his evening stubble. He loved the little shiver that produced and knew her nipples had tightened. His tongue tingled with the memory of how they'd felt and tasted against it. He wanted more.

"I have," Harper said, a little breathlessly.

"What have you told her?"

"That you're a firefighter," she said with a little smile that made his cock harden.

"Knew it." He gave her a grin.

She laughed then leaned in closer. "And that I want you. That I know I probably shouldn't. That you're young and love to go out and that we have nothing in common. But that I have dirty dreams about you and that you make me laugh and that I think about you when you're not around and that the sound of your boots on the steps always make my heartbeat speed up."

James's own heartbeat sped up with that, and he lifted a hand to the back of her head and brought her in. "Fucking love that." He kissed her, hot and hard. But then he pulled back. "I'm not too young for you, Professor."

She nodded. "I think that was just an excuse to keep from getting involved."

"Why did you want to keep from getting involved?"

"Seemed easier not to."

He took a breath and looked over his shoulder at the baby in the back seat. "Well, that was for damned sure." He'd sucked her into all this. Inadvertently, but still, she was now smack dab in the middle of a lot of craziness. None of which was her responsibility and that she hadn't chosen.

He felt her hand on his chin, turning him back to look at her. "It's okay."

"You sure?" He wanted it to be okay, but he did want her to be sure. It was probably too late to really be asking that, though. He should have asked that, thought of all this, before she'd gone to the store for formula that first night.

But he really didn't want her to bail now.

He would do this on his own if he had to.

He really didn't want to, though.

He had to give her a chance to get out. If they found Isaac's mom. Or if they didn't.

He hadn't told her that one of the women he had on his list was a *real* long shot. It was possible he'd never be able to track her down. Especially if she didn't want to be found. Whether that made things easier or harder was yet to be seen.

"I'm... pretty sure," Harper said after a long moment.

He appreciated her honesty.

"It's a lot," she admitted. "But I don't regret getting involved."

"It's the endorphins from the orgasms," he teased. He was only half teasing. Why this was all hitting him right now, he couldn't say. But he'd been so damned glad to have her there for all this and thinking about how amazing it was that she'd just step up like this for him and this baby that he hadn't really thought about what a huge deal it was that she was actually doing that.

"Oh, I'm sure that's part of it," she said with a smile. "And the fact that I want about a hundred more of those from you."

His body reacted in spite of his brain trying hard to be reasonable and decent.

He wanted her. In his bed. Every fucking night. He wanted her in his apartment, the scent of her shampoo in his bathroom, her coffee cup in his kitchen sink, her shoes by his front door. And yeah, he wanted to come home to find her rocking his son to sleep.

That was not reasonable.

"Harper, you don't have to do all of this. I... should have said this before. I should have *thought* this before. You don't have to take all of this on."

She frowned slightly. "What do you mean?"

"Isaac. Looking for his mom. The late-night feedings. The diapers and..." He shrugged. "Everything. This isn't your responsibility."

"I want to."

Did she? Or was she just a good person who couldn't say no? Or was she an uber-responsible person who didn't quite trust him to not screw it up? Did she still see the guy standing in front of her with a tree that he didn't even know produced olives, using it as a way to hit on a woman?

"Because you're worried about me and Isaac?"

"Yes." She didn't even blink. "This is a lot for you to handle, James. You don't need to do it alone."

"I have a lot of friends who will step up." As they'd proven.

"But I'm right there. And we're a good team," she said.

He could tell she was confused by this sudden resistance on his part and the way he seemed to be trying to push her away. She should be confused. He wasn't sure where all this was coming from exactly, either.

On the heels of hot sex? Where the hell were *his* endorphins?

But that was it. He'd now had the best sex of his life with the bookworm professor across the landing, who was turning out to be so much more than that. He was already so comfortable with her in his life. He was already coming to depend on her in crazy ways. This all felt good. Great. Perfect.

He wasn't pushing her away. At least he hadn't been. But he maybe should be. If not pushing, *offering* her a way out.

"What's going on?"

He looked into her eyes. "I'm just realizing that I've gotten very comfortable with you using the word "we." I love it. I want it. And that's not fair. This isn't really a we thing. This is me, and I've been cajoling you into it from the beginning. Just like the tree and Henry and Fred."

Harper looked confused and concerned. "This is sudden."

He looked up at Bea's front door. "It just hit me. You're usually at home in your chair reading at this time of the night. It would be one thing if we were just at my apartment finally having hot sex, but we're also here picking up my son from the babysitter's and collecting casseroles from my friends."

"Oh." Harper sat back in her seat. "Oh."

He wasn't sure what the *two* ohs were for. But it didn't sound good.

"What?"

"It just all got real and domestic to you."

He frowned. "More real and domestic than changing poopy diapers? No."

"Yes. The first night was all just crazy, and you were shocked he was even there, and you were—*we* were—kind of just going on instinct and making it through. Not to mention the being in bed together the first time and the shower and everything. It wasn't routine or normal. But now this"—she gestured at the truck and the casserole dishes on the floor at her feet—"is a lot more normal, and you're realizing that it's happening really fast."

"I'm trying to give *you* an out," he said with a frown.

"Sure," she said. "Because if I take an out, you'll have an out."

"Why would I want an out?"

"Because now we've finally had sex."

Her words hit him hard in the chest. "That is *not* what this is." Then it really sank in. "You think now that I've fucked you, I'm over it all? That's what I've been going for and now that I got it, I don't want you around anymore? Or that it wasn't good enough, and now I'm trying to get out of doing it again?"

"Shh!" She glanced into the back seat. "You'll wake him up."

James shifted the truck into reverse and backed out of Bea's driveway. She thought he was over her now? Fuck that.

"You really think that all of this has just been my way of getting you into bed?" he asked as they drove the dark streets back to the apartment. "This is pretty fucking elaborate, isn't it?"

"I don't think you had someone deliver a baby to your front door as a ploy to get me into bed, no."

She said it calmly. Which further irritated him.

"So what do you think? I'm an opportunist who thought, 'Well, hell, now I have a kid, but at least maybe the professor will take her panties off this time?'"

She sighed. "Of course not."

"Then what?" He looked over.

"I told you. This all got real at Bea's. We've been playing around at the apartment, in the shower and everything. You and your friends were hanging out after that. At the restaurant, it was more of a date than it was about Isaac, really, especially because it turned out not to be Megan. But now, you pulled up to pick the baby up from the babysitter, loaded the car seat, got the casseroles, had to think about things like the fact this is long term and how hard it's going to be to even make meals and clean the apartment and do laundry and... it got real."

"Okay, it got real," he said. "And I realized that you didn't sign up for this. Something's been happening between us for six months—and don't fucking say it hasn't been."

She didn't say a word.

"I realized that all of this chaos is mine and that I love having you in the midst of it and that the sex with you was the best I've ever had, probably because I fucking *like you* more than I've liked any other woman, ever. You make everything easier. And more fun. I've loved having Fred with you, and well, gee, a baby will be even more of that, right? Then it hit me that holy shit, that's unfair. I should tell you that I want to *date* you and take you out and dance with you and yes, fuck you in every position, on every surface, over and over and over again, and you don't have to change one poopy diaper at all. I'll figure out a way to do all of that."

She said nothing, and he didn't take his eyes off the road. He just let all those words hang in the air between them, his heart pounding, as he finally pulled onto their street and into his space in front of the building.

He shoved the truck into park, shut the ignition off, and

started to turn toward her. But before he'd even shifted his weight, his lap was full of woman.

Harper straddled his thighs, took his face in her hands, and kissed him.

He gripped the back of her shirt, holding her in place, opening his mouth, not sure who was devouring who but feeling her rocking against his cock, her tongue tangling with his, her hands in his hair, almost desperate to be against him.

He knew the feeling. He pressed her down against his instantly hard cock, wanting to take her right now, hard and fast. The baby was asleep in the back seat, the street was quiet and dark, and hell, he didn't care if someone saw them. This woman was everything, and if she wanted him right here and now, she could have him. She could always have whatever she wanted from him, whenever she needed it.

Her thoughts seemed to be going in the same exact direction because a moment later, her hands were at his fly, unbuttoning and unzipping. He reached down and hit the lever to send the seat shooting back, giving her plenty of space to move. She opened his pants and freed his erection, her hands squeezing and stroking.

"Fuck, Harper."

"Yes. God, yes. I need you."

"Right-hand pocket."

She dug for the condom, opened it and rolled it on then hiked her skirt up, pulled her panties to one side and then guided him home.

She sunk down on him, and they groaned together.

She wasn't naked. He couldn't see anything but her face. But this was perfect. Her face said it all. Her gaze was hot and locked on his. Her mouth was open as she breathed fast, her hair was escaping the messy bun. The frantic pace, the way she'd climbed into his lap, was all too damned good. This was about more than the pleasure and sex, more than their bodies.

This was a connection. A promise. An I'm-here-for-this moment. After everything he'd laid out, his buttoned-up linguistics professor was fucking him in the front seat of his pickup. It was the hottest, most important sex of his life.

"James."

He gripped her hips and thrust up into her. She was so tight, so perfect, so fucking hot and wet. "Harper."

She gripped his head, her fingers sunk deep in his hair, and started moving. Up and down, taking him deep, the sweetest pussy he'd ever felt milking him, sucking everything from him.

"God, this is so good." She breathed out. "So, so good."

He squeezed her ass. "You are amazing."

He couldn't wait to spread her out and really see what he was doing. He'd put her back on his bed, legs wide, every gorgeous inch on display as he made her come again and again. Or he'd lay her out on his kitchen table, push her knees to her chest, and watch his cock move in and out of her. He'd bend her over the back of his couch or put her on her knees, gripping his headboard and take her from behind. So many ways to take her.

And none of it would be quite like this. This felt like a commitment.

He needed to cool it. He needed to slow down. Take it easy.

He couldn't.

She started moving faster, her deep muscles gripping him. He met her with upward thrusts, loving the breathless gasps and little moans.

James felt his climax building, and he reached under her skirt, finding her clit and circling with his thumb.

"Oh fuck. Yes, James."

That was pretty damned close to what he'd wanted to hear from her. He put his thumb to his mouth and sucked on it. She watched, her eyes wide, clearly turned on. Wet and slippery, he returned his thumb to that sweet spot, rubbing and pressing.

"Fuck me, Harper," he said gruffly.

She did. Riding him hard and fast, making sure she kept the angle that would keep her clit against his thumb, she took him deep over and over, until she cried out, clamping down on him and making his balls tighten hard and his own climax rip through him.

"Harper. Fuck. Yes. Holy hell. Yes." He chanted and praised as the pleasure overtook him.

He wrapped his arms around her waist, putting his forehead to her shoulder, dragging in deep breaths of her scent and the scent of them together.

They stayed like that for several long moments, ripples of pleasure fading slowly.

Finally, she stirred and pulled back to look down at him.

He looked up.

Fuck. He was in love with her.

It hit him in that moment, and he had to bite his tongue, literally, to keep from blurting it out.

"And as I was saying," she told him, still a little breathless. "Everything just got a lot more *real*."

Well, that was the biggest understatement ever. He nodded. "Agreed."

"But you let me go that first night, James," she reminded him. "I went to the store and got the stuff, but I went back to my apartment. I was the one who came over and climbed into your bed. So you need to stop with this crap about you *making* me be there for all of this. I'm very capable of telling you when I don't want to do something."

He didn't totally believe her. He didn't think she would be able to say no to Isaac. Or him, honestly. If he needed her, she would be there. But if she understood that he knew she didn't have to be doing any of this, then that was a good place to leave all this. Probably.

It was very hard to think straight with his cock still buried inside the body he never wanted to leave.

"Say okay, James," she told him, her voice soft. "Say you trust me to tell you if I'm not okay."

"Okay."

"And say that you'll tell me if you're not okay. Because this is going to be hard sometimes."

"I'll tell you."

She smiled. "You won't. You're the guy who takes care of things."

He liked that. He liked that she thought that. That she didn't think he'd been showing up at her door because he was a fuck-up. "I do. But I also know that I can't always do it alone. The fire station has taught me that. The band has taught me that. I'm a great piano player, but it all sounds a hell of a lot better when everyone is playing."

Her smile grew. "I like that. Okay, then. We're on the same page."

"I like this page," he said honestly.

"Me too."

"And I *really* like the make-up sex." He squeezed her ass.

"Me too," she said enthusiastically.

If he'd liked her before with her books and tea and the pencil that was sometimes tucked behind her ear when he'd interrupted her in the middle of correcting student essays, he *loved* her when she was wanton about sex with him.

And when she was lifting his baby boy out of his car seat and cooing to him as she carried him inside, and when she was loving up his dog that had been left alone far too long—in the dog's estimation, anyway—and when she was letting his bearded dragon sit on her shoulder while she made two cups of tea.

"ONE OF THE WOMEN YOU... DATED... IS A PHOTOGRAPHER?"

James grinned at Harper's hesitation over the word *dated*. They both knew he hadn't dated this woman. He thought her name was Kylie, but it might have been Kaylie. He hadn't told Harper that part.

"A photographer's assistant," he corrected as they headed down the sidewalk toward Angie's photography studio.

"And you met her how?"

"Shooting the firefighter's calendar for next year."

"Of course." Harper didn't roll her eyes.

But he could hear in her voice that she wanted to.

"I'm Mr. July. That's an important one," he said, inserting just enough cockiness into his voice that she'd know he was joking.

"Wow, I'm shocked," Harper said. "Hottest month of the year? That just doesn't fit at all."

They were holding hands, and he pulled her close, kissing the top of her head. "Oh, yeah? Because Caleb is August, and he claims August is the hottest month of the year."

"Hmm..." She seemed to be thinking about that. "Caleb is— I mean *August* is—really hot."

James looked down at her with an eyebrow up.

He was exhausted. So was she. Isaac had decided that his nap at Bea's and in the car had been enough to sustain him until about one in the morning. James needed to work tonight, and Harper had tried to insist they could put this visit off. She'd also offered to go to the photography studio alone and find out if anyone there had been pregnant in the past few months as she had at the restaurant so he could sleep. But he hadn't been able to let her go.

So not only were they on their way together, working on very little sleep, but they had Isaac in tow. He was currently in the sling carrier across James's chest. In part because they hadn't wanted to leave him with a sitter again so soon and in part because, as James had mentioned last night, if they walked in and the mother saw the baby with James, they would get a reaction that would be hard for her to cover, and it would give her away before they had to ask many questions. It hadn't felt fair to do that to Megan in such a public place, but Kylie-Kaylie's workplace was a lot less crowded. And honestly, this would really cut down on the time it would take tiptoeing around the issue with subtle questions.

Even though they had both been yawning their way through breakfast, and he had a long shift ahead of him tonight, he felt energized. Having Harper there while they'd tried to get Isaac to sleep again last night and lying in bed with him while he fed the baby at four a.m. and waking up with her this morning—even if it was to the sounds of an angry, wet baby—had been awesome.

"Be good or I won't reenact my pose for the calendar for you," he told her.

"What was the pose?" she asked.

"Me in my uniform pants, unzipped, kind of sagging on my

hips, shirtless, wet from a hose—of course, because we always run around half-naked and spraying each other with the water hoses—and..." He trailed off. "Nah, I don't think you could handle it."

Now she looked up at him with an eyebrow raised. "You'd be surprised what I can handle."

He wouldn't, actually. There was nothing he'd put past her. She was capable and smarter than hell and willing to just take a deep breath and go for it. He loved that about her.

He was also getting more comfortable with the L word in relation to this woman. Very quickly, as a matter of fact.

"Okay," he said. "Remember—half naked. Wet. Glistening, even."

"Got it," she said with the eye roll she'd hidden earlier.

"And holding a Dalmatian puppy."

She stopped walking. Right in the middle of the sidewalk. A dangerous undertaking on even most of the side streets in the French Quarter. The people a few steps behind them dodged them, one shooting them a frown.

"You okay?" he asked her with a smug grin.

"I think my panties just melted off," she told him.

"Yeah, I thought that might be a problem."

"I mean, seriously. How am I supposed to walk around the rest of the day like this?"

He nodded, trying to look solemn. "I warned you." He glanced around. "I mean, I could put you up against a wall here and take care of you, if you need it. Maybe we could get that guy to hold the baby."

There was a street performer standing on a beat-up milk crate, juggling a shoe, a plastic bowling pin, and a rubber chicken. He wasn't bad. The chicken was a nice addition.

"But he'd have to put his stuff down," she said. "Those three minutes could cost him a buck or two."

No one was dropping money in the guy's jar. But that

wouldn't stop him. A lot of the performers on the corners in the Quarter did it for money, for sure, but they also did it because they enjoyed the attention and being in the heart of the fun craziness that was the French Quarter. They were part of the ambiance, and a lot of them actually felt as drawn to that as they were to the money.

"Three minutes?" he asked. "You think that's all I can last?"

She eyed the building beside them. "Against those rough bricks? I think that's all I can take, big guy. You're gonna have to just get to it and get it over with."

"Big guy," he repeated. "I like that." He stepped close. Of course, Isaac was fast asleep now. Now, while they were wide awake. Which was clearly an instance everyone had been telling them about where they should have been sleeping along with him. But that simply didn't always work. They had stuff to do. Maybe they should try to wake him up and show him the world. James honestly didn't know. At the moment, however, the fact that the baby was sleeping worked well, because it allowed him to pull Harper in and run a hand up the back of her leg to her ass, pulling her skirt up a bit with it. "How about we revisit the wet and glistening conversation later when we're back home? Maybe see which of us can get the other wet first."

Her pupils dilated a little even though she said, "You'll be at work."

Dammit. This would be his first work shift since Isaac had showed up. Which really did seem to indicate that whoever had brought him to James knew about his work schedule. "We should go home now," he said.

She laughed, put a hand on his chest, and pulled back. "We need to go to the photography studio."

They did. They needed to get to the bottom of all this. If Kylie-Kaylie wasn't the mom, he was going to take Harper to the club when he was off again. One of the bartenders there had introduced him to the third woman on his list. James didn't know how well Marcus knew Caroline—he was sure of her name, thankfully—but he was hopeful Marcus would at least know how to get ahold of her. She was from Wisconsin. Or Wyoming. One of the W states. Fuck, Washington. It could also be Washington.

"How many states start with W?" he asked Harper as they started walking again.

"Four," she answered promptly.

"Wyoming, Wisconsin, Washington, and?" he asked.

"West Virginia," she said. "The closest one, by the way."

Right. Yeah. But no, it wasn't anything with a direction in it.

"Why?" Harper asked.

He sighed. She already knew a lot about him and his previous sexual habits. He wasn't proud of it, but she was still here, helping, so maybe she wasn't *horrified*. Though *he* was starting to feel a little horrified.

He was ready to be a one-woman man.

With Harper.

"The girl we need to find if this one isn't her," he said. "She's from somewhere that starts with a W."

"Ah."

"Ah? What's that mean?"

"That's maybe a little more complicated."

"To find her? Yeah."

"Not that. She's here. Or at least she was a couple of nights ago," Harper said. "But the fact that she's from another state might make custody difficult." She shrugged. "Though I don't know. If she's just willing to drop him off, she might be willing to sign over rights, and it won't matter where she's from."

He hadn't thought of all that. Dammit. Whoever the woman was, when he did finally find her, she was going to get a piece of his mind. This was their *child*. Didn't she realize he might need to know a few things? That if she wanted James to take care of him, he'd need at least a few details? He looked at Harper. At least his taste in women had improved. Harper would have never just dropped the kid off like that.

"Maybe she wasn't the one who dropped him off," James suggested. It bugged him that a woman he'd been involved with would do that. But he hadn't really *known* any of these women. He'd probably spent the most time talking with Megan. Kylie-Kaylie would have been second on that list. They'd gone to dinner after the photoshoot and talked for an hour before she'd suggested going back to her apartment. Of course, once they hit that doorway there hadn't been much talking, and he'd headed back out of that door about two hours later.

"I think the mom dropped him off," Harper said, interrupting James's thoughts of what a man-whore he'd been. "Whoever did it, dropped him off right at your door, so she knew where you lived. She did it right before you got home. And she did it right before you had two days off. It's someone who knows those details. And it's not easy to explain to people why you're pregnant and then suddenly have no baby. I'm guessing she kept it all as secret as possible. You don't just ask someone to take your baby from Wisconsin or Wyoming to New Orleans to an apartment in the Quarter and leave it."

He frowned. "I guess."

"She could have left him at any safe haven in this city or in any city between here and wherever she's from," Harper went on. "She also could have given him up for adoption. She specifically chose to give him to you. With a note. That means that she knew you well enough to know that you're a good guy and she cared enough to at least give him to his father."

That made James pause. Had he really known any of these women well enough to convince them that he was a good guy who'd be willing and able to be a dad?

It only took about a minute of really thinking about that question for him to groan. If the woman hadn't just panicked about not wanting to be a mom and had specifically decided that he'd be good at this, then it wasn't Megan or Kylie-Kaylie. They didn't know him well enough. It also wasn't the girl from the W state. He was sure she'd been willing to spend the night with him because Marcus knew him and could vouch that he wouldn't kill her and put her in his freezer. But she hadn't *known* him. Marcus didn't really know much about James except that he could play the hell out of a piano. That meant that if Harper was right—and Harper was always right—then Isaac's mom had to be Emily.

He hadn't really thought about it being Emily.

Because it being Emily made this all a lot more complicated.

Emily was Ethan's little sister. Ethan was one of James's firefighter brothers. One he didn't get along with all that well. Emily had been in town for Ethan's wedding. The wedding James had been invited to only because Ethan had invited the entire firehouse. That's just what you did. They were a brotherhood even if they weren't best friends in their off time. When they were on the clock, they had each other's backs and would risk their lives for one another. That gave them a bond. Even if, after hours, they thought the other guy was a prick.

So James had met Emily at Ethan's wedding, and they'd spent the evening talking and dancing and drinking champagne, and he'd made the mistake of *not* going up to her hotel room that first night. Because of Ethan.

But he'd known that Emily trusted him because he was her brother's coworker in a career that required men who were brave and self-sacrificing and who would put their differences aside when it came to getting the job done. Ethan and James were a lot alike actually, which was probably why they rubbed each other the wrong way sometimes. It had been clear Emily admired her brother. Then, in the course of conversation, he'd learned that Ethan had actually talked highly of James. Not highly enough that he'd want him banging his little sister, maybe, but highly enough that Emily clearly respected James and even went as far as to say that her brother had called him funny and upstanding.

That had all been enough for her to show up at his apartment the next morning with muffins and coffee and enthusiastically toss her panties onto his bedroom floor.

It was Emily.

James felt like someone had just slapped him on the forehead.

It had to be Emily.

They'd been together during the right window of time. She lived far away from all her family, so it wasn't impossible to think she'd avoided them during the months when her pregnancy would have been most obvious. She knew where James lived and what he did for a living. She knew how fire stations ran and how theirs in particular worked. She would have known she could call and find out when James was on and off shift. And she would have known enough about him to think that he was a decent, upstanding, take-care-of-others kind of guy.

Holy shit. He now knew who Isaac's mom was. He wasn't sure exactly how to find her or get ahold of her, but there had to be a way since he knew her brother.

"She wouldn't risk someone taking him to the wrong apartment or at the wrong time and leaving him out alone. She'd bring him herself."

Harper was still talking about how the person leaving the baby with James had to have been the mother.

James glanced at her. Harper was attached to Isaac. It was more and more obvious the more time she spent with the baby and the more James observed them together. *Harper* couldn't imagine just leaving the baby there, taking a chance it was the wrong apartment. That didn't mean the mom would feel that way, though.

He was guessing that after Harper had the baby to herself for the next twenty-four hours—minus the hours she'd be in class and Bea would be watching him—they would be even more bonded.

"And besides," Harper went on. "If it *wasn't* the mom dropping him off, wouldn't that person just come to you and hand him over? They wouldn't have had to leave him in a basket with a note. You wouldn't have known them. They could have played dumb about details. They could have just waited until you were home and given him to you."

That was a decent point.

"Yeah, I think it was her, too," James admitted. It made sense. Now that he knew who she was, it made even more sense. Emily would know that fire stations were all safe havens. He was sure Ethan had told her about the baby that had been left at theirs about three years ago.

Harper nodded. "Gut instinct."

Paternal instinct, maybe. "I think I know who it is."

She looked up at him. "Really?"

"Yeah. What you just said makes a lot of sense. I think it's Emily. She's the sister of one of the other firefighters. Met her at his wedding."

"Oh." Harper seemed to be thinking about that. "How sure are you?"

How sure could he be? He shrugged. "Seventy percent?"

She seemed surprised. Probably that it was that high. "Okay. So..."

"Should we go home? I need to figure out how to get ahold of her. That might take a little time."

Harper blew out a breath. "We're already almost to the studio. We might as well cover all the bases, yes? If you're not one hundred percent."

He nodded. "Okay."

"Okay."

They walked a few more blocks before stopping in front of the photography studio.

"This is it," James said.

He was ninety-percent sure that Kylie-Kaylie wasn't Isaac's mom now. He looked up at the sign over the door and then down at Harper. He didn't mind that this outing had given him more time to hang out with her, though. Searching for the mother of his child with the woman he was falling in love with —and they were definitely not the same person—was a strange way to date her, but he was enjoying their time together.

He reached for the door and pulled it open for her.

Harper preceded him into Angie's studio, and since it was early afternoon on a weekday, a typically less busy time for her, Angie came out from the back room almost immediately.

"James!" she exclaimed, clearly surprised but pleased to see him.

"Hi, Angie."

A shorter, younger woman stepped into the room a moment after Angie. Her long, blonde hair was pulled into a high ponytail, and it still almost brushed her ass. Her bright green eyes lit up when she saw him. "James!"

Seeing her again made her name click in his mind instantly. "Hey, Kylie."

"What are you doing—" But that was as far as Kylie got before she noticed Isaac. Her eyes went wide, and her mouth dropped open.

For a second, James froze. She looked stunned. Was it her after all? And not Emily?

"Oh my God, you have a *baby*?" Kylie hurried forward. She put a hand on Isaac's back and leaned in to get a better look into the sling. "Oh, wow, he's so beautiful." She looked up at James, a bright, sincere smile on her face.

She looked young suddenly. And sweet. He did not remember her being sweet. She'd been cute and flirty, but once he'd gotten her to her apartment, she'd been very dirty. And when he'd pulled his pants back on and said he had to get going, she'd given him a big smile and said, "Okay. Thanks. Have a great rest of the night." As if he'd just brought her a pizza and she couldn't have cared less what he was doing after he left her.

"Congratulations," Kylie said enthusiastically. Then she glanced at Harper. "You must be the mom." She sighed. "I love babies so much. Wow, I'm so happy for you."

It didn't seem to phase her a bit that she was gushing over the baby that belonged to the man she'd had a very hot, sexy night with not *that* long ago.

For just a second, James was a little annoyed. Really? Not even a hint of jealousy? Not a flicker of awkwardness remembering what they'd done to one another, while standing in front of the woman she was assuming he'd just had a baby with? Maybe Kylie was really bad at math and didn't realize how close to their night together this baby would have had to have been conceived.

But when Harper stepped closer to him and put her hand on Isaac just above Kylie's in a very possessive, protective, this-is-mine gesture, James immediately stopped caring about Kylie completely.

Kylie wasn't Isaac's mom. Thank God. James clearly hadn't meant much to her, and she definitely hadn't been anything more than a hot night to him. At least he and Emily had had muffins.

And he and Harper had a hell of a lot more than that.

"Thank you," Harper said, her voice calm and sincere. "We're very happy."

James heard the unspoken *that you're clearly not the mother* tacked on to the end of Harper's sentence and he grinned.

"We just stopped in to see about maybe getting some pictures of him done," he said, directing the statement to Angie as Isaac began to stir. Baby photos actually hadn't been his intention at all, but it made sense. Why would he not want to get photos of Isaac done? Everyone had photos of their newborns done. They even sent out announcements. "You do birth announcements and things like that, right?"

He was going to send out a birth announcement?

Harper looked up at him quickly, obviously thinking that same thing.

But yeah, it seemed that he was. He was a dad now, and he wanted to let everyone know.

Of course, he should probably tell his parents before he did a mass mailing to everyone, he supposed. And his grand-mother. And the guys at the fire station.

Including Ethan.

Which meant, he needed to track Emily down. Soon.

Isaac wiggled and stretched, his eyes opening.

"I do," Angie said. She moved behind the counter and pulled a huge binder out, setting it on top and flipping it open. "Come show me what you're thinking. We'll get the session booked, too." She smiled at Isaac. "Yes, congratulations, James. That's really awesome."

"You think so?" He looked down at Isaac. Awesome. Huh. Yeah, it kind of was. Then he looked at Harper. Yeah, it defi-nitely was.

"I do all kinds of invitations and announcements," Angie said. She looked at Harper. "What are you thinking?"

Harper blinked at her. "Of?"

"For the announcements?" Angie pointed to the book. "Oh."

James had thrown her—or pulled her—into all of this so far. Why not this, too? He put an arm around her, hugging her close and said, "I know you'll want something simple and clas-sic. Nothing too cute. Nothing too gender specific."

He shifted Isaac as the baby began squirming, lifting him out of the carrier and to his shoulder.

Harper looked up at him, then to Isaac, then at the page Angie flipped to, then up at him again. "Um."

Professor Broussard never said, "Um."

He patted Isaac's back and studied the pages Angie was showing them. The baby was wet, no doubt, and probably getting hungry.

"That's really her style," James told Angie. "Classy, pretty, sweet. Nothing dramatic or too loud or fussy. Focus on the photo, not a lot of decoration around it."

Angie nodded, flipped another page, and then looked up. "Something like this?"

There was a white card at the top. The center of the card was where the photo would go. There were tiny yellow and green decorative curls at the corners and a space for information like name, weight, and birth date at the bottom. Simple, classy, focused on the photo. Exactly as he'd asked. Angie was good.

He glanced at Harper. "What do you—"

He frowned as he noticed that her eyes were shiny. As if they had filled with tears. Oh, shit. James turned. "Harper?"

She sniffed. "Those are perfect."

He liked that he'd gotten it right. But something was going on. He looked at Angie.

"I'll give you a second," she said. "Kylie and I have some things to do in back. Ring the bell when you're ready." She gestured toward the little silver bell sitting on the corner of the countertop.

"And here, let me take him for a little bit," Kylie said, coming forward and reaching for Isaac.

"He's wet," James said.

"Then give me the diaper bag, too," she said with a smile.

He must have looked surprised, because she shook her

head. "I have three younger siblings. I've changed lots of diapers. This is fine. Is there a bottle, too?"

"Yeah." James surrendered it all to her.

"You don't have to," Harper started to protest.

"It's fine. I love it," Kylie said, slipping the diaper bag over her shoulder and cradling Isaac with a smile. "Honest."

A moment later, she'd disappeared into the back room with the baby.

James focused on Harper. She was frowning after Kylie.

"You want me to go get him?"

She shook her head. "It's just... weird."

"What is?"

"That I know there are all these women in your past. I mean we've been specifically looking for two of them in the past two days, and clearly, Kylie isn't his mom, so we're going to have to keep looking. And I want to hate them and feel like I should be jealous." She looked up at him. "And I am, a little, but mostly I'm just happy to know that the women you've been with are nice women. Hardworking. At least one was happy to see you. Megan might have been too if you'd talked to her. I just..." She trailed off, shaking her head.

"You just what?" James prompted, wanting to hear this for some reason.

"I know you said that none of these women were serious or long term and yes, I'm glad about that. But you're also not just..." She took a deep breath. "You're not just fucking around with these women either. I know they might have just been one-night stands, and you might not know what W state one of them lives in, but you were sweet and funny and made sure they had a good time, and they all walked away from you—or watched you walk away—feeling good about things."

He'd liked to think so. But it meant even more that Harper would assume all that. Not because one of the women had told her that, but because she knew him. He lifted a hand to her face, running the pad of his thumb over her cheek. "Would this be easier if I'd just banged them in the storage room and didn't even know where any of them were from or worked?"

"No. Because that wouldn't line up with the guy I know you are."

"Why the teary eyes, then?" He stepped in closer.

"Oh." Her gaze flickered to the book of invitations and announcements. "I realized that if we really were ordering birth announcements, we didn't have any information to fill in. We don't know how much he weighed or even what day his birthday actually is." She gave him a wobbly smile. "And we don't know if he had another name or what to put for his mom's name."

"He has a name, though," James said. "And I think we just make the day he came to us his birthday. And... we could fill his parents' names in."

"We could fill his dad's name in, I guess," she said. "Single dads are hot."

He smiled. "Or we could give him a mom."

She frowned.

He hadn't prepared to say this today. Or this week. Or maybe for a few months. But hell, a week ago he hadn't been prepared to be a dad, yet here they were. "I looked some stuff up. Her abandoning him essentially terminates her parental rights. We go get a lawyer, show up before a judge, and make it official."

"You mean declare you as his father and to make it official that she's out of the picture?"

"Well, yes."

"You'll need the DNA test."

"Right. But I should have that in a couple of days."

She nodded. "I mean, it doesn't solve the problem of medical history, but I guess we just do the best we can."

"But I was talking about showing up in front of the judge to make something else official."

"What's that?"

"We get married."

She just stared at him. Her eyes didn't widen. Her mouth didn't drop open. She didn't gasp. She just stared at him. As if she were still waiting for him to speak. Or maybe explain himself.

"If we're married, then you can adopt him. He'll have a mom and dad."

She wet her lips, then took a deep breath, then pressed them together.

"Professor?"

She closed her eyes and took another deep breath.

"Harper?"

"Yeah?" Her eyes were still closed.

"Did you hear me?"

She nodded.

"What do you think?"

"About getting married so we can adopt Isaac?"

Finally, he couldn't take it. He took hold of her wrists and leaned in until she opened her eyes. "Say something."

"I... I really wasn't expecting that. At all."

"When was the last time I brought something up with you that you *were* expecting?"

She seemed to think about that for a second. "The sex," she finally answered.

He gave a little laugh. "Okay, fair enough."

"But you're right," she added. "I never know what's going to happen when I answer my door."

"So this being unexpected should not be a reason to say no to it."

Harper took a deep breath.

"We have a little situation." Kylie breezed back into the

front of the store just then, Isaac in hand. In both of her hands. Which were outstretched, holding him away from her, and the baby puke that was covering the front of her. "I didn't burp him soon enough."

"Oh my gosh!" Harper rushed forward.

The moment was completely shattered, and James pulled in a deep breath. Holy shit. He'd just proposed.

But as he watched her scoop Isaac up and apologize to Kylie, who laughed it off very nicely and said she didn't live far and could easily go home and change, James realized he barely remembered a thing about his night with Kylie. But he remembered every smile Harper had ever given him.

Before Isaac. All these things he felt and thought about her were *pre*-baby. Had it all come rushing forward now that they were doing this huge, crazy, over-the-top thing of caring for a newborn together? Yes. But it had all been there before.

Now he just needed to figure out what to do about Emily, and everything would be great.

He needed to call a lawyer.

And maybe buy a ring.

No, for sure buy a ring.

———

"He *proposed*," Harper said to Celia. For the third time.

"You mentioned that," her friend said dryly.

"I mean, that's *insane.*"

Celia shook her head. "I'll give you that it's a little crazy, but it's not *insane.* You've known each other for six months. As he said, you *like* each other. Now you know the sex is amazing. You practically live together. There's a dog and now a baby." Celia took a sip of her tea. "It's not really insane at all."

"So that's all you need? To like each other, have great sex, and get a dog and baby?" Harper asked.

Celia seemed to think about that. "Well, I'd say those are a pretty great place to start. I mean, there's also stuff like kindness and trust and respect, of course."

They already had those, too. Harper realized that she was *not* winning this argument. Why was she arguing again? She looked down at the stroller where Isaac was reclining, happily watching the brightly colored stuffed lion toy that hung from the stroller's canopy. She wanted this little boy, and surely her and James being married would make that easier. The state or a judge or whoever decided these things probably liked giving babies to married couples. Right?

"Are you hung up on the fact that James is young?" Celia asked, sipping again.

"He is young," Harper said.

"He's not *young*," Celia disagreed. "He's *younger* than you. But it's not like he's barely legal."

"He's..." Harper trailed off.

"He's what?"

Young. She'd been about to say young. But it wasn't true. She sighed and looked at her friend. "He used to *seem* young. I wanted him to be too young. I thought he was this party guy who just went out all the time and loved to joke around and didn't take things seriously. But he's none of that." Which meant all her excuses to not fall for him were gone.

Probably a good thing. Since she'd fallen for him about three months ago.

"He does hang out at the jazz club a lot," Celia said.

"He plays there," Harper said. "I think just because he really loves it. I'm guessing it's the people as much as the music. There are probably guys there who he buys meals for or waitresses he overtips to help them out with their bills or something."

"I was trying to be helpful," Celia said with a little laugh.

"But yeah, he's a great guy. So for the record, I'm on Team James."

"Team James?" Harper said. "Who's the other team?"

"Team Stay Single and Celibate," Celia said with a grin. "I guess I could call James's team Team Orgasm Central or Team Happily Ever After."

Harper shook her head. "Those seem like two kind of different things."

Celia gave her a look that said she knew Harper knew better. "But they're really not, are they? They're the perfect combination."

Harper stirred her now cold tea. Finally, she nodded. "Yeah, they are."

"Is he the forever type?" Celia asked. "I mean, that's really the question. Can all of this stuff... the stuff you've fallen for and talked about *a lot* over the past six months... last? Is this the real him, or do you think it will change?"

Harper knew the answer immediately. "It will last. It's the real him." She sighed. "But this is about Isaac. And the idea of losing him. He's thinking this will make it easier to keep him."

"It probably will."

Harper nodded. "He wouldn't have proposed without the baby in the picture."

Celia shifted forward in her chair to rest her forearms on the tabletop. "Well, so what? It's not like you're a total stranger. It's not like you don't already like each other. You have chemistry. The baby has fast-forwarded things. So what? 'Life is what happens when you're busy making other plans.'"

Harper rolled her eyes. As a planner, she'd always hated that quote. "You think it's okay to get married because of the baby?"

"I think there are worse reasons to get married."

Harper sighed. "I'm not sure you're being helpful."

Celia laughed. "It's incredibly helpful to tell you to relax and to follow your heart."

"Unless it ends up getting broken."

Celia reached out and grabbed her hand. "Honey. Look at that baby."

Harper looked down at Isaac.

"How is that baby going to break your heart?"

Harper shook her head. "Not him. James. I've never felt this way about a guy before," she told Celia. "I've never been in love before."

Celia rewarded her with a bright smile. "Well, I have a feeling being in love with a hot, charming, funny firefighter and jazz musician, who's a softie for dogs and babies and who knows how to find your G-spot in point three seconds is going to be really, really easy."

In spite of the butterflies swooping in her stomach, Harper nodded. "You have a point." Too easy really.

Celia gave her a sly smile and leaned in farther. "So he did find your G-spot in point three seconds?"

Harper couldn't have hidden her satisfied grin if she'd tried. Which she didn't. "Point two seconds."

Celia sat back with a sigh. "Oh my God, that's awesome."

"It really was," Harper agreed. "I'm starting to understand why new parents don't have a lot of sex, though." She shot the baby an affectionate look. "It's been a whirlwind, and I don't think we've slept more than about five hours at a time."

"Then it's extra good that James can find that spot so quickly. No need to waste time looking around."

Harper couldn't *disagree*. They both laughed and sipped their nearly cold beverages, and Celia turned the conversation to wedding venues.

But Harper couldn't ignore the little niggle in the back of her mind. *She* was falling in love with James. But he was in love with the idea of… them. But them as a group. Making this work. Making this family happen. For Isaac.

She loved Isaac, too. Yes, being a family with him, for him, was great. But she would love James without the baby in the picture. Was that true of how James felt about her? Had he even thought about that?

That question was easy to answer.

No.

He hadn't really thought about how he was feeling, or why. James just rolled with things as they came. He charged through doors in buildings that were, literally, on fire, not knowing what was on the other side. He came home to a door that often had surprises outside of it. Surprises that never made him even blink. Not really. No matter how he tried to pretend when he knocked on her door. He was fine with spontaneity and surprises and adventure.

This might just be another surprise that he was dealing with as things came. Like Henry outgrowing his first tank and Ami needing major bathing after he'd gotten off the leash and rolled around in a pile of trash. James grinned through it all and just dealt with it.

A baby showed up on his doorstep? James took him in. The baby has an explosive poopy diaper? James jumped in the shower. The baby needs a mom? James marries the woman who's already coming into the apartment to feed the lizard and dog. Pretty efficient, really.

Harper fought the urge to laugh hysterically. Suddenly she leaned in and unstrapped Isaac, lifting him out of the stroller and cuddling him to her shoulder, rubbing his back. He nuzzled in against her neck in a way that was becoming very familiar and felt completely natural.

"Professor Broussard?"

Harper looked over her shoulder. The one not occupied by

a baby who needed help holding his head up but who was checking the world out from his perch.

"Sophie. Hi." She gave one of her favorite students a smile. "How are you?"

"I'm fine." Sophie was staring at Isaac. "You, um, have a *baby*?"

Harper had known bringing Isaac to campus today would be cause for some questions. But she hadn't wanted to leave him with Bea today, after all. The other woman was available, and Harper had been in her car with him on her way over there, but with every passing block she'd been less and less okay with the idea. He'd been with Bea the other night, and everything had been fine. Harper and James were both going to continue working, so they'd have to figure out a plan with care for Isaac during their work hours.

But today Harper had wanted him with her. It was the first time she'd had him on her own. This was all still new. And it was the first time she'd really, truly considered the idea that he could be hers long term. In her mind, he'd been James's son all along, but she hadn't really let herself think about how she fit into it beyond the next day or so. Now she had. And she wanted the baby with her. She knew her boss would be okay with it. She had a class and then a long break, then another class, then a break. Isaac was still young enough that he was sleeping a lot, and if she planned feedings and changings just right, he might sleep peacefully to the side of the classroom while she lectured.

The first period had gone perfectly. She just had two more to get through.

But now she had to answer the question about who he was. Celia knew. Her boss knew that she was dating Isaac's dad—she'd given her department head that much information, at least. She supposed she could tell Sophie the same.

"Kind of," she said with a smile, turning him so Sophie

could see him better. "This is my... boyfriend's son." Nope, she just couldn't use the term fiancé yet.

Sophie looked surprised then frowned. "Oh. You're dating someone with a baby?"

Harper had recognized early on that one of the things that had drawn her to Sophie was how much she'd seen herself in the girl. Harper had appreciated Sophie's color-coded planner and that she'd attended office hours nearly every week and had volunteered to tutor other students. Harper had found her intense and interesting and incredibly relatable.

But in spite of her buttoned-up, perfectionistic, clearly ordered personal priorities, Harper was sure Sophie knew people sometimes got pregnant without meaning to, and she knew that people who made babies together didn't always stay together. She surely knew lots of kids had four parents because of divorce. Or grew up in foster care. Or were adopted. While Sophie clearly avoided all things unpredictable herself, she had to know that life sometimes threw curveballs that people couldn't dodge.

There was something about making Sophie understand this fact that suddenly seemed important to her.

Because Harper *was* Sophie. Or had been. And she would have been very judgmental about a favorite professor, a woman who had worked for a doctorate degree and had her eyes set on a department head position and authoring research papers and getting tenure, who suddenly found herself tied to a jazz musician with a baby who had been dumped on his doorstep.

"Yes. I'm dating his dad." Harper gave Sophie a smile. She shot Celia a look. Her friend was watching with interest. "It's a little complicated," she told Sophie.

"I didn't even know you had a boyfriend," Sophie said. But then she smiled. "Not that I expect I would have known, I guess. It's none of my business."

Harper didn't share things about her dating life with her

students, but she had shared where her love of languages came from and her family history. She'd thought it would make them feel more able to connect with her if they understood her passion for what she taught. So yes, she'd been a little personal with them and had encouraged them think about what the class—what all of their classes—really meant to them and how their chosen major mattered and was influenced by their personal stories. That was how Sophie had ended up in her office sharing about her dedication to her education and how hard she'd worked to get where she was.

"Oh, I don't mind you knowing," Harper said. "It's all kind of new."

Sophie took a step closer to their table, and Harper turned more fully in her chair.

"He seems really little," Sophie said. "How old is he?"

"Only a couple of weeks." If James and Isaac were going to be a part of her life then she needed to get used to telling people about them.

"What's his name?" Sophie asked.

"Isaac." Harper felt that same surge of pride and love go through her saying his name.

"Oh." Sophie gave her a smile. "I like that name."

"It means 'God laughed,'" Harper said. "Or, 'He laughed.' And that makes me think of words like 'joy' and 'happiness' and 'delight.' Those are all things he makes me feel." James did, too. She couldn't avoid that thought.

"Wow." Sophie nodded. "I should have expected you to know the meaning of a name."

Celia gave a soft laugh at that.

Harper smiled at them both. "I helped pick it out."

Sophie smiled again. "I'm glad."

"You are?" That seemed like a strange thing to say.

"That means you're really involved, right? That's great. You'll be a great mom."

The compliment shocked Harper. No one had ever said that to her before. People rarely asked her about having kids since she wasn't married. Her parents didn't even ask. She supposed they just assumed it would come up when it was time. But she hadn't been around kids much in her life, so she'd never had anyone comment one way or another about how she'd be with one. "You think so?"

"Of course. You're so patient," Sophie said. "And, of course, a great teacher." She smiled. "But you're also so smart and clearly driven and goal oriented. Those are important things to pass on to a kid. And you have a steady job and a family you care about a lot who are really supportive and all of that." Sophie shrugged. "Seems like you're in a great place to be a mom now."

Harper looked at Celia again. Celia nodded with a smile.

Harper thought about all of that. It was all true. She was stable in her job. She wanted more out of her career, but her goals were things that would take years, and that could be accomplished while having a family. Many women had done that before her. She did have a supportive, loving family. They were far away, but she could imagine that her parents would fall in love with Isaac right away and would be emotionally supportive even from a distance. And her propensity for organization and planning would only be an asset when it came to being a working mom. She'd have to be organized to handle work and soccer practice and sleepovers. But she and Isaac could sit at the table at night and work together—him on his homework, her on grading her students' homework.

And it didn't surprise her at all that the table which came to mind when she pictured that was James's.

"Thank you, Sophie," she said sincerely. "That is really nice of you to say. I didn't realize that I needed that little confidence boost."

Sophie smiled. "I can't imagine you ever feel less than fully capable."

"Oh, I do." Harper laughed. "I definitely do. But—" She looked down at Isaac's head and ran a hand over his hair. "I think when you do something that you really care about, then your love for it helps make up for the nerves about doing it."

Sophie nodded. "I like that."

Harper smiled. It was good for young women to see women a bit older, women they admired, dealing with real life, and she was thrilled to be able to do that for Sophie. Harper did know that Sophie was from South Dakota so was far from home and any positive female role models or support she might have there. If there were any.

"How many brothers and sisters do you have?" she asked on impulse.

Sophie seemed surprised, but she answered, "An older sister and a younger brother."

"Are they back home in South Dakota?"

Again, Sophie seemed surprised that Harper had remembered that. "They are," she said. "My sister is older than me, but she... needs a lot of help from my parents. She makes a lot of bad choices." She sighed. "And my brother is still in high school and at home. But he's a handful. So my mom is pretty busy worrying about them."

"Meaning she doesn't worry about you much?" Harper asked.

Sophie pulled herself up straighter. "I don't give her anything to worry about."

"You're far from home, in college, working hard. I'm sure she worries some," Harper said.

Sophie shook her head. "Really, no. It's a relief to her that I'm gone, and she has one less kid around."

Harper frowned slightly. Surely that wasn't true. But she really had no idea. "Well, I'm sure she's very proud of you."

Sophie just shrugged. "I hope so. I'm trying really hard not to be like my sister and just constantly be in trouble and needing help."

Harper couldn't imagine the straight-A, always-on-time, hardworking, bright young woman being any trouble, but again, she didn't know her *that* well. Younger Harper had a lot in common with what she had observed about Sophie, but there were always layers.

"By the way," Sophie said, "I love babies, and I'm very responsible. And I could always use a little extra cash." She smiled. "If you ever need a babysitter, I'd love to do it."

Harper hadn't been expecting that, but it immediately sounded great. The girl was the epitome of responsibility, and, of course, as a college student, a little extra money, maybe a home-cooked meal, a big comfy couch with a TV she didn't have to share with a roommate for a night, probably sounded perfect.

"You know what? I'm going to take you up on that," Harper said. "We actually need to go out tomorrow night."

They still needed to hit the jazz club to find some woman James had met through the bartender there. They had planned to ask Lexi and Caleb to do it, but they had their own kids, and Sophie would be able to come over and take care of Isaac in James's apartment, so they wouldn't have to transport him back and forth.

"I'm available," Sophie said. "What time?"

"Why don't you give me your number, and I'll let you know for sure?" Harper said. "James works until seven, so it will be after that. Is that too late?"

"Not at all. Is it okay if I bring my laptop and work on a paper after he goes to sleep?"

"Absolutely."

"Great."

They exchanged cell numbers, and Harper watched Sophie head off across campus toward her next class.

"Well, that was very maternal," Celia mused.

"Setting up a sitter so we can go out?"

"Yep."

Harper grinned. "It was, wasn't it?"

"I think you're going to be just fine with this," Celia said.

Harper's heart thunked against her rib cage. She hoped so. She really did.

8

———————

"YOU *PROPOSED*?"

James laughed at Caleb's incredulous expression even though he felt just as incredulous really.

"Listen, I don't need two years with an amazing woman to realize she's amazing and that I want to keep her around forever," he said, referencing the fact that it had taken his friend two years to realize that his feelings for his now girlfriend were more than friendship.

Caleb opened his mouth, clearly to protest. But quickly shut it again. Because he had no argument here. He nodded. "Fair enough."

"So yeah, I proposed. I didn't really mean to, but it felt right. I mean I wasn't really ready for the dad thing either, but I'm in the midst of it and I like it. Might as well jump in with both feet, right?"

They were lounging in the living room area of the fire station. James was in an armchair, one foot propped on the coffee table, a bottle of water in hand. Caleb was in a recliner across from him, tipped back, his attention half on the ballgame on TV. It had been a quiet night so far, thankfully. James

185

was operating on less sleep than usual, but even more, his mind was miles away from Engine 29. He'd be ready instantly if a call came in. That stuff was ingrained, and he took his job seriously. But for now, he was grateful to not have more on his mind than the woman and baby who had taken over his heart in just a few days.

Who was he kidding? Harper had already been there, and it had taken Isaac about an hour to get to him.

"Hey, if you can get a woman like the professor to marry you, hell yes, you should go for it," Caleb said. "She's way too good for you."

James grinned. He knew Caleb didn't actually mean that. Well, he maybe did mean it—and he wasn't wrong—but he thought James was a good guy, too. He'd been impressed with the way James had stepped up with Isaac. And that meant a lot. James looked up to Caleb. The other man was older and had been a firefighter for years. He was James's lieutenant, and he ran Engine 29 with a firm command but also a sense of true concern and care for every firefighter. He demanded a lot, but he also gave a lot. He never asked anyone to do something he wouldn't do himself, and he definitely supported the men all having lives and loves outside of the station as well. Caleb was also raising his niece, Shay. He'd lost his sister and brother-in-law in a car accident and immediately stepped up as Shay's guardian. He was a great dad, a great boss, and a great friend.

"Yeah, I'm not above using her affection for that baby to make her stick around," James said lightly. He knew Harper felt more for him and that Isaac wasn't the whole reason she was around, but he meant it. If the baby allowed him to press forward with her a little quicker than he might under normal circumstances, he was going to take advantage of it.

Caleb nodded. "Well, I can personally attest to the fact that four hands make things easier than just two." He gave James a sincere look. "It's great to have a partner. Seriously. Single parents are amazing. I know several. They deserve all the kudos. But if you choose to do it on your own, know that you have a whole bunch of people who will be there for you," he said. "Of course, if she'll stick around and make your life easier and happier, then, fuck yeah, go for it."

"Thanks," James said. "I appreciate it."

"So you're just giving up on finding the mom, then?" Caleb asked.

This was where it got tricky. Because James was actually hoping to ask Caleb for some help here. "No. I think we still need to talk to her."

"Makes sense. If you can anyway. Get as much info as possible."

"Right. So..." James trailed off.

Caleb looked away from the TV, eyebrow up. "So, what?"

"I need to tell you something."

Caleb sighed. "Shit."

"You don't even know what it is."

"Is it something I'm going to like?"

"Um..."

"So, shit."

"It's not *bad*," James protested, dropping his foot to the floor and leaning to rest his arms on his thighs. "But I could use some help."

"What did you do?"

James wasn't sure if he should be offended that Caleb assumed he'd screwed up somehow or relieved that his friend and boss wasn't already shooting down his "I need some help" request.

"I slept with Ethan's sister after his wedding." He kept his voice down. Ethan was on shift tonight, and even if he wasn't, everyone in the station knew him, of course.

Caleb groaned. "Dammit, James. Emily?"

"He's only got one sister?"

"Yes."

"Shit."

"Exactly."

A sister was bad enough, but his *only* sister? He might be even more protective of her.

"Does he like her?" James asked. Maybe they had a horrible relationship. Maybe she was the black sheep. Maybe they hardly spoke.

"Adores her."

"Dammit."

Caleb shook his head. "Why did it have to be Emily?"

James shrugged. "She's gorgeous and brought me muffins."

"God, you're easy."

"Chocolate cream cheese muffins from Marci's. You have to get up *early* to get those before they sell out. The girl put some real effort into it."

Suddenly Caleb sat up, the footrest of the recliner thunking into place. "Shit. Are you telling me about Emily because you think *she* might be the mom?"

James nodded.

"Oh, *no*." Caleb scrubbed a hand over his face. "Oh, shit, no."

"But if she is, either Ethan doesn't know she had a baby..." James shot a glance toward the doorway. The other guys were busy playing pool, sleeping, or were on kitchen duty and were cleaning up after dinner. But soon enough they'd start filtering into the room with the big screen. "Or he doesn't know it was me."

Caleb shot up from his chair and started pacing. "Fuck. Fuck, fuck, fuck." He swung to glare at James. "You know how this is going to affect the whole house if you two have this kind of issue? *Dammit!* You didn't even fucking use a *condom*?"

"Of course I did!" James shot back, again looking at the door then frowning at his friend. "Jesus. I'm not an idiot."

"Was it old or something?"

"I don't have old condoms," James said. "I go through them plenty fast."

Caleb ran a hand through his hair and blew out a breath.

James just waited. He knew his friend would process the fact that not only had Logan, one of Caleb's best friends, knocked his now wife up on their first and supposed-to-be-only night together, but Lexi had accidentally gotten pregnant as well. It happened.

"Sorry," Caleb finally said. "I'm just worried about the house."

"I know. Me too."

"So that means you don't say a fucking word," Caleb told him, hands on his hips.

James shook his head. "I have to talk to her. He's the only one who can give me her number."

"You cannot even *hint* that something went on between you," Caleb said. "She didn't tell him. You can't be the one to tell *her* brother about a baby that she gave up, James."

James thought about that. "So, what do I do?"

"Let me handle it."

James sat up. "You? How are you going to handle it?"

"I have access to his personnel file. Maybe she's listed as a contact. If not, his mom or wife surely is. I can come up with some reason that I need her number."

James was amazed. "Like what?"

"I don't know," Caleb said, clearly exasperated. "But I'll think of something."

"You'd do that for me?"

Caleb met his eyes. And nodded. "Yeah. I'd do that for you. You're my friend. I'll always have your back."

James swallowed hard. "Thanks, man."

"And you're trying to do the right thing. Being a dad is hard enough when you *do* know everything about the kid from day one. Starting in the dark doesn't help you or Isaac."

James knew that Caleb was going out on a limb here. He wasn't doing anything unethical, exactly. He was going to find a phone number and was going to try to avoid lying directly to his friend if possible. He was helping another friend out. But this was a gray area about how he was using his power and access to records.

"I don't want you to get into trouble," James said.

"She dumped the baby on your doorstep," Caleb said, frowning. "I know you and Ethan don't get along all the time, but I know him. He'd be pissed at her for that. And I have to believe that he'd want to help the people caring for his nephew however he could. Especially if it was to give them access to his sister's information so they could make good decisions. That's not a big ask of him. If he could, you know, separate all of that from the fact that *you* fucked his sister."

"Whose sister?" Daniel Abrams came into the room, followed by three other guys.

Caleb and James's alone time was over.

"Hey, guys," Caleb said. "James is engaged."

Caleb's obvious attempt to change the subject worked. Daniel stopped with his hand on the refrigerator door. He looked over, clearly shocked. "No shit?"

James liked the idea of being engaged to Harper. There was the little detail of her not saying yes yet. But she hadn't said no either. Words mattered to this woman, and there was no way she was going to give him the biggest one of her life without thinking about it hard first.

But he really wanted that yes.

"No shit," Caleb answered for him. "He's a one-woman man now."

"Who's a one-woman man?" Ethan asked as he came into the room.

James looked over at Caleb.

"James." Caleb was watching Ethan closely.

Clearly, Caleb had seen Ethan coming and had timed his comment for Ethan to hear.

"Really." Ethan gave James a look. "You find Jesus or something?"

Well, Isaac was a biblical name, and he'd more or less found him. "Yeah, something like that," James told him.

"Huh. Well, good for you. A good woman is what most of us need," Ethan said, grabbing an apple out of the bowl by the sink.

"Speak for yourself," Mark Lebers said. "I'm looking for a good man."

"Or a few good men, right?" Daniel joked.

Mark saluted him with his soda can.

"So we were talking about when James should introduce Harper to his family," Caleb said. It seemed he was talking to the room at large, but he was looking at Ethan.

"She hasn't met your family yet?" Ethan asked, taking a seat on the end of the couch closest to Caleb.

"Not yet, but they've heard about her." That was true. James had told his parents about the cute professor who lived across from him and shared custody of his dog. More than once.

"When did you introduce Brianna to your family?" Caleb asked.

James wasn't sure where they were going here, but they were now on the subject of Ethan's family. Which included Emily.

"Man, I don't remember exactly," Ethan said. "After we'd dated a few months, I guess. When I knew it was serious. Way before I proposed, though."

"James has the same thing that you do with his family not living close," Caleb said. "Makes it a little tougher."

"How often do you see them?" James asked.

Ethan shrugged. "Every few months."

"So when you go home to visit, you see them all at once?" Caleb asked. "Do your siblings all live close to your parents?"

"It's just me and my sister," Ethan said. "And she's in Oklahoma City. About four hours from my parents."

"So you don't see her as often?" Caleb asked.

"Nope. We talk a lot, though."

"Man," Caleb said. "Try to see her as much as you can. I know that siblings sometimes grow apart when they get to be adults, but I'll tell you from personal experience, you never know what might happen, and you will regret not staying close."

There was a moment of total silence.

Everyone knew about Caleb's sister dying. Many of them had been working at Engine 29 when it had happened. Those who hadn't been, knew all about Shay and how he'd come to be raising his niece.

James stared at his friend. Wow. Caleb had played the dead-sister card for him.

Ethan cleared his throat. "Yeah, you're right. I see her as often as I can. I just saw her a couple of months ago."

Caleb shot a look at James.

James frowned. A couple of months?

If that was true, that would mean that Ethan would have seen her pregnant. He would have known she was having a baby. There was no way he knew James was the dad—evidenced by the fact that James was alive and had no black eyes or broken bones—but Ethan couldn't have missed the pregnancy.

"A couple of months?" Caleb said. "You sure? Time goes fast. You need to try to see her every other month at least. It's important to stay close."

Brotherly advice from the guy with the dead sister could

seem a little over the top, but Caleb would be given a little leeway if he seemed to be pushing the topic.

"Yeah, actually more like six weeks," Ethan said. "It was my dad's birthday."

Damn. Six weeks? She would have been *very* pregnant. James supposed he owed Emily for not telling Ethan that James was the father. Maybe she'd known what a huge rift that would cause at the station. The guys here had to work together and work well. Lives depended on it. He appreciated that she got that.

But what about the suddenly-not-there nephew? What story had she given Ethan about the baby?

Caleb nodded. "Good. That's good. So, do you have a brother-in-law? Nieces or nephews?"

James gave him a frown. *Ease up there, dude.* But Caleb was trying to help James. He was Ethan's boss. And his sister had died. James supposed he could get away with this.

"Nope. Not married. No kids."

"She ever planning to do either of those things?"

Ethan shrugged. "Yeah, I think so. She's dating a guy right now that she likes a lot. I think she wants to be a mom."

"My sister got pregnant with Shay before they got married. They were headed that way anyway, so it worked out, but she was a little freaked out for a bit." Caleb leaned in, pinning Ethan with a look. "You the kind of brother she would confide in? Would she tell you if something like that happened?"

Ethan nodded. "Yeah, man, I think so."

"You need to be sure. You need to be that kind of brother." Caleb sat back and looked around at the other guys. "You all need to be that kind of brother. If you've got sisters, for sure, but if you've got brothers or even just friends. Be someone they can come to and admit their fuck-ups and know that you'll have their backs anyway." He looked at Ethan again. "You wouldn't want her keeping a big secret from you, would you? You wouldn't like knowing she was worried she couldn't tell you something that was going on with her because you'd react badly, right?"

Ethan shook his head slowly. "No, I definitely wouldn't."

"Good," Caleb said.

James was watching him with wide eyes. Caleb had really gotten into that for a minute there. Yes, he'd been trying to help get information for James, but he meant every word he'd just said.

Caleb looked over at James. He lifted a brow.

James frowned. Then it hit him.

Emily wasn't Isaac's mom.

She hadn't been pregnant.

She would have told Ethan if she was. And Ethan had just seen her six weeks ago. It sounded like she wanted kids, too. She had a boyfriend and a good job. Not really a classic candidate for abandoning a baby in a basket.

James sat back in his chair as that realization sank in.

It wasn't Emily.

It wasn't Megan or Kylie, either.

That left one woman. The woman from the W state.

The hardest one to find, of course.

Just then the alarm went off, and all of the guys jumped into action.

James was relieved. He definitely needed something to take his mind off of the woman from the club. The woman who, by process of elimination, *had* to be Isaac's mom.

Not that taking his mind off her took much.

He remembered her least of all the women on the baby-mama list.

———

"Wow. She's... great."

Harper laughed as she and James made their way down the steps.

"She is."

"She... showed up with a binder," James said.

Sophie had indeed showed up with a binder. With dividers. Where she'd written down all of her notes about caring for Isaac tonight. In fact, she'd made James and Harper feel a bit inept when they'd been unable to answer some of her questions. Like how many ounces he ate at a time. "Until he's done," had been James's answer. And what time they put him down. "When he falls asleep," James had told her.

She'd given a little, "hmmm," sound and noted it in the binder.

Then she'd offered to leave the binder with any notes she made while they were out and for them to add to over the next few days until they needed her again.

It was a not-very-subtle-at-all hint that they really needed to start paying more attention.

It was also pretty clear that Sophie had been mildly disappointed that Harper hadn't had a binder already started.

Well, Sophie didn't know what it was like to be a new mom to a two-week-old who had showed up, literally, without warning. The nine months of pregnancy would have been heaven to a planner like Harper. Everything would have been in its place, she would have had a plan B *and* a plan C for everything, and damn right she would have had a binder. A whole shelf full of them.

Harper grinned. "She's the perfect choice for babysitting."

James opened the gate that led out of their courtyard to the street. "Yeah, it's really nice that she can come to him rather than us needing to take him somewhere."

Harper nodded. "That will be easier on all of us."

They turned toward Frenchman's Street, the famous street where the oldest and best jazz clubs in the city sat nestled together. They held hands and chatted casually as they wound their way through the crowds in the Quarter.

He told her about the two calls they'd gone out on. She told him about her first night with Isaac alone.

It had been hectic but fine. They'd done the eat, sleep, diaper, repeat routine throughout the evening, interspersed with some reading out loud and singing. There had been about forty-five minutes of fussiness, but she'd gone to the piano and plunked out the melody of "Heart and Soul," the only song she knew, while holding him. He'd quieted right down. The look of happiness on James's face when she'd told him about it had been enough to melt her heart and panties at the same time.

The guy really was into this baby.

And she was really into both of them.

He hadn't asked her about getting married, again. She was surprised but appreciated that he was giving her time. He'd been at work, of course, and the first thing they'd talked about when he'd come home was that Emily was not the mom. Then he'd gone to bed. So they hadn't had a lot of time to talk about things like committing their lives to one another forever. But Harper found herself anxious to have the conversation. If he didn't bring it up tonight, she would.

But right now, he seemed excited to be on his way to the club, and she found herself caught up in his enthusiasm. She knew it wasn't about finding this next, most mysterious woman. It was about the club. The music. Clearly, this was a great love of his and she was excited to see him in his element. The fact he'd stayed away from it since Isaac showed up said a lot about his commitment to his son. He was willing to put his second job —that was clearly more of a passion than work—to the side, to be there for Isaac.

Just one more thing to like about him. As if she needed any more.

"I've never been to the clubs down here," she said as they crossed over to Frenchman's.

"Never?" he asked, clearly shocked. "Why not?"

"It's intimidating down here," she admitted, looking around.

Overall, the vibe here was different from the neon and craziness of Bourbon Street or the touristy feel of Decatur and Jackson Square. This area was clearly all about authentic people, food, and music.

The streets were narrower here, and the buildings were crowded together. People milled about from one doorway to the next, but the pace was a little slower here. Some of the doorways led to clubs, some to restaurants or bars. Some were restaurants with the club upstairs. There was limited capacity in all of them, so there was spillover onto the sidewalks and streets, but there was no escaping the trumpets and pianos. For those who couldn't make it into the clubs or didn't want to pay the cover charges, there was a jazz band on the opposite corner playing live and seemingly having the time of their lives.

For those who did make it inside, there was always another place calling to them. People came and went in a steady stream it seemed.

"Nah, nothin' to be intimidated about," James said, his grin wide. "Everyone's the same here. You love music and food, you fit right in. Come on."

He turned them into a doorway that was painted dark blue. It was narrow and almost hidden between an art studio and a café. The big man at the door—clearly the bouncer—cleared a path for him. "Hey, Reynaud," he greeted.

"Hey, Bill, what's up?"

"Not much. Been a bit."

"Been a little busy," James said, tucking Harper up tightly against his side.

"Nice." Bill gave her a wink. "You've got your hands full with this one."

She nodded. "You have no idea." She doubted that Bill knew this one came with a dog and baby.

"He don't bring ladies here to see him play," Bill said.

"No?" Harper looked up at James.

"Always plenty inside waitin' on him, though," Bill said.

"You tryin' to get me in trouble?" James asked him with a grin.

"Absolutely," Bill told him.

"After I brought you beignets last time?" James asked.

"Beignet. One. You ate the other two on your way over," Bill said with a chuckle. "Payback, man."

"Wow, really glad I didn't eat all three. Who knows what you might spill to her," James joked.

"I might tell her how you washed dishes for Betty last week," Bill said with a nod. He focused on Harper. "No girl wants a guy who's had his hands in dirty dishwater so an old lady with bronchitis can go home and get some extra rest, right?"

Harper stared at him. "I—"

"And I might tell her about the time you saved someone's life."

"Come on, now," James said, starting forward.

Harper stopped. "You saved someone's life here?"

"He sure did."

"Wow."

"Ah, I do that life-savin' stuff all the time," James said, almost looking embarrassed. "Firefighter, remember?"

"Of course, I remember," she said. "Why do you think I'm sleeping with you?"

He gave her a grin that made her heart flip. He seemed proud of her teasing him. "Right."

"So what was it? A heart attack or something?" she asked Bill.

"Nah. Dragged her in, made her eat dinner and listen to the band, then got her up on stage. Got her a job cleaning up. Got her off the streets."

Harper processed all of that. Then she turned her attention to James. "You didn't jump in and carry someone out of a fire or do CPR or something? You got someone off the streets?"

He shrugged. "She's incredibly talented, and we needed a female voice. I really did it for the band."

Harper tipped her head. "Uh-huh."

He sighed. "She's just a kid," James said. "Sixteen. Foster home was terrible. She kept running away."

"So it really wasn't about you being a firefighter. It was about you being an amazing guy."

"But I would never tell a girl he brought around all of that," Bill broke in. "She just wants a good time in the bedroom, so she doesn't want to hear all of that."

Harper gave him a smile. "Yeah, I'm really glad you didn't tell me all of that. Might make me look at him as more than just a hot guy with a big hose."

Bill snorted. "Yeah, and how you react might show me what kind of person *you* are."

She nodded. "Might act as a test or something."

"Might."

"Okay," James broke in, finally nudging her through the doorway. "Thank you so much for protecting my virtue," he told Bill. "But I've got this."

"Of course you do," Bill said, giving Harper a wink. "I wouldn't dream of getting involved."

"Yeah, yeah."

Harper stepped into the dark club, feeling James right behind her. He had to be. There wasn't a lot of space on the other side of the threshold. But she really liked when he was close.

"I love that you have such close friends."

He chuckled, and she felt it vibrate through her. "He's never done that before."

"No?"

"Well, I've never brought a woman here before." He brushed her hair to the side and put his lips against her neck.

She shivered. "Right, you meet them once you're *in* here."

He chuckled again and wrapped his arms around her. "I don't remember a single one."

She smiled and turned in his arms. She wrapped her arms around his neck. "You're so sweet. And... such a liar."

He ran his hands down to her ass and brought her up against him. "I'm serious. You're the only one now."

She loved that he'd said that. She didn't believe him totally, of course. It was the kind of thing a playboy charmer would say. But she did believe she was different. She did believe he wanted to be with her. She did believe all of this was different for him. He didn't have what he had with her with anyone else. They were parents together.

That thought rocked through her.

They were *parents*.

This did not just happen to feel different from the other people they'd dated. It *had to be* different. *They* had to be differ-ent. Isaac needed them to be different. That meant doing things differently, in every way, than they'd done before.

Harper pulled back and looked up at him. "Yes."

"Yes, you're the only one?" he asked with a grin.

"Yes. I'll marry you."

He froze. His eyes widened. Then his eyes got even wider. She felt his hands squeeze her ass, and he leaned in. "Say it again."

"Yes, I'll marry you."

"Harper..." He trailed off, shook his head, then kissed her. Deeply. Hotly.

She arched into him, tightened her arms around him, and kissed him back.

He didn't lift his head until someone bumped into him. "Damn, Harper. That's amazing."

She grinned, a thrill shooting through her. "It feels right. I know neither of us really expected any of this, but this is where we're supposed to be. You and me and Isaac. A family."

His smile spread. "I said the very first night with him that he's the best wingman I've ever had."

She laughed and hugged him. "I want this. I want you. And him. All of it. So much."

"It's all yours. *We're* all yours."

She took a deep breath. "I love that." Then she took his face in her hands. "I love *you*."

He gave a little groan. "God, I love you, too, Harper. I really do." He kissed her again, hot and deep.

But a moment later, they were pulled apart by a hand on his shoulder. "James!"

He gave her a hot look that spoke all kinds of promises about what he wanted to do later now that they'd confessed their feelings, and she'd said yes to his proposal. But he turned. "Hey, Ray."

A tall, lanky man with dark skin and sparkling brown eyes clapped James on the shoulder. "You're playin' with us tonight."

"Nah, I'm just here to hang tonight." James pulled Harper up against his side. "Wanted to show the place off to my fiancée."

Fiancée. Wow, she really loved that word suddenly. Two weeks ago, that would have freaked her out, but now it made her feel hot and possessive and like he'd just staked a claim. She would have never guessed that she'd like that, but she really, really did.

"I wasn't asking," Ray said with a huge grin. He looked at Harper. "But nice to meet ya."

"Nice to meet you too."

"Ray's our bass player," James said.

"And I can tell you that you want to hear this one play," Ray said. "I mean, me too. I'm awesome. But James, too."

Harper grinned. "I'd love to hear it."

"Be careful," Ray said. "James gets whatever he wants after he plays. Drinks. Other gigs. Panties."

"I'm really regretting bringing you here tonight," James broke in.

Harper laughed. "I'm willing to lose a pair of panties in here tonight."

James leaned in to growl against her ear. "Don't tease me, Professor. I know the way to the back office, and it's got a lock."

"You ever take anyone else in there?" she asked.

"Never."

"Then why don't you get up on that stage and try to impress me?" she asked. "We can talk about the panty status when you're done."

"*Try* to impress you, huh?"

"Well, you did have to get a *baby* before I'd really date you."

He nodded, his eyes narrowed, but his lips were curling. "You are a little harder than most."

He gave her one more quick kiss then steered her toward a table up front. There was another woman already seated there.

"This is Neveah," he told her, pulling out a chair at the table.

The other woman gave her a huge smile. She had gorgeous, long, jet-black hair and deep, chestnut-brown skin and was wearing the most beautiful multicolored wrap dress. She extended her hand. "Hi."

Harper took it as she slid into the chair next to her. "Hi. It's nice to meet you."

"You too. I'm so glad to see James back playing tonight."

James leaned in and kissed Neveah's cheek. "You didn't miss me," he teased. "You've only got eyes for the big brute with the trumpet."

Harper checked out the trumpet player. The guy was definitely big. And extremely good looking. He was a few years older than James and looked like he could have played football with his build. The trumpet looked like a toy in his huge hands. He glanced over at them and smiled when he noticed James. Then he gave Neveah a wink. The other woman laughed.

"Yeah, well, I thought it was polite to mention that I noticed you were gone," she said to James.

"I appreciate that," James said with a laugh. "That's Anthony. Nev's husband," he told Harper. "I think she's with him because of the lips. God knows he's not as funny as he thinks he is, and he's an accountant when he's not here." He rolled his eyes to show what he thought of that.

Neveah laughed again. "Oh, those lips are definitely part of it."

Just then another man joined them. He was tall and lean and at least in his sixties with plenty of white peppering his short dark hair.

"And this is Joseph," James introduced. "Anthony's dad."

Harper shook Joseph's hand, too. "It's really nice to meet you all."

Joseph took the chair across from her. "You too." He gave James a look. "You better get up there." He inclined his head toward the stage.

"So you can start talking about me to Harper?" James asked.

"Yes," Joseph told him without hesitation.

James shook his head. "Maybe I'm not playing tonight."

Joseph scoffed. "Even if you don't start out up there, you'll be there two songs in. Just get your ass up there now."

James grinned and looked down at Harper. "You sure you're okay?"

"Of course." She looked at her table companions. It was really interesting meeting people who knew and hung out with James. She was sure she was going to enjoy this. "I mean, you've been talking really big about this piano for months, but all I've heard is you tinkling on it through the window."

"Tinkling, huh?" he asked. He straightened, nodding. "Okay, Professor. You asked for it."

She grinned watching him get up on stage, shake the hands of all the other men, exchange a couple of hugs, and then take his place on the piano bench. He shot her a look that was part flirtatious and part challenge. Oh, she was ready for whatever he thought he had to show her.

"So how do you know James?" Joseph asked as the other men took their spots.

"Oh, we're neighbors," she said. "I live across the landing."

"You're the lady taking care of Amos's olive tree," Joseph said with clear surprise.

"Yes." Harper smiled. "Helping, anyway."

Joseph nodded. "Yeah, we've heard about you."

"You have?"

Neveah smiled. "I'm not sure James even realizes how much he's talked about you, actually."

Harper felt her heart give an extra beat at that. "Really?"

"You also take care of Fred," Joseph said.

Harper didn't even bother correcting the dog's name. "Yes, I do."

"And you teach at Loyola, and you speak French, and you drink tea, and read romance," Neveah said. She laughed lightly. "Yes, we've heard of you."

Harper shot James a glance. He was laughing with one of the guys who was leaning on the piano. He looked completely at ease behind the instrument, and she felt a little flip in her stomach. She knew he was a musician, and she had heard him on the one in his apartment, but she was about to see yet another side of him. She couldn't wait.

"Of course we pressed him," Joseph said.

"Pressed him about me?"

"Well, about what it was that had changed," the older man said. "But it became clear quickly that it was you."

"What do you mean what had changed?"

"A few months back he stopped flirting—" Joseph looked at Neveah and shook his head with a chuckle. "Well, he never stops flirting. He can't help it entirely, you know. But he stopped taking women home, stopped so much of the partying. He still came in and played. He'll never stop doing that. But he changed. And when we asked him about it, he talked about you."

Harper took all of that in. James had told her he hadn't been with anyone since he'd met her. She'd believed him. Kind of. She wasn't sure she'd believed that he'd totally stopped flirting and going out and everything. That was... something.

"Wow."

Neveah covered Harper's hand and gave her a sincere smile. "James Reynaud has one of the biggest hearts of anyone I know."

Harper nodded. "Me too." She paused, more words on the tip of her tongue. But she wasn't sure she should say them. Still, these people seemed to really care about him. Honestly, she had yet to meet someone who knew James who *didn't* really care about him. It seemed wherever he went he made deep, loyal friendships and connections. "It surprises me a little that he came to me for help so many times," she finally said.

"What do you mean?" Joseph asked, leaning his elbow on the table.

"Well, with the olive tree and Am—Fred," Harper said. "And there's a lizard and..." She glanced at James again. He was talking to another member of the band, but as if he felt her eyes on him, he glanced over and gave her a quick smile. "There's a baby," she told Joseph and Neveah. She wasn't sure she should be spilling that, but Isaac was a fact, and these people clearly knew James and cared about him. "The baby's mother just left him on James's doorstep. Literally. He doesn't even know who she is."

Joseph's eyes didn't even go wide. He just thought about all that for a moment. Then he said, "He takes care of people. He always has. His mother was like that."

"You knew his mother?"

"Of course. His father played in here," Joseph said. "I sat on a stool playing trombone next to his piano every weekend for almost forty years."

"You're a friend of his parents," Harper said. "Wow."

Joseph smiled. "I am. Wonderful people. It almost killed his father to leave the city, but he had to take Katherine out."

"But you said she took care of people," Harper said. "I'm surprised she'd want to leave after Katrina when so many people needed help."

"They stayed to clean up," Joseph said, his eyes sad. "But that's what almost killed her. Her soul, you know? Because she took care. She loved so much. She empathized so easily. It was just almost too much. She wanted to stay. Part of her did. But her husband saw what it was doing to her. In the end, it was his idea to go. And we all encouraged it. It was like her light was slowly going out. We couldn't stand that."

Harper swallowed hard. "I'm so sorry."

"No one was truly the same after Katrina," Joseph said. "Whether you stayed or went. If you stayed, you wondered why. You faced the fact that the city was different, a little broken. If you left, you felt guilty. There is no winning."

Harper nodded.

"Anyway," Joseph said, "James is just like his mama. He

takes care of people. And things. He fights fires and adopts dogs. And babies." Joseph shrugged. "I don't think anyone who knows him would be surprised to find him with an abandoned baby."

"I'm flattered that he keeps coming to me for help, then," Harper decided. "I've never... been like that. The person that people come to for things." She frowned as she realized that. "I'm capable, of course. I can figure almost anything out. I just am not the person that someone would think of handling something huge like that. At least, not as a surprise." She realized most of the people who really knew her would probably describe her as smart and adept, but probably not all that flexible.

Joseph nodded, studying her. "You sure that he's coming to *you* for help?"

"What do you mean?"

"Maybe he's coming to help you."

"To help me with what?"

"Laughing. Loving. Having a dog. And a baby."

Harper felt herself nodding. "Yeah, maybe," she said softly.

Maybe James had been taking care of her all along, bringing all those things into her life because he thought she needed it. Just then the first notes from the stage hit her, she turned in that direction. Or, more specifically, toward the piano.

It was just James, with a bit of bass and a little cymbal behind him.

And holy crap. He was good. Already.

Sure, she was biased. But the entire bar quieted, and the music filled the room. It was a slow, jazzy piece that mesmerized her. She couldn't take her eyes off him and the way his fingers moved over the keys. Confidently, easy, with no music in front of him, just his eyes on the ivories.

Yes, she wanted to be that person. The person who people knew, just knew without much thought or contemplation, just *felt* could be counted on. Someone who they could come to with the things that needed taking care of, that they couldn't handle themselves, but needed to be done. A man who needed to know things would be taken care of as his health was fading had thought of James. A little boy panicked about a home for a lizard had thought of James. All the men who worked with him and knew him, who trusted him to have their backs in life and death situations, had thought of him when a dog needed someone. And a woman, who had spent only a few hours with him, and hadn't been getting to know him all that well, probably, had still sensed he was the kind of guy she could trust her child with.

Harper wanted to be that person, too. Someone who others could depend on when things seemed desperate.

And because of James, she was seeing she could be.

He'd helped her realize that.

She felt a tear on her cheek and quickly dashed it away. She couldn't believe all this had happened in the course of a few months. And honestly, without the last few days with the baby, she wasn't sure this all would have come to light so quickly or clearly.

Just then the music shifted, the trombone and trumpet came in, and the tempo picked up. James's fingers flew over the keys faster, with skill and confidence, and his face lit up as the band hit their stride, and the light and the temperature and the very air in the building seemed to be turned up a notch.

It was very familiar, actually. From the first time she'd opened her door to James Reynaud, everything around her had seemed liked it had been turned up a notch.

9

————

He played for almost an hour.

James kept looking over to where Harper was sitting to gauge when it was time to call it a night. But she was into it. She was watching them constantly, her fingers tapping on the table along with the beat, smiling, seemingly absorbing it all. Her smile would grow when she saw him looking at her, and at one point she'd fanned her face and winked.

He loved it.

He'd wanted her to love all of this. He'd wanted her to enjoy the club and the music. It was a huge part of him, and it would have felt strange if she *didn't* like it. But he hadn't been *sure*. She didn't go out. She liked to be at home. Alone, as far as he could tell.

He knew he'd been challenging her and her usual routines and habits over the past few months. But she'd risen to every challenge and surprised him at every turn.

And every time she did, he fell a little deeper for her.

Earlier, hearing her say she loved him and would marry him had been the biggest thrill of his life. He'd had no idea how that would feel. He'd had no idea how it would all play out at all. But having her say it to him in the middle of the club where he poured his heart out into the music so often, where he'd grown up watching his father do the same, had meant everything to him. He didn't know if Harper realized that or if it had truly just been a spontaneous moment that had felt right— which he also loved, considering spontaneous was not a word he'd use to describe Harper Broussard—but it had been perfect.

Finally, he called it a wrap. As much as he loved playing, he wanted to be with her. Marcus was working tonight, so James needed to go and ask him about how to get ahold of Caroline from the W state, and then he needed to get Harper home.

He made his way to the table where she was nursing her second glass of wine.

"You read—"

Before he even got the words out, she was on her feet and had grabbed his hand. She pulled him through the crowd and around the tables. Toward the back office.

"You know where you're goin', Professor?" he asked.

"Neveah filled me in," she told him over her shoulder. "She said there's a bow tie to hang on the doorknob."

James chuckled. "I didn't know about the bow tie."

"I'm glad you didn't." She pulled him down the short, dark back hallway to the closed door at the end near the back exit. She turned to face him as she twisted the knob and stepped back into the room. "Neveah said she'd run interference for us."

He'd never brought a woman back here. He knew a few of the guys had hookups in the club, but he hadn't asked for details. He followed her into the room that was lit only by a small lamp on the corner of a messy desk. There was a dusty file cabinet in one corner, a coat rack with a blazer jacket that could have easily been there since the forties, and a brown leather sofa that had also, clearly, been there longer than James had been alive.

"You sure this is your kind of place, Professor?" James asked, settling his hands on her hips. "'Cuz I'm happy to take you home to not just one big, comfy bed, but *two*. Hell, we've got two couches and two kitchen tables to choose from, too."

She ran her hands up to link them behind his neck. "This office has been used for decades as a rendezvous spot," Harper told him. "I love the idea of being a part of this club's history."

"Well, that's as much arguing as I'm going to do on the subject," he said. He fucking loved that she was the one who had pulled *him* down the hallway. He reached over and turned the lock on the door. "How are your panties?"

Harper's voice was husky when she answered. "Wet."

Lust swept through him. "So you like jazz piano?"

"I like *you*," she said. "I like watching you in your element like that. I like being surrounded by people who get you and think you're amazing. I like realizing that you had no reason to be interested in me but that something brought you across that landing to knock on my door."

He wasn't sure exactly what the right thing to say was, so he just went with his gut. "Take them off, Professor."

She immediately reached under her skirt and pulled her panties down and off. She moved as if to toss them away, but he snagged them. She watched, eyes round, as he lifted them to his nose and breathed in. They were, indeed, wet, and they smelled like heaven. Like her.

"Unzip me."

He was vaguely aware of the sound of his phone ringing in his pocket, but there was nothing that was going to make him stop this.

Her cheeks were pink and she was breathing hard. This woman made him weak in the knees. Her fingers went to his fly, and she unbuttoned and unzipped him, spreading his jeans open.

"I've never given a jazz musician a blow job."

Definitely weak in the knees. James clenched his fists. He was going to fucking stay on his feet. Even if it killed him.

"Harp—"

She went to her knees, pulled his boxers down, and slid her tongue up and down his length.

James braced his legs and worked on breathing. He squeezed his eyes shut but then quickly popped them open to focus on the sight of Harper Broussard taking him into her mouth.

He groaned. "Professor."

She looked up at him from under her lashes. And took him deeper.

He swallowed hard. He was going to die.

She sucked and licked for several minutes, and James tangled his fingers in her hair, absorbing every second. But finally it was too much.

"On your feet, Harper," he growled, his gut, balls, everything, tight.

Licking her lips like a damned siren, she got to her feet.

"Come here." He pulled her in, his hand at the back of her head, plundering her mouth with his tongue.

She kissed him back, enthusiastically. He turned her and backed her up against the door. He ran his hand up under her skirt, relishing the silky, hot skin of the back of her thigh, the lower curve of her ass, then the sweet, wet heat between her legs. She moaned as he slid a finger deep and ran his thumb over her clit.

She gripped his arms. "Please, James."

He should tease her, play a little, make her beg. But he couldn't take one more second not being balls deep. He rolled a condom on and lifted her against the door then bent his knees and thrust.

They moaned together, and he started moving immediately. He thrust again and again, taking them both higher and higher.

He felt her clamp down around him just seconds before he roared her name as he came hard.

Panting, he leaned into her, resting his head against the door over her shoulder.

Slowly he became aware of her hands and knees gripping him. He pulled back and looked down her. She gave a big sigh and smiled up at him. He squeezed her ass, then let her legs swing to the floor as he stepped back and dealt with the condom.

They both worked to straighten their clothes then moved in to kiss again. As their lips touched, James's phone dinged with a new text message.

He pulled his phone out, kissing her, glancing down to swipe the screen to open the message, then kissing her again. He lifted the phone and peered at it. Then he frowned.

"Everything okay?" Harper asked.

"It's Lexi. She has the DNA test back. She wants to meet us at the apartment."

Harper frowned, too. "That doesn't sound good."

No, it didn't. James punched the button to dial Lexi's number. "Lex, what's going on?" he asked the second she answered.

"I was called into work tonight and just checked my mailbox, so I didn't realize I had the results here," she said.

"That's okay. What do they say?"

"Let's just meet at your apartment, and I'll tell you both everything," Lexi said. "I assume you're with Harper."

"I am." James looked at the woman whose hair was a mess and whose lips and cheeks were pink. She looked well fucked. And happy. Why did his gut tell him that the happy look was going to be temporary.

"I'll meet you there in ten minutes," Lexi said.

"Just tell me now."

"There's... quite a bit to tell you," Lexi said. "It really will be easier in person."

James blew out a breath. "This doesn't sound good."

"I know," Lexi agreed. "I'm sorry."

Well, shit, that *really* didn't sound good. Feeling like he had a cement block in his gut, he said, "Fine. See you soon."

It took him a second to meet Harper's gaze.

"What's going on?" she asked quietly, obviously sensing something big was happening.

"I'm not sure exactly. Lexi got the DNA results back and wants to talk to us. She said it would be easier to explain everything in person."

Harper frowned. "Oh."

Yeah, oh.

"I haven't asked Marcus about Caroline," he said. He knew Harper would put the pieces together and realize Caroline was the girl from the W state. The final contender for Isaac's mom.

Harper nodded. "I guess we could ask him quickly if he's got her contact information."

James nodded.

"Or we could come back." Harper frowned. "I'm worried. I just want to get home to Isaac right now."

James blew out a breath. "Me too." Then he held out his hand.

Harper hesitated for just a second. But that second was long enough to make the ball in his gut tighten further. They both sensed something was wrong, and they knew it was going to change everything. Was Isaac sick? Did he have a genetic condition that was going to cause a disability or long-term problems or even be terminal? James felt cold suddenly. None of that had occurred to him. It had all seemed so easy to this point, actually. The baby had shown up, James had headed over to get Harper, she'd jumped in to help, they'd fallen in love with Isaac and each other, and they'd planned a future. It had all seemed to be falling into place. Yes, not knowing and needing to find the mother had seemed liked a complication, but he'd fully expected to offer her whatever she wanted to have her turn over all of her parental rights and for him and Harper and Isaac to ride off into the proverbial sunset together.

A moment later, Harper took his hand. Her pause had really only been for heartbeat or two, but it had felt like a year in some ways.

They stepped out of the office and turned down the hallway, heading out of the club without speaking. James pulled his phone out and called up his Uber app. There was a car available a couple of blocks over. They weren't far from the apartment, but a car would get them there faster than walking, and while a part of him wanted to put off whatever Lexi was going to tell them, suddenly James needed to know what was going on. It was a burning in his gut.

He reserved the car and started up the side street. Harper didn't ask a single question. Not even when he stopped by the car and opened the door for her. They didn't talk on the drive back to the apartment or as they climbed the steps.

But he paused outside his door.

"You okay?" he asked Harper.

"No."

He nodded.

"You?" she asked.

"No."

She also nodded.

Finally, he inserted his key and opened the door. He knew Lexi wasn't here just yet, since he hadn't seen her car downstairs, but if she was coming from the hospital, she wasn't far. She might have gone home to get Caleb, though. If this was really bad news, she might want James's friend there to help break it.

He pushed the door open, letting Harper step in first, then

following her, but she came up short. He bumped into her and looked up to see what had caught her attention.

It was Sophie and Isaac and Fred. Isaac was propped up in his car seat, sitting on the middle couch cushion. Fred was right beside him. They were both listening to Sophie read from what appeared to be a thick textbook. In French.

She gave Harper and James a little wave and smile but kept going, her voice almost singsong as she read the text out loud.

When she got to the end of the page, and what sounded like the end of the chapter, she stopped. "Hi," she greeted.

"Hi," Harper said, finally stepping fully into the apartment.

"I needed to finish reading that chapter, and he will just *not* go to sleep," Sophie said, looking at the baby with a soft smile. "So I thought I'd combine studying with entertaining."

"Looks like you have a rapt audience," Harper said, moving to gaze down at the baby and the dog.

Fred gave a soft woof and wagged his tail. Harper ran a hand over his head and back and then let him lick her hand.

"Has Isaac been fussy?" she asked Sophie.

"No, not really," Sophie said. "A bit when he was wet and hungry. But mostly he's just been awake. Alert. Like he just wants to hang out and not miss anything."

James swallowed hard and tossed his keys on the table by the door, trying to seem like everything was fine. Trying to tell himself everything was fine. But it wasn't. Lexi wouldn't be coming over to deliver the DNA news in person if everything was fine. He almost wished he'd insisted she just tell him what was going on over the phone, but honestly, now that he was home, he was grateful he hadn't. If it was bad news, he wanted to be here, in his home, with his dog and Harper, to deal with whatever it was.

"Well, great," Harper said. She was looking at Isaac with a strange expression.

James wondered if she was debating about picking the baby

up. He was feeling the same way. He was torn. He wanted to cuddle the little guy. Hug him and hold him and assure himself that Isaac was fine. On the other hand, he was afraid he might not ever put him back down if he picked him up now.

"Thanks so much for coming over tonight," James said, pulling his wallet out and withdrawing money for Sophie.

She took it, though for just a moment he thought she was going to turn it down. She slid it into her pocket and gave him a smile. "I enjoyed it. Thanks for letting me do it. I'm happy to help out any time."

"We'll remember that," James said. Hell, part of him would love to make plans right now to take Harper out for a romantic dinner that weekend and wanted to ask Sophie to plan to come over, but something held him back. He needed to know what was going on first. He had a nagging feeling that Lexi was about to tell them something that was going to change all of their plans.

Sophie gathered her stuff, said goodbye, and even went over and gave Isaac a kiss on the head. "See you soon, sweetie," she said to him. Then she patted Fred and headed out.

James went to Isaac. "I guess I'll change him and see if we can get him down before Lexi—"

There was a knock on the door just then.

Harper sucked in a quick breath. Clearly, she was feeling the same touch of dread he was.

He looked down at her. "Here we go."

She nodded.

He pulled the door open. Lexi wasn't alone. But it wasn't Caleb. Another woman was with her.

"Hey."

Lexi gave him a little smile. "Hey. James, this is Shelly. Shelly works at the hospital with me. Shelly, this is James." She leaned in. "And that's Harper."

"Hi." Shelly extended her hand.

James took it. "Come on in."

It was not a good thing that Lexi had brought a coworker with her.

Harper had already gathered Isaac out of his car seat and was holding him, rocking gently side to side, as if to comfort him. But James knew it was her who needed the comforting. He felt the same way.

"Are you a nurse, too?" he asked Shelly. Maybe she specialized in genetic disorders or something.

"No. I'm a social worker," Shelly said. Then she lifted a hand. "But I'm only here to provide information tonight, I promise. I'm here as a favor to Lexi."

"Information?" Harper asked. "Why would you be here to provide information about the DNA test?"

Lexi shook her head. "That's not why she's here. But let's start at the beginning. Do you guys want to sit down?"

"No." James knew his tone was sharper than it needed to be, but his emotions were swirling now. He braced his feet apart and crossed his arms. "Just tell us what's going on, Lex."

She took a breath. "Okay. The test results came back as I said. And... you're not the father."

There was a long pause where no one said anything or even moved.

"Wait. What?" Harper finally asked.

Lexi shook her head. "James is not Isaac's father. We can't tell who is, of course, but we can tell that there is definitely not a match between the two of them."

Her words rocked through him. His throat tightened, and his heart thundered.

"James?"

He vaguely heard Harper's voice filter through the static in his ears.

Harper came closer, reaching for his arm. James couldn't

make his muscles work to uncross them. Hell, he couldn't make his lungs work to take in oxygen.

She laid her hand on his arm but looked at Lexi then Shelly.

"So you're here to help us with what? How to find his parents?"

James looked at the two women. Fuck. His *parents*. Not just his mom—who was even further out of reach now—but *both* of Isaac's parents were now a mystery. Well, at least he didn't have to get Marcus to try to find Caroline for him.

James waited for a feeling of relief or humor or even anger to go through him, but he felt nothing. He was numb.

He hadn't realized just how deeply, and how easily, it had sunk in that Isaac was his. From the moment Harper had suggested it, it had just felt right.

Now nothing felt right.

"Not... exactly," Shelly said. She was watching them with some concern. "Maybe we should sit down. I can tell this is a shock."

Lexi was frowning at him. "You had to know there was a chance he wasn't yours," she said. "That's why we did the DNA test."

"No," he said flatly. Well, he'd found his voice. "No, I didn't really know that. We did the DNA test to prove to everyone *else*, like doctors and teachers and whoever else would need proof, that he was mine. But no, Lexi, I guess I didn't really believe that he wasn't mine. Someone *gave him to me.* Why would they do that otherwise?"

Yeah, he'd definitely found his voice. By the end of that, he was almost shouting.

Harper squeezed his arm. Shelly nodded.

"That's a good question. And maybe a good place to start," Shelly said. "Why would someone leave the baby with you?"

"Because if you have something that needs taking care of

and you've met James, he would be the first person to come to mind," Harper said, her voice scratchy.

He looked down at her, but she didn't meet his gaze.

"James is a natural protector. He's a caregiver. He's warm and loving and loyal and dependable. If you had a baby that you couldn't take care of but that you loved and wanted to be sure was in a safe and loving place, then yes, James's doorstep would be on the top of your list."

His heartbeat thundered, and he was finally able to move. He uncrossed his arms and put one around Harper, pulling her and Isaac up against his side, hugging her close. He looked at Shelly. "What do we need to do now? Apply to be his guardians? Foster parents? Start an adoption process?"

She held up a hand. "Okay, slow down. That's why Lexi asked me to come—to talk to you about all of this. What happens next, where things stand. All of that."

James sighed. "All right." They needed answers, and it seemed that Shelly had them. "Let's sit."

Shelly and Lexi looked relieved. Everyone took seats around the living room. Harper and James sat together with Isaac on the couch, right against each other, his arm still around her.

"I want to reiterate that I'm here tonight as a friend of Lexi's," Shelly started. "I'm not here in an official capacity."

"What does that mean?" Harper asked. "If you *were* here in an official capacity, what would be happening?"

"I would be taking Isaac with me when I leave," Shelly said simply.

James felt his gut clench and his heart thump. "That's bullshit," he said sharply. "His mother—or father," he added, realizing that was a possibility now, "left him with *me*. They wanted him to be with *me*."

Shelly nodded. "I understand that. And that's a consideration, to an extent."

"To an extent?" James said, his voice rising a bit again. "What the fuck does that mean?"

Isaac started and his face wrinkled. Harper rubbed his back and cooed to him softly while James worked to regulate his blood pressure.

"From what I understand, there was a note," Shelly said, totally keeping her cool.

James supposed that she encountered plenty of emotional, angry people in her line of work.

"There was."

"Do you still have it?"

"I do."

"Can I see it?"

James went straight for the area of his kitchen counter where he kept his stack of bills to pay and a shopping list. He pulled the note out and handed it over to Shelly before settling back on the couch with Harper. He was sure she could feel the tension in his body. He didn't think he'd be getting rid of that any time soon, no matter how hard he tried to relax.

Shelly glanced at the note—it wasn't long and didn't take long to read—then looked up. "This is a bit of a problem."

"Why?"

"There's no name. This could have been written by anyone. You could have written it."

James glared at her. "I didn't fucking write it."

"I believe you," Shelly said. "But a judge might not."

"A judge?" Harper asked.

"This baby has been abandoned," Shelly explained. "Lexi said she didn't think that you're already foster parents?"

"No," James confirmed, knowing where this was going.

"There's a process for all of this. If you want to work on becoming a foster parent or look into adoption, all of that is fine, of course."

"But," Harper prompted. "In the meantime..."

"The baby will go to a foster home."

"The mother fucking *gave* him to *me*," James said through gritted teeth. "She wanted him with *me*. That should matter."

"And it might," Shelly agreed. "I'm sure the court will take that into consideration, but"—she shrugged—"it would be so much easier if you knew who she was, if she could be a part of this."

"How could she be a part of it?" Harper asked.

"It could be arranged as a private adoption," Shelly said. "There would need to be lawyers involved, of course, but if the mother chose you as parents and could sign over her rights officially and testify, this would all be much easier."

"And the foster system could be avoided," James said.

"Yes." Shelly leaned forward. "But I assure you that he will be placed in a good home, James. There's no reason to be afraid of that."

"Of course there is," James said, trying to keep his voice down. "Because it's not *here*, with *us*."

Shelly pressed her lips together and nodded.

"James—" Lexi started.

"Why did you tell her?" James asked. "Why did you bring her into this?"

Lexi frowned. "You need to know what your options are now. He's not yours. You can't just... keep him."

"Why not?" James felt frustration and anger and fear all coursing through him, burning in his veins.

"There are processes and laws in place for a reason," Shelly said. "Becoming parents to a *child* is not like adopting a kitten. You can't just pick one up out of a box with a sign that says *free to a good home*." She held up the note that had been in the basket with Isaac. "That's not how it works, and that's for the protection of the child *and* for you. If the mother decided to come back in a month or a year or five years, you'd want to have all of your ducks in a row, right? You'd want to have gone through the correct legal procedures to protect Isaac, and make sure everything happens in his best interest."

"*We* are in his best interest," James insisted. "What will happen if I do just keep him? What if we just keep doing things just as we've been doing them?" He looked at Shelly. "Will you turn us in?"

"All of the things we talked about the other day will still be issues, then," Lexi said before Shelly could answer. "Just medically speaking, this is complicated, not to mention legally. You don't know anything about her pregnancy, his birth, the family history. You can't just show up at a doctor's office without any of that and not raise suspicion, James. And you don't even have *your* half of the medical history to refer to. You can't claim that you're the father and she just left you with the kid. You have no rights here."

James could tell this was hard for Lexi, but she was trying to be a good friend and be honest.

He didn't care.

He was angry. And scared. And sad.

He was losing his son. Isaac might not be his biologically, and therefore, legally, but dammit, James felt like the baby was *his*.

"I can come back tomorrow. I can handle the case personally and keep you as updated on things as I'm able," Shelly said. "I will keep you in the loop as much as I can."

"I could just take off with him tonight," James said.

"You won't," Lexi told him. "You wouldn't do that. You have a job, family, friends." She shot a look at Harper. "You have lots of reasons to stay. Don't do anything stupid."

"And that would be kidnapping. And then the police would get involved. And you don't want that," Shelly added.

James glared at her. She didn't even blink.

He could only imagine some of the shit she'd seen and

done in her line of work. He saw plenty just in what he did as a firefighter.

He didn't say anything more. He didn't have to confirm that he wasn't going to go anywhere with Isaac tonight. But he also didn't have to act happy and agreeable about any of this.

Shelly stretched to her feet. She laid a business card on the coffee table. "If you have any questions, even later on tonight, please feel free to call me," she said. "That's my cell number. I answer twenty-four seven."

James just nodded. Shelly started for the door. Lexi stood and stepped around the coffee table. She paused beside the couch and put a hand on his shoulder.

"I'm sorry."

He looked up and forced himself to give her a nod. She hadn't done anything wrong. She'd given him a DNA test. It had turned out he wasn't the father. That wasn't her fault. It wasn't her fault that he'd so easily accepted the idea that Isaac was his without waiting for proof. It also wasn't her fault that he'd immediately started looking for one of his past hookups to be the mother, further enforcing the idea in his mind that he was now a dad.

"I know," he told her. "It's okay."

She looked like she wanted to say more but then like she wasn't sure what to say. She nodded. Finally, she added, "Shelly is a good person. She'll take good care of him."

She wouldn't take care of him as well as James and Harper would, but James didn't say that. He just nodded.

Lexi followed Shelly, and they left, pulling the door shut quietly behind them.

James and Harper sat together on the couch in stunned, pained silence for several long minutes. Eventually, Isaac started to fuss and Harper rose. James followed. Both without speaking. Together they changed him, fed him, rocked him, and when he was asleep, put him down in the bassinet next to the bed.

Harper stood staring down at him for a long moment, then she reached out and ran a hand over his head. The baby took a deep breath and let it out with a little, contented sigh.

That was when she broke.

A sob escaped. She put a hand over her mouth, squeezing her eyes shut. But she couldn't keep it in. Another sob, then a shuddering breath, then another sob. Tears started.

James reached out and pulled her in, feeling his own eyes burning. His throat was tight. His chest was tight. He had no words.

He couldn't comfort her. He couldn't say it would be okay. He couldn't say that he'd fix it. He couldn't say they'd make a plan.

So he just held her. Tightly. Feeling her tears wet the front of his shirt, feeling his tears track down his cheeks. Sharing the pain.

He turned them, sitting on the edge of the bed and pulling her into his lap. They sat like that, holding each other and crying until, finally, they lay back and eventually fell asleep.

At some point in the night, he pulled the comforter up over them both. But neither of them moved out of the other's arms.

Isaac didn't stir all night, and in the morning, when James woke up and realized that, it made him sad, too. He would have loved a few extra stolen hours with the baby in the night.

Then he rolled over and realized that Harper was no longer in his bed, and the huge, cold ball of dread got even bigger.

———

THE POUNDING ON HER APARTMENT DOOR DIDN'T SURPRISE HER.

It frustrated her a little because she was only about ten

minutes away from walking out and heading to work, and she could have avoided this.

But it didn't surprise her.

She also knew there was a good chance he would have come to the campus to find her if she'd tried to sneak out and avoid him, so this was maybe for the best.

Harper took a deep breath and pulled her door open.

Ami ran past her feet and headed for the food bowl in her kitchen.

The hot-firefighter-jazz-musician-wannabe dad from across the hall was standing in her doorway looking the opposite of flirtatious and charming and laid back.

"I don't suppose you know anything about why my fiancée snuck out this morning without waking me up after the hellish crap we went to bed with last night?" he asked, his eyes stormy.

She flinched.

She couldn't help it.

It was the fiancée thing. That just drove it all home hard and fast, like a right hook to the jaw. It was ridiculous that she was even kind of, sort of, his fiancée. And after the news last night, she really didn't need to be anymore.

It was also the way this was so like all the other times he'd come across the landing, knocked on her door, and asked if she knew something about what was going on in his life.

But it simply magnified the fact that she didn't. She didn't know crap about what to do about this situation.

The only good news in this mess was that she didn't need to know how to fix it. James had never really needed her help, and he would just roll with this like he did everything else.

"I have to go to work," she said simply.

"You couldn't kiss me good morning and tell me that?" he asked.

She noticed his apartment door was open, so James could hear the baby, and she assumed that meant Isaac was still asleep. Good. She knew she couldn't see him this morning. Not knowing that James was going to have to take him to meet Shelly. And turn him over to the State of Louisiana. Her heart felt like it was being shredded all over again. She hadn't thought there was anything left to hurt. She'd had nightmares all night long after crying in James's arms for almost an hour after Shelly and Lexi left.

"I knew you'd figure it out," she said.

"What's really going on?"

"You know what's really going on," she said.

She looked up at him. She was exhausted. She was feeling beat up. She was grieving. And she didn't want to dance around all of this and pretend it was all fine or that everything would go back to how it had been. Everything was different now. She'd fallen in love—twice—in the span of just a few days.

She'd tried rolling with it. She'd tried just going with it and getting caught up in the adventure. She'd said yes to his proposal but *mince!* she'd made a plan. Automatically. The plan had been for them to be together, for it all to work out, for the happily ever after to happen. And now, surprise, they had something new to deal with, and the plan was all different again. She didn't think she could keep up with this.

"I don't," he said. "I thought we were in this together."

"There is no *this* anymore," she said, throwing up her hands.

"What the fuck does that mean?"

"Isaac isn't yours. He certainly isn't *ours*. You are taking him to foster care today. So *this*"—she waved her hand between them—"isn't a *this* anymore."

"What did you think *this* was, exactly?" he asked, his voice low and almost ominous sounding.

Harper took a deep breath. "We were taking care of a baby together. We were planning for a future because we suddenly had a baby. Now… we don't."

"So everything else is just over, too?" he asked incredulously. "Nothing else means anything without him?"

"It doesn't mean... the same thing," she said truthfully. "It will go back to how it was before. Fred. Ami. All of... that."

"I see." The muscle along his jaw tensed. "So you're not interested in fighting to get him back? In applying to be foster parents or to adopt him? You're just done?"

She blew out a breath. She was interested in that. But it would take a lot of time, and it might be a long shot anyway. "You think that we should get married on the *chance* that they'll let us have him?" she asked.

"Yes. Don't you?" he asked.

Of course, he was ready to just dive in anyway. James always dove in. He didn't worry about tomorrow. He was Mr. Right Now.

She took a deep breath. "Having a baby wasn't part of the plan. Losing him once we had him certainly wasn't part of the plan. Becoming a foster mom right now wasn't part of the plan. *Trying* to become a foster mom to him and having that not work out"—she sucked in a breath as that painful thought went through her mind—"is not part of the plan."

"What of *any* of this has been part of a *plan*?"

"Exactly."

James gave her an exasperated but affectionate look. "You're good without a plan, Harper. I know you don't think so. I know you think you want binders and lesson plans and to know what's going to happen two hours from now and tomorrow and next week and next year. But you can roll with it. You've been showing that over and over again."

She was shaking her head by the time he finished.

"Listen, James, I think that you're feeling a little guilty. For getting me all involved in all of this and then having it turn out like this. You're a fixer. You came across my landing because you saw someone who you thought was lonely or needed to get out more or who needed, at least, to be flirted with a little. But you don't have to feel responsible here. It's not your fault this didn't work out. I got caught up, and I'm sad and upset, and I'm going to miss him, but I don't need fixing, and I don't need an adventure. There doesn't always have to be a dog, or a baby, or a mystery to solve, or a mission. This is all... chaos. It will always be chaos. And I don't want that. I'm very happy with my books and my tea and my schedules and my classes. So you don't have to worry about me. And you definitely don't have to marry me."

And while he was still, clearly, flabbergasted, she slipped past him and headed off for class, leaving her apartment wide open for him and their dog whining by the empty food dish.

James would take care of it.

That was what he did.

10

———————

Four nights later, four bottles of wine later, four nights of crying herself to sleep later, there was a pounding on her door.

Harper glared at it.

She was mad at him for staying away for four nights. Of course, he'd worked two of those four nights. Still, James had left her completely alone. She hadn't pegged him for the leave-her-alone type. Unless, of course, he realized she was right about everything, and he'd only been trying to fix the quiet, tea-drinking bookworm that he thought needed a little excitement and romance in her life.

She was also mad at him for *not* leaving her alone now. Because the moment she saw him, she was going to burst into tears. And probably climb him like a tree.

God, she missed him.

She missed Isaac. She missed Henry. She'd seen Ami, of course. But James had even been considerate enough to come and get the dog, and return him, while she was at class.

Things were pretty much back to how things had been before Isaac.

And it all sucked.

Turned out, she *did* need to be fixed. She needed to be dragged into adventures.

She didn't want him to be considerate. She wanted him pounding on her front door, demanding she let him in, so he could tell her she was crazy and that he was madly in love with her, and he wasn't just trying to take care of her, all while stripping her clothes off and putting her up against her front door.

Harper didn't even bother to pull her glasses off or the tie out of her hair. She marched to the door and yanked it open.

But it wasn't James.

Well, it wasn't James that had been pounding on her door anyway. Because he was sitting on the ground, propped against *his* front door, looking exhausted, and very pouty.

The pounding had come from Caleb and Logan.

"I don't suppose you would be able to keep *that* off the streets tonight, would you?" Caleb asked without even a hello. He jabbed a thumb in James's direction. "He needs a babysitter, and we both have to work. I know you don't want to talk to him, and hey, I get it, but seriously, he has to stay in tonight and get some sleep. He's a fucking mess, and I'm gettin' damned sick of him."

She blinked at the big man, then at Logan, then peered around them at James again.

He did look like a fucking mess.

"What is going on?" she asked.

"He's been out looking for Isaac's mom," Caleb said. "He's tryin' to figure out if someone he knows or he's helped in the past had a baby recently they might have dropped off with him. He's talked to a bunch of the homeless kids he helps out once in a while, talked to people he knows from the club, interrogated the firefighters, went through records of the fire calls we've done in the past few months, was harassing Lexi in the

ER about medical calls we've done. She had to have security throw him out last night."

"He was at Trahan's tonight tryin' to figure out if any of the people he's met there have had a baby," Logan added.

"Oh boy." Harper sighed. Then she nodded. "Yes, of course I'll take care of him. Bring him in."

Caleb and Logan hoisted James to his feet and led him to her apartment. Harper stepped back to let them in. James's eyes were glued on her the entire time.

"Is he drunk?" she asked.

"No, actually," Caleb said. They half-lowered, half-dropped him onto her couch. "Exhausted. I don't think he's slept more than three hours at a time over the past few days. The chief sent him home from the station the last night because he was clearly not worth a shit."

Her eyes widened. "That can't be good."

"Nope. He's in trouble. But he can't handle that until all of this with Isaac is figured out, I'm guessing."

James had his head tipped back against the back of her couch, his eyes shut. He hadn't shaved in at least two days, he had dark circles under his eyes, and he was wearing jeans and a rumpled hoodie. He looked terrible. And wonderful. She'd missed him so much.

She missed Isaac, too. She ached with worry. But Shelly had told her he was with a very nice family with two little girls and that he was doing fine. He was healthy, sleeping well, eating well. The family was even interested in possibly adopting him. That made her ache even though she knew she should be happy. Isaac deserved a warm, stable family with sisters and a mom and dad and all of that. Harper still wanted him.

"You got this?" Logan asked, looking at her.

She nodded. "Definitely."

"Call us if you need us," Caleb said. "We're headin' to work, but you know how to get ahold of us."

"I do."

"Call me first," Logan said. "I can get away easier than Caleb."

It was true that leaving the bar, that he owned, would be easier than getting Caleb away from the fire station. "Got it."

They left, and she closed and locked the door behind them. Then she turned and regarded James.

"Missed you, Professor," he said, his eyes still shut.

"Missed you, too," she confessed. She wasn't sure she should. They should just cut ties. She didn't want all the craziness James brought into her life. It was too hard. It was fun when it was fun, but when it hurt... it really hurt. He'd acknowledged, himself, that his life was crazy. He'd tried to give her an out. He'd told her she didn't have to be involved with Isaac. Even he'd realized this wasn't really her thing.

"Come here." James held out a hand.

His head was still back, and she thought he was only minutes away from falling asleep. But she went. She slipped her hand into his, and he tugged her down onto the couch beside him.

"Isaac is okay," she said softly, unable to keep from reaching up and brushing his hair back from his forehead.

"I know. Shelly called me."

"So why are you killing yourself to find his mom?" she asked.

"Because I want him." James took a deep breath, rolled his head toward her, and opened his eyes. "I want him, Harper. And I would have thought that it was because someone trusted me with him and wanted me to have him, and I like feeling like someone people can depend on that way—and that is true. But it's also because I love him."

Harper's heart flipped in her chest. James wasn't just accepting that Isaac was gone. He wasn't just rolling with this.

He lifted her hand to his mouth and gave the back a little

kiss. Then he linked their fingers, resting their hands on his thigh, looking at them. "I do want to take care of you, Harper. That *is* what took me to your door the first time. You're right. I didn't really realize that, but you're right about that. I... thought you needed something. It was subconscious on my part, I swear. But yeah, I thought you needed something, and I couldn't not try."

She swallowed and nodded even though he wasn't looking at her. "I know. It's who you are. I wouldn't really want you to change," she said. The way he cared about other people and took care of things was one of the reasons he was most attractive to her. "You're a natural-born hero, James."

He nodded, running the pad of his thumb over the back of her hand. It gave her tingles, but it felt like more than desire. He needed comfort, and he was here with her. Yes, his friends had brought him here, but he seemed like he was relaxing, like maybe he was content to stay here and not beat the streets for information tonight.

"I've learned something, though," he said after a long moment. "I like taking care of things *with you* even more than taking care of them alone. It feels good to have a partner. To have someone that cares about everything as much as I do."

Harper felt her throat tighten. She swallowed. "Do I, though?" she asked quietly. "I don't think anyone cares like you do, James."

He looked up at her quickly. "Why? Because you don't initiate it all the time?" he asked. "That doesn't matter."

"Doesn't it? I'm not someone who jumps in. I can't just go with whatever happens. I need plans. I need to think things through. I need to analyze and research."

"Well, no. You don't jump in, but you're... a door opener."

She shook her head.

"Yes. You are. I might be the one who knocks. But you opened your door to me. And not because I was a hot firefighter." He gave her a little smile. "The first time you opened the door was because you thought I needed help and that the tree needed help because I didn't know what I was doing. But you figured out that I didn't really *need* help. You still kept opening the door because you wanted to."

He paused. "You don't charge in like I do. I sometimes even kick doors down—figuratively and literally. You're softer about it. But you open doors for your students to explore new languages and places and stories. And now, you've seen a grittier side of it—drunk girls and stray dogs and lizards that need to be rescued and..." He took a deep breath. "Abandoned babies. You've seen tougher things. More real things. Raw things. And you're fucking *glowing,* Harper. I've wanted you since I first saw you, but you've never been more beautiful than you are now that you've literally and figuratively flung your door wide open." He paused and gave her a goofy grin. "That sounds dirty. I don't mean it that way. Exactly."

Harper tried to take a deep breath, but it lodged, almost painfully, in her lungs. She felt her eyes stinging with tears. No one had ever seen anything like that in her. "People always see me as classy and sophisticated and quiet and studious. Not someone who will get gritty and who will take chances."

"Well, those people aren't giving you a chance to take a chance," he said simply.

She leaned in quickly and pressed her lips to his. She pulled back after only a moment, but he cupped the back of her head and brought her in for a longer kiss. Still, it was relatively chaste and sweet. When she did sit back, she said, "Thank you. For seeing what I could be—what I want to be—even if I'm not quite there yet."

He gave her a soft smile and then leaned back into the cushions. "You're there, Professor. Trust me."

His eyes slid shut, and he took a big, deep breath.

"You should sleep," she said softly.

"Yeah, maybe for a little bit."

"Do you want to go to bed?"

"Yeah, maybe in a little bit."

The next thing she knew, he was asleep. On the couch. Shaking her head, Harper got him tipped over and his feet up on the cushions. She took his shoes off and covered him with a blanket. If he woke up, he could come into the bedroom. She knew he'd know that was fine.

"Ami," she called softly.

The dog came trotting over from his dog bed.

She patted the cushion beside James. "Keep him company, okay?"

The dog jumped up and curled up next to one of his favorite humans immediately. She patted the dog. "Good boy. Love you." Then she smoothed a hand over James's head. "Love you, too."

———

SHE'D LEFT AGAIN BEFORE HE WAS AWAKE, BUT THIS TIME SHE LEFT a note.

Now she was ordering a chai latte with Celia before heading to class. Not because she needed a drink but because she needed her friend to tell her if James was right. Or not.

"He said I'm a door opener," she said, watching the barista write her name on the side of the cup. "Do you think that's true?"

"Skinny white mocha with whip," Celia ordered, then she said, "I think so. Sometimes," to Harper's question. She swiped her credit card.

"Just sometimes?"

"Yeah."

They moved down the counter to wait for their drinks.

"He said that he thinks I do it a lot. Sometimes in small

ways, like with my students when I encourage them to try new things, but that now that I've seen the bigger ways, how rewarding *actually* opening my door and letting people and things in can be, I'm glowing."

Celia looked at her, seeming to consider that. "You have definitely been happier. I thought it was the sex."

Harper glanced around. No one was really paying them any attention. "Well, that's probably part of it."

"Listen, yeah, you're a person who is very willing to help others who need you," Celia said. "But what you really are is an enabler. For your students. You always encourage them to try new things and do what's calling them. For me. You tell me to take chances and risks. For James. You help him take all of this on. And that's a really great thing to be," she added quickly, when she noticed Harper's frown. "We've talked several times about how great James is. Having someone support and encourage him is awesome."

"You think so?"

"I absolutely do," Celia said firmly as they picked up their cups. "You are smart and put together and organized and calm. When you tell the rest of us that we can and should do something, we believe it." She shrugged. "You're an amazing cheerleader. And with James, you're actually getting your hands dirty. You're helping him do these big things. He might kick the door down, but having you walk in with him, makes him more confident going in there. Figuratively." She smiled. "And literally, I'm sure."

Slowly, Harper nodded. "I'm like a quieter, smaller, better-dressed firefighter." She looked at Celia. "Those guys have his back. They make it easier for him to be confident going in to do his job helping people in a fire. I'm like that, but at home. In a skirt."

Celia laughed. "Yes. Exactly. James absolutely knows all

about how important it is to have people to depend on. You're a great team."

"Professor Broussard?"

Harper turned with a smile, to find Sophie behind her. "Sophie! Hi!"

"Hi." The girl gave her a big smile. "I was hoping to run into you here before you headed to class."

"I do like my habits," Harper admitted. She did. But maybe there was a way to balance that with the craziness of a life with James. Because she had to accept the fact that life with James would always be full of unexpected adventures.

"I left my hoodie over at your place the other night. I was wondering if I could stop by tonight and get it," Sophie said. "And I'd love to say hi to Isaac."

Hearing his name unexpectedly like that caught Harper by surprise, and she felt a jab in her chest. Her smile fell away, and she sucked in a quick breath.

"Are you okay?" Sophie asked, looking concerned.

Harper swallowed and nodded. "Yes. I... of course you can stop by for your hoodie, but... Isaac won't be there."

"Oh. If it's not a good night—if you're going to be out or something—I can come another time."

"No. It's not that." Harper blew out a little breath. "He's... It turned out that James isn't his father. The DNA test came back. Actually, the same night you were there."

Sophie frowned. "Oh, I see. But... what does that mean? Why isn't Isaac with *you*?"

"He was taken to a foster home," Harper told her, blinking against the tears. "Since he's not James's son, he doesn't have any rights and can't keep him. But he's been looking for the mom and applying to be a foster parent and... it's just complicated and will take some time. So he has to be in an already approved foster home for now."

Sophie looked pale, and she was shaking her head. "No. That's not right. He's supposed to be with *you*."

"We want him," Harper said. "We're going to try to get him back."

"You *are* still together?"

"We... are. We're not getting married right now. But we're seeing each other." She assumed that was true. Last night was the first time they'd talked about anything since Isaac had been taken away. But it had seemed good. She couldn't marry him right now, but she loved him. She wanted to be with him. Wanted to see where it would all go without the forced togetherness. And panic and exhilaration that Isaac had brought to them.

"Why aren't you getting married?" Sophie asked, frowning.

"We were going to get married to make things easier with Isaac. But that's not necessary now." She shrugged. "It was really fast, and we just need to take some time."

"But you need to be together to get him back."

"It's not that simple."

"The mom wanted you to have him," Sophie insisted. She was breathing hard.

"We don't really have proof of that," Harper said. "If she actually *said* that, turned over her rights, worked on a private adoption with us, something, it would be easier. But as it is, the state has no proof of... anything, really."

Sophie started shaking her head. "No. This is wrong."

Harper reached out and took her hand. "I know it feels wrong. I've been sick and sad ever since it happened, but the social worker said that he's doing well, and the home is great and—"

"How do you know the social worker?" Sophie broke in.

"Um... through the hospital. St. Michael's. Through a nursing friend of ours."

"What's her name?"

Harper frowned. "Shelly Welsh."

"I need to go." Sophie turned and started across campus.

Something niggled at the back of Harper's mind.

"Wow," Celia finally commented.

"I need to go after her," Harper said. "Something's not right."

Celia nodded. "Looks like maybe you're going to have to be the one to knock on this door."

Harper gave her friend a quick hug. "Talk to you later."

She started across the grass toward the parking lot where Sophie was headed. As she walked, she sent a group email to her students canceling class.

She got to her car as Sophie was pulling out of the lot. Harper caught up with her three blocks later. She didn't even mind if Sophie saw her following.

It only took four more turns for Sophie to confirm what Harper had suspected.

At the next stop light, she texted James.

Need you to meet me at St. Michael's.

He responded almost immediately. *On my way. What's going on? You okay?*

I'm okay. Sophie's on her way there. Shelly's office.

———

JAMES STEPPED OFF THE ELEVATOR ON ST. MICHAEL'S SIXTH floor, his heart thundering.

He wasn't sure why he was here. But he had an idea.

Raised voices became clear as he turned down the hallway. He picked up his already fast pace.

"He's mine! I get to decide what happens!"

James arrived to find Sophie squaring off across Shelly's desk from the social worker. There was another woman standing on Shelly's side. Harper was on Sophie's side of the desk.

"It's complicated now, Miss Duncan," Shelly said.

"I have his birth certificate. I'm his mother. This shouldn't be complicated," Sophie said.

Sophie was Isaac's mother. That sunk in faster than James would have expected. Not that it made sense, exactly, but it made sense that they were here now. And at least there was a connection between them and Isaac's mother.

Though it was between Sophie and *Harper*, not him.

Harper noticed James first. She gave him a wide-eyed *oh, shit* look followed by a relieved smile. "Shelly, please," Harper said to the other woman. "Help us here."

"She abandoned him," Shelly said. "That essentially terminates her rights."

"I didn't!" Sophie protested. "I left him with a friend who I knew would take care of him!"

"But you *left* him," Shelly said.

"But the statute says that it has to be for four months without making myself known or six months without providing for his care at all or maintaining any contact," Sophie said. "It's only been a few days, and I was going to tell Harper and give her the birth certificate and everything as soon as I knew she was in love. And I helped take care of him the other night and planned to keep helping babysit."

Everyone stared at her for nearly a whole minute.

"You know the child abandonment statute?" Harper asked.

But James wasn't surprised. This was the girl who'd showed up to babysit with a binder.

"Of course," Sophie said. "I looked it all up ahead of time." She frowned. "I wouldn't just drop my *baby* off on a stranger's doorstep. I knew you were home. I put him there, I knocked, and I ran."

James was starting to understand that this girl had not

really *abandoned* her child. She'd... provided another home for him when she thought she couldn't give him a good one.

"You volunteered to babysit as a way to see him?" James asked, to make the point with the social workers.

Sophie shrugged. "Of course. It was perfect. I could see him, but he would be with you. I was confused about Harper thinking he was your son," she admitted. "But then I realized it didn't matter, because you both loved him. I was going to come over tonight and tell you the truth."

"You left your hoodie at James's house on purpose, too?" Harper asked.

Sophie nodded.

"How do you know Mr. Reynaud?" Shelly asked.

Sophie shook her head. "No, I didn't leave him with James. I left him with Professor Broussard. Harper."

James nodded. Yeah, that made more sense, too. "But he was in front of *my* door," James said.

Sophie swallowed. "I didn't know that. I followed Professor Broussard home one day after class and saw her go into that apartment."

Harper looked at James. "I must have gone in to check on Ami that day when I got home." Then she frowned at Sophie. "Wait. What? You left him with *me*?"

"Of course. I've never admired someone like I do you. I knew that you would take care of him."

"But... how did you know I would keep him?"

"Because you're that kind of person," Sophie said simply. "You help people with whatever they need from you."

Yeah, she did. James knew that Harper thought she needed everything to go according to a plan, that she didn't like chaos, that she couldn't just roll with things.

She was wrong.

"You're a door opener." James stepped forward as he said it.

Sophie looked at him and nodded. "Yes." She focused on

Harper. "You are. You would open your door to anyone who needed you."

"Why not just ask me?" Harper asked.

James could hear her voice was thick with emotion, and he moved in to put his hands on her shoulders.

"Why not just tell me you needed help?" Harper asked again.

Sophie's bottom lip trembled. "I was scared. I was pregnant while I was in your class last semester but not far enough along for you to notice. I thought about telling you a couple of times but... I just couldn't. I don't let things like this happen." She took a breath. "I'm organized. I'm on top of things. I don't mess up like this."

Harper stepped forward. "Like you think your sister does."

Sophie nodded. "Like my sister *does*. She doesn't think. She just goes with her heart. And it causes problems and makes things complicated—for her and my mom. So, when this happened, I knew I couldn't tell them either. I just messed up. It was this dumb one-night, stupid thing, and I should have known better. But I do know I can't handle being a mom. I'm only nineteen. I have huge plans. I have a lot of school to get through. Isaac deserves more than I can give him."

She looked at Shelly. "I really don't want to be a mom, and his dad doesn't want him. He's willing to sign over any rights, too. We hardly know each other, and he wants to pretend this never happened." She took a shaky breath. "But I love Isaac. I want him to have a great life. A *wonderful* life. And I knew Harper would do that. She's just like me, but she's older and has money and has her plan already in place."

"You can't just give me your baby because we're both really organized and like schedules and planners," Harper said weakly.

Sophie looked back toward Harper. "It's not just that. That stuff's great, of course. I want my son to know how to take care of his business, how to be responsible, and organized to be productive, and to contribute to the world around him."

James assumed that was another shot at her sister who, apparently, did not take care of her business.

"But you're also someone who looks at the big picture and thinks long term, and you want what's best for all the people around you. And you help them get whatever that is as much as you can," Sophie said to Harper.

James saw Harper's eyes were filled with tears.

"Why didn't you just come to me and ask me to take him?" Harper asked Sophie.

Sophie looked a little sheepish for a moment. "I knew that you would have to fall in love with him first. If I'd told you ahead of time, you might have thought about all of the reasons not to do it. But I knew that you would feel protective if you just found him there with a note and that you'd take care of him for at least a couple of days, and by then you'd be in love with him."

Harper took a shaky breath.

Sophie faced Shelly. "I want her to have him. Please."

Shelly was watching the whole thing quietly.

James wanted to say something, but he wasn't sure what. This was clearly all in Harper's court.

Finally, Harper stepped forward, and she took hold of Sophie's upper arms. "Thank you for trusting me like this."

Sophie nodded.

"But you're his *mom*," Harper said. "If you want him, we'll help you. We will do whatever we can to support you and help you two be together."

Sophie's eyes got wide, and she shook her head quickly. "No. No. Really. I can't be good for him right now. The best thing I can do is give him a fabulous mom." Her gaze skittered to James. "And Dad."

James felt his heart thump hard in his chest.

Everyone was quiet. Clearly, they were all waiting for Harper to take the lead here.

After several long moments of her studying Sophie, Harper nodded. "If you're sure, then, of course, we'll take care of Isaac for you." She glanced over her shoulder to James then back to Sophie. "And if you want, you can move into my apartment and keep helping us with him and be right there across the hall to see him whenever you want. We can make it a wide-open adoption. You can be as involved as you want to be."

Right across the hall. That sounded a lot like he and Harper were going to be living together. He was on board with that. James nodded. "Absolutely. Whatever you want, Sophie."

But Sophie was shaking her head again. "I don't know. You don't have to do that. I don't want to be in the way."

Harper just paused for a long moment. Then suddenly she pulled her into a big hug and just held her. It took a second, but Sophie seemed to melt into her, wrapping her arms around Harper and taking a huge shuddering breath with tears streaming down her cheeks.

James glanced at Shelly and saw that the social worker's eyes were shiny, too.

After a long moment, Sophie pulled back and sniffed. "I'm sorry. I'm sorry to make this all so crazy for you."

"Don't be sorry," Harper told her. She looked at James. "We do pretty well with crazy."

His heart turned over in his chest. God, he loved her.

Harper looked at Shelly. "Now what?"

"Do you maybe want to take her to the coffee shop downstairs to talk some more?" Shelly suggested.

"No," Harper said. "I want to take her to her son."

Shelly shook her head. "I can't—"

James stepped forward and put his arm around Harper. "Or a judge. Whoever you think we need to start with."

Shelly opened her mouth then closed it. She glanced at the woman next to her. "What do you think?"

"Can you produce the birth certificate today?" the woman asked.

James assumed she was another social worker.

"Yes," Sophie said quickly. "And hospital records. I had him here."

Everyone looked surprised for a moment. Then Harper said, "Okay, what else do we need to do?"

"It's not like she dropped him off at a drug house or with an abusive ex or something," the other woman said with a sigh.

James winced. He was sure they'd seen both of those things. And worse.

Shelly nodded. "And she's right about the statute," Shelly said. "There is a time frame applied. And she left him with people she knew." She finally smiled at Sophie. "He can go home with you for now, and then we can help you get started on an adoption process when you're ready. Let me make some calls and see what the next steps should be."

Sophie took a deep breath and lifted her chin. "As long as my baby is back with me and Harper and James tonight."

Shelly opened her mouth, but Harper said firmly, "*Tonight*, Shelly."

Finally, Shelly took a breath. "Yes. Tonight."

It took twelve hours. Twelve very long, stressful hours.

But they were finally home. All of them. Together.

Sophie was asleep across the landing in Harper's apartment —where she was going to be staying full time now. Part of her concern with keeping Isaac had been that she lived in the dorm. She had to. It was what she could afford with her scholarship. She couldn't have kept the baby in the dorm with her.

Now she had an apartment. For free, for now. She didn't like the idea of taking charity, but Harper had convinced her that even if she didn't think she could be a full-time mom, Isaac would benefit from having her around. Harper was referring to it as a live-in-nanny situation. But James knew she was betting on Sophie being head over heels for her son, and once they removed all the pressures that had made her believe she couldn't keep him, her perspective would change.

Right now, though, James and Harper sat on his couch with Isaac lying lengthwise on Harper's thighs, looking up at them. He was dry, fed, and apparently not that sleepy.

"He's starting to stay awake longer already," Harper commented.

James nodded. "He's changed a lot just in the time we've had him."

Isaac had his hands wrapped firmly around Harper's thumbs. He gave them a little smile. James couldn't help but return it. It might have just been gas, but it still looked sweet.

"Do you think this will work?" James asked, reaching out to give the baby's foot a little squeeze.

"Yes," Harper said simply.

"How?"

"However it needs to." Harper looked up at him. "She needs us, too."

"Yeah." Sophie clearly had a complicated relationship with her family. What she needed right now was support. Period. Day to day, what that looked like, might change. But James and Harper were nothing if not flexible. And a great team. "So if she decides to keep him, we're okay?"

"Not exactly."

He knew what she meant. He wasn't *okay* either. But they could handle this. Together.

"If I can keep *you*, I'm okay." Harper leaned over to put her head on his shoulder.

James wrapped his arm around her, feeling his chest warm.

"We will just take care of whoever or whatever comes to us," Harper said. "Right now, we're kind of fostering a baby and a teenage girl. And whatever happens tomorrow, we'll deal with it."

James kissed the top of her head, feeling his heart swell. "You're going to be okay with that? Not being able to schedule and plan everything?" He didn't need Harper to change. He loved her just as she was. But he had to admit that she'd blossomed and seemed so much happier since she'd just started going day to day and taking care of things as they came.

Harper shifted so she could look up at him. "You know what I realized? About opening that door?" she asked.

"What?"

"That I never knew what was going to be on the other side. But I kept opening it. Because I knew *you* would be there. Whatever else came along with that didn't really matter." She gave him the most beautiful smile he'd ever seen. "I think you're the only constant I really need."

James felt everything in him tighten. With need. He looked down at the baby. He couldn't do all the things he suddenly needed to do to, and with, Harper because they had a baby. Kind of. For now. But for now was enough.

He could, however, kiss the hell out of her. James cupped the back of her head and pulled her in. "I still want to marry you, Professor. But this time, you can tell me when you're ready."

Just before he kissed her, she said, "I'm ready."

James pulled back, looking into her eyes. "Are you sure? Is it because we have the baby back?"

She shook her head. "I know we might not be keeping him. Or maybe we'll have him for a year or two and then Sophie might be ready to be on her own. Or maybe we'll send our girl off into the world after she graduates, and she'll come back and visit all three of us. I don't know. But... there will be so many other adventures and people and things that need us. We're really good together and all of this—the dogs, the babies, the teenage girls, the lizards, and trees—they all orbit around us. We're the center. Us. Together."

He kissed her before she could say anything else. This woman... she still made him weak in the knees. She was starting to see how amazing she was, and he was so damned grateful to get to be around to watch her discover all her kick-assedness.

Their kiss was interrupted, however. He supposed that if their life was going to be full of pets and kids, he should get used to that.

Though a loud baby fart followed by the unmistakable sound of that baby filling his diaper—and then some—would never be romantic.

Harper laughed and looked down at Isaac. Who was grinning up at them. "Wow."

The smell hit him a second later, and James shook his head. "I was wondering how to get you naked again."

"To the shower, then?" she asked.

"And this time you don't need to keep your pj's on," he told her with a wink.

"Our hands are going to be kind of full," she said, tipping her head toward the squirming baby boy who was starting to get uncomfortable in that diaper.

"Yeah, until he's asleep. But you can just stay wrapped in a towel until then." James scooped the baby up from her and stretched to his feet.

Harper rose as well and started for the bathroom, stripping her shirt up and over her head. She tossed it to the side and looked over her shoulder. "I'll get the water warmed up."

James watched her go then looked down at the baby. "Seriously. Best wingman ever."

———

Six months later...

Harper sat next to James on the folding chair, watching Sophie and Isaac. He could stand up if she held his hands, and he was bouncing, holding on to Sophie's fingers, watching the other kids play.

It was the monthly family get-together for the support group that Caleb, Lexi, Bea, and all their friends were a part of. James, Harper, and Sophie had all started going to the group meetings at Caleb and Lexi's invitation. Together.

Sophie lived across the landing and spent a lot of time with Isaac. But so did Harper and James. The baby was always with at least one of the three, and they parented him as a unit. They hadn't started a formal adoption process yet, and James and Harper were happy to give Sophie whatever time she needed. Maybe she'd never decide to give him up. That was okay. They were a family. An unconventional one, for sure, but still a family.

The support-group members hadn't even blinked at their unusual situation, and over the past few months, they'd learned that every member of the group had a different parenting setup themselves. Some had lost their spouses, some had divorced, some had never had a spouse to start with, and some had spouses who were gone for long periods of time, like Lindsey's husband, Matt, who was stationed overseas with his army unit. The thing they all had in common was wanting to be the best parents they could be and the need for support from other parents.

"Wow, he's getting so big."

Harper looked up at Dana Trahan, Logan's wife. She had their youngest daughter propped on her hip. Harper had quickly figured out that Logan Trahan was just meant to have girls. Lots of girls. Everyone thought it was hilarious, but it was obvious that he was a fantastic dad and embraced everything about raising his girls.

"I know. I can't believe how much they change and learn in the first few months," Harper said.

"It's crazy," Dana agreed. "So, hey, us moms are going out next week for a spa day. Massages, mani-pedis, and lunch. Addison, me, Lexi, Lindsey, Ashley, Roxanne, and Bea, if she can make it. We'd love to have you and Sophie join us."

Harper smiled at the other woman. "Thank you. It's so nice that you include us both."

"You're both his mom, right?" Dana asked with a shrug. "One thing that we know very well in this group is that families are formed in all kinds of ways. As long as there's love and support, it really doesn't matter how the people in the family come together or if they share blood."

Harper felt tears prickle at the backs of her eyes. "I love that."

James had told her that all of this was just one more way she was proving she was good at rolling with things, just like he was. She was starting to believe him.

Sometimes she thought she was Isaac's mom. Sometimes she thought she was *Sophie's* mom. Sometimes she didn't think either of them really needed her. Some nights they both needed her. And having two kids—three if she counted James, which she definitely did sometimes—meant never knowing exactly what the next day would bring.

She loved every bit of it.

James's phone rang just then, and he glanced down at the number. He frowned slightly.

"So that's a yes?" Dana asked.

Harper pulled her eyes from James. "Yes, definitely."

She and Sophie had enjoyed the evenings together when James had been working. Harper had loved getting to know the younger woman better, and Harper really did feel that she was mothering Sophie, too, sometimes. She'd taken care of her when she'd had a sinus infection a month ago. She'd helped with homework. She'd taught her a couple of recipes. It was fun having a new friend-daughter figure. Harper would never have expected that. Nor would she have discovered it if she hadn't been open to bringing Sophie into their lives.

"Saturday?" Dana asked.

"James, do you work Saturday?" Harper asked. Celia had offered to help sit Isaac anytime they needed someone, but so far they hadn't needed to take her up on that.

"Uh... no," he said, clearly distracted. "Hang on." He lifted his phone to his ear. "This is James Reynaud."

Harper watched his face go from frowning to surprise. He glanced at her.

"I, um... yes." He paused. Then he nodded, holding Harper's gaze. "Yes. Definitely yes." He listened again and then smiled widely. "Great. We'll be right there." He disconnected.

"What's going on?" Harper asked.

"You might not be available next Saturday," he said. "You're going to be a little busy."

"Why?" Harper felt a little thrill shoot through her that she didn't understand. She didn't even know what was going on, but she could sense James's excitement.

"They have a foster kid for us."

She felt her eyes go round. "What?" They'd just completed all of their paperwork and interviews two weeks ago.

He nodded. "A girl."

"Oh." Harper reached out and squeezed his hand. "Wow."

"Yeah. And... she's thirteen."

Harper stared at him. "A teenager?" She hadn't been expecting that.

His gaze went to something over her shoulder. "Apparently one of the people they interviewed about us said that we'd be awesome with teenage girls."

Harper didn't have to look to know he was watching Sophie. She felt those tears prick her eyes again. "She did?"

"I guess so. What do you say? Think we can handle a teenager whose mom just went to jail for child endangerment because her boyfriend was dealing drugs out of their house?"

Harper shot to her feet. "Yes. Come on. Let's go get her."

James grinned and got to his feet. "That's what I'd figured you'd say."

Harper grabbed her purse. "I'm sorry, Dana, I don't know about next weekend."

"It's fine," Dana said with a big smile. "You guys go. We get it. Spa days can happen anytime."

"Sophie!" James called.

The girl swung Isaac up to her hip and came over to them. "Hey, what's up?"

"We need to go meet our new foster daughter," Harper said, her heart pounding. "Can you get Isaac home all right?"

"Of course," Sophie said with a nod. "A new foster daughter?"

"Yeah. What do you think?"

"I think that's amazing." Sophie gave them a big smile. "I'll make cookies."

Harper grinned. "That would be perfect." She loved that Sophie wanted to be a part of this. A part of making all of this work for whoever needed them, even while *she* needed them.

"Logan and I will get them home," Dana offered. She waved to her husband. "Logan will come out and get the baby's car seat out of your car."

Instinctively, Harper leaned in and gave Sophie a quick hug, then she kissed Isaac on the head. "We'll see you later. At home."

"Yep." Sophie looked a little overwhelmed but happy.

Exactly how Harper was feeling.

James took her hand and lifted it to his lips. He kissed it and said, "I feel like I should go get her and show up at your door and say, 'I don't suppose you know anything about thirteen-year-olds?'"

Harper smiled. "Well, the answer would be the same as it basically was all the other times—'no, but I'll learn.'"

He laughed. "We'll learn together."

"Yeah." She nodded. "I really like opening these doors together."

"Me too, Professor. Me too."

———

Thank you so much for reading Getting Off Easy! I hope you loved James and Harper's story!

And now you can head down to the bayou for more sexy, Louisiana fun in the companion series, **Boys of the Bayou!**

Small town, hot-country-boys-with-Louisiana-drawls, crazy-falling-in-love fun!

My Best Friend's Mardi Gras Wedding
Sweet Home Louisiana
Beauty and the Bayou
Crazy Rich Cajuns
Must Love Alligators

———

If you want more sexy, single dad romances, check out these titles from Erin!

Best of Three
Forever Mine

**No Matter What
Just A Kiss**

———

Other books in the Boys of the Big Easy series include:

Easy Going (prequel novella-FREE everywhere!)
Going Down Easy
Taking It Easy
Eggnog Makes Her Easy
Nice and Easy
Getting Off Easy

———

Find all of Erin's books here!
www.ErinNicholas.com